Love

IS A NUMBER

Also by Lee Monroe

Dark Heart Forever
Dark Heart Rising
Dark Heart Surrender

LEE MONROE

Hodder
Children's
Books

A division of Hachette Children's Books

A Catalogue record for this book is available
from the British Library

ISBN 978 1 444 91056 8

Typeset in Berkeley by Avon DataSet Ltd, Bidford-on-Avon, Warwickshire

Printed and bound by CPI Group (UK) Ltd, Croydon, CR0 4YY

The paper and board used in this paperback by Hodder Children's
Books are natural recyclable products made from wood grown in
sustainable forests. The manufacturing processes conform to the
environmental regulations of the country of origin.

Hodder Children's Books
a division of Hachette Children's Books
338 Euston Road, London NW1 3BH
An Hachette UK company
www.hachette.co.uk

for all you romantics

PROLOGUE
Eloise

When my grandma died I was in an art lesson at Parkway Juniors, intent on a messy self-portrait, dabbing random colours everywhere and feeling kind of happy. When there was a knock, and my mum appeared behind the glass of the classroom door, some of my happiness drained away. Your mum only turns up to school when something serious has happened. She was very pale and hadn't bothered with make-up. Her brown hair was scraped back in a short ponytail and she had the kind of expressionless look that I now know comes from shock. It was probably one of the few times that she looked like the rest of us mortals. Not a shred of polish.

The rest of it happened in slow motion. Mum coming into the classroom, our teacher frowning in concern and glancing over at me. As my child's mind put things together I thought it must be about Dad. Something had happened

1

to Dad. And then things speeded up. I stood up quickly, sending my self-portrait wafting up into the air before floating to the floor. The tray of paints slid off my desk.

But it hadn't been Dad. As Mum talked to me, explained how Grandma had been very ill for a while and this was really sad, but she was peaceful now, and that she had loved me very much – even though Mum's face was ashen and her eyes were damp I struggled to feel anything. I loved Grandma, didn't I? Why couldn't I cry?

It's something you're not warned about when someone close to you dies. That sometimes you don't feel a thing. Nothing. You feel weird and as though you're hovering above yourself and life is going on around you. And a bit of you feels this odd excitement. Adrenalin. It is nothing like you imagined it would be.

'It's the shock,' Dad told me later. 'And sometimes, feelings are so big you have to put them away. Deal with them another day.'

And he had stroked my hair back from my face and I saw in him something really sad. As though he was all too familiar with putting things away, and dealing with them another day.

'It sounds heartless,' he'd told me next, 'but sometimes terrible, awful things happen and you think they might break your heart. But we're designed to move on, darling. And learn to be happy again.'

'I could never be happy knowing Grandma isn't here,' I told him miserably. 'How can you carry on loving people, trying to be happy, when they're gone? It hurts too much.'

'It does . . . but it gets easier.' He smiles distantly. 'One day you will suddenly feel yourself again; happy, when you never thought you would.'

I stared up at him then, disbelieving, and his smile this time was broader as he nodded.

'Something . . . or someone will bring it all back to you, Eloise.'

Daniel

I am feeling . . . homesick. And just slightly over the company of my travelling companions, Syd and Jamal. When we'd first planned this trip – our last 'hurrah' before uni and real life – it had seemed like a great idea. I've known them since we were all ugly, snotty-nosed four-year-olds at kindergarten. I thought I knew them inside out, that nothing they did could grate on me that much. Not after all the three musketeers had experienced together: primary school, the ruthless pecking order at the local comprehensive, dire Scouts trips to the New Forest, shared, oppressive family holidays, festivals, pointless band practice during our 'let's be rock stars' phase. They're just Syd and Jamal: a bit annoying, and about as physically attractive as I am (average to awkward on a good day). Syd and Jamal didn't laugh when I'd started wearing glasses at the age of seven. They haven't laughed (at least not in front of me) at my dad's pigeon fancying, or at the fact that my mum is a formidable karate instructor and not a home-made cakes and fresh flowers kind of lady.

Syd and Jamal have always just accepted me for who I am. In return I don't bat an eyelid at Syd's obsession with *Baywatch* re-runs and Alphabetti Spaghetti, or Jamal's fixation with old footage of Fascist demonstrations during the Second World War.

Me, I have no extreme tendencies. I read a lot more than I admit and I have not much interest in football. I like girls, but have not yet developed the necessary skills to approach them with anything like a well-constructed sentence. I admire them from afar and, like a lot of other emotionally immature boys my age, I admire the wrong ones. Girls way out of my league, but if I am being honest none of them have yet been interesting enough to let that really bother me.

That sounds arrogant. It's not. It's just that experience and good sense have not yet intervened to help me find my soulmate. And I am beginning to realize that I am not a casual relationship kind of guy.

Syd and Jamal aren't great with girls either, and this works well to maintain the camaraderie between us. None of us have ever posed a threat to each other.

But it's getting to the point where their little idiosyncrasies are tiring and I want them to go away.

Like tonight, in this heaving club in a still sweltering Madrid, Syd appears to have reinvented himself as a ladykiller. It worked at first. The lights are quite low and Syd has drunk six bottles of beer, which make him fearless and perhaps deluded. Whatever it is, a female volleyball-player type is dancing with him – while Jamal and I stand stunned by the bar.

Then one of Syd's contact lenses falls out and all his composure evaporates in his frantic efforts to feel the damp floor around her feet searching for it.

'Should we step in?' I venture to Jamal, whose mouth is frozen around the lip of his beer bottle. 'I think the game's up for Syd.'

Jamal considers for a second. 'Syd's a big boy now. He needs to find his own way.'

'Or his own contact lens.' My eyes flicker around the room. Great-looking people everywhere. Spain does nothing for your self-confidence.

'We should see if those guys are here . . .' says Jamal, after a bit. 'The ones we met last week in Granada. Didn't they say they'd be here this week?'

I frown. 'You mean the Abercrombie and Fitch models?'

Jamal is chuckling. 'The very same,' he nods, Yoda-like. 'But they were OK. Obviously higher up the food chain. But, Dan, they could make things happen for us.' He finishes his beer, placing it on the counter behind him. 'Did you notice how they were followed by beautiful babes wherever they went?'

'I see. You think that by association we will suddenly

become babe magnets?' I say drily. 'I'm not sure it works like that.'

'It's our only chance, Dan.' Jamal shrugs. 'Let's face it, Syd's not doing our rep any favours. I'm socially awkward. You . . . well, you're cripplingly shy . . .'

'I wouldn't say cripplingly,' I reply, wounded. 'I'm picky.'

'Fine,' sighs Jamal. 'Oh God . . . what on earth is he doing?'

I smile as a hunched Syd staggers out of the crowd. The female volleyball type is craning her head in all directions, wondering where he's disappeared to.

'Crap,' mutters Syd uncharacteristically. He's a well-brought-up kind of nerd and doesn't often swear. 'Just when things were starting to happen for me.' He straightens up, scratching at his hair and squinting.

'But think of the humiliation you've saved yourself for later,' I tell him, laughing. 'You know, when the lights come on . . . or she sobers up.'

'Funny,' Syd says grumpily. 'For your information we were having a very interesting conversation. Ella was telling me how gutted she was at not making the Olympic team.'

'So she *is* a volleyball player?' I nod. 'Thought so. Her shoulders are probably twice the width of yours.'

This raises a laugh from Jamal. The two of us are now trying to control ourselves in front of poor Sydney.

'Mate . . . It would never have lasted,' Jamal pulls himself together, trying to be comforting. 'You belong with a comic book nerd kind of chick. Like that Sophie girl who hangs out at Ventura Legends back home.'

Syd sighs melodramatically. Together with his squint he is a picture of failure. I almost feel affectionate towards him.

'I know. But I wanted to experience the thrill of reciprocal romance just once in my life. If only for two hours.'

'Hey.' Jamal lifts his head, staring over at the entrance to the club. 'There's that Marcus kid . . . and the other one, Henry or Hugo or something. There, by the door.' He practically stands on tiptoe in his eagerness. 'What is that guy's name?'

Syd and I exchange a look and – I am certain – a mutual internal groan.

'Huck.' We supply in unison.

'That's all I need. A member of One Direction, raining all over my parade,' Syd says miserably. 'That's it. We're finished around here.'

'Just fake confidence.' I turn to Syd, realizing how futile this instruction is, given that one of his eyes is leaking fluid. 'They're not better than us.'

'I know.' He sniffs, lifts his chin and twists his mouth into a gruesome-looking smile.

'Hey,' says Marcus, closely followed by Huck 'the male model', with Jamal bringing up the rear. Next to the brothers Adonis, Jamal looks like Lurch from the Addams family.

'Hey.' I raise a hand, then am unsure what to do with it, so lower it again.

'Evening,' says Syd, looking even more demented than a minute earlier, if that were possible.

'Love it here,' Marcus says breezily. 'We were here last night as it happens. Or was that this morning?' He grins at Huck, who just has to stand there mute to look good.

'Dan, right?' Huck gives me the full beam of his smile. Perfect teeth, floppy brown hair, evenly tanned skin, interesting green eyes.

'Yep. How long are you two staying around here?'

'Not sure.' Huck looks coolly around him. A gorgeous brunette with legs up to the ceiling gives him a coy little wave and when he turns back to us his interesting green eyes are dancing in a not-very innocent way.

'We're staying in a hostel round the corner,' Huck continues. 'We were staying further in town, but there was a dispute . . .'

Marcus rolls his eyes.

'He means we were sent packing by the owner. She didn't like the rapport that Huck and her sweet little daughter were enjoying.'

Huck shrugs. 'She totally overreacted. We were just talking, that's all. Nothing happened.'

'Nothing ever does, does it,' Marcus says cryptically.

Syd is looking puzzled. 'Didn't you say you had a girlfriend in England?' he asks Huck.

'He does. He has a beautiful princess of a girlfriend,'

supplies Marcus. 'You should see the two of them together. It's nauseating.'

Huck's face changes then. It loses some of its assurance, and his eyes dip. He rubs at them with his fists.

'You're obviously missing her,' Syd goes on, straight-faced.

To his credit, Huck does give Syd a smile, approving the sarcasm, shaking his head a little. 'Actually, I am missing her. She's . . . she's amazing. But, you know, we're here to have fun, right?'

Syd is nodding so hard his head practically falls off.

'Totally,' he breathes. He looks unsubtly over at the pretty brunette. 'Any chance you could help me in my pursuit of fun by introducing me to your platonic friend over there?'

There is a second's bemused silence, before all residual awkwardness evaporates. None of us can help cracking up at Syd's ridiculousness.

'Sure I can.' Huck slaps him on the shoulder.

As Huck and Marcus make their way towards the dance floor, I grab at Syd's shoulder.

'Are you sure this is wise?' I hiss. I point at his half-closed eye. 'You're practically blind. Why don't we go back to the hostel and get your glasses.'

'I can't wear my glasses!' Syd hisses back. 'It's not my look at the moment.'

'So, what is your look? Mentally impaired?'

'Give me a break. I don't think she'll notice. And I can

see through that eye. A bit.'

'Righto.' I push him at Huck's departing back. 'Don't say I didn't warn you.'

I am woken up by the ceiling falling in on me. Or at least that's what it sounds like when I jerk into consciousness.

It sounds as if someone is trying to break down the door. Grabbing a hoodie I move quickly but cautiously to the door.

'What the hell's going on?' I shout over the noise. 'Who is this?'

'Dan, open the freaking door!' It's Syd, sounding more forceful, more masculine, than I have ever heard him.

I open the door and face him. He looks a total mess. His dirty-blond hair is sticking out in every direction and his Judge Dredd T-shirt has a massive stain across the chest. He also seems to have lost a trainer.

'What happened?' I pull him inside and realize that his arm is shaking. 'Syd?'

'Crap, crap, crap.' Syd starts hugging himself.

'Syd. You're frightening me.' It's true; I can feel my heartbeat going like the clappers. 'What happened? Where's Jamal?'

'He's with the police . . . with the other two . . . or the ambulance,' Syd gibbers.

'Ambulance? Is someone hurt? Is Jamal hurt?'

'No. Not Jamal.' Syd takes a massive deep breath, finally his breathing slows down, and he walks unsteadily over to my bed, and crashes down on it.

'Sorry. I'm just . . . I can't believe what happened,' he says, slowly now. 'One minute we were all in the club, having a laugh. Maria was hanging off my every word . . .'

'Maria? Who's Maria?'

'The lovely brunette goddess, who I will never see again. Obviously. Because of course something had to happen to thwart the course of true love.'

'Syd,' I push him gently. 'Stick to the salient points, please.'

'Yeah . . . Yeah. Well, we're hanging out, the four of us, and Maria, and her friend Ella, and Marcus went off to get some beers, and I'm chatting with Maria and I look up and I can see Huck's face is, like, completely pale. Like a ghost. And sweat's just kind of pouring off him. And Jamal is talking to Rosa, but then he looks up and sees it too. And we both say at once, "You all right, mate?"' Syd takes a breath, starts tapping his legs with his palms, which is what he does when he's nervous or freaked out.

'And?' I prompt him.

'And he opens his mouth to say something, but then his face gets all loose and floppy and when he speaks he sounds like he's out of it. Drink or drugs or something. And Jamal takes his arm, but then Huck just collapses. He folds up. He just folds up and kind of floats down to the floor.'

I put my hand to my mouth then. I think I am trying to fit my knuckle in my mouth. But then I recover myself. 'Jesus. Did he have some kind of fit? Is he OK?'

13

Syd doesn't reply. He tucks his hands under his thighs. Like he used to when he was a little kid. And he's chewing on his lip, trying to find words, I suppose.

'Syd? Is Huck OK now? He's OK now, isn't he?'

Syd stares blankly into my eyes. 'He's . . . well, the paramedics came eventually, and he was just rigid and they did all the stuff like you see on TV. They were doing it for ages. But he never opened his eyes. He never woke up.'

'Jesus,' I repeat. 'Don't tell me he's dead.'

Syd nods manically as though someone else saying it is what he's been waiting for.

'Dead, yeah. Dead.'

We sit in stunned silence for a long time before I get up and walk to the bathroom. I turn on the shower and then walk back to Syd.

'Have a shower,' I tell him. 'It'll help.'

Syd nods. He gets up and starts taking off his clothes, before registering me watching him in a daze. 'Privacy, please,' he says, and I obediently turn and move towards the window, sticking my head out, looking down at the street below. People are still walking home from their nights out. Behind me I hear the clunk of Syd's belt, and his belongings falling on to the floor, before the sound of the bathroom door shutting and locking.

I am seized with the urge to call my mum. I really need to speak to my mum. I have no idea what time it is in Manchester. She'll go mad if I wake her up. She gets up at about four in the morning for karate training. I chew on my lip and decide to leave it a while. I'll just freak her out anyway. She'll probably demand I get on the first plane home. She might be a lapsed Jewish mother. But she's still a bit of a Jewish mother.

Syd is still under the shower, and I pick up his clothes, his phone and his belt. I straighten out his jeans, and I chuck his dirty, damp T-shirt in the bin. I pull one of mine out, and lay it over the jeans, together with his wallet, phone and the belt.

Then I sit on the end of the bed, my head hanging down between my knees. I try and imagine my future. Huck must have imagined his. His would have been full of good times, of good luck. In a few years he'd have graduated from Oxbridge, or Yale, or Harvard and he'd be this great guy who everyone would like because he's just so great, even though he would be basically sickeningly better than anyone else. He'd get married eventually to a beautiful girl with perfect skin and impeccable genes. Probably the amazing girl he left back in England, who is probably sleeping a dreamless, perfect sleep right at this moment.

My future is not going to be much like that. My future will probably be working in the accounts department of my dad's struggling hardware stockists. Or I'll be the unfanciable male school teacher who is ignored by the younger female teachers and flirted with by the menopausal school secretary. Or I'll try and write a book and it will never get published and I will live a sad, deluded life and all my friends will pity me and never come and visit me in my bedsit because I'm such a downer.

I force myself to stop imaging the worst-case scenarios for my life. At least I'm not dead. At least I have a future, even if it is grim.

I continue to stare down, listening to the sound of the shower and the odd shout from outside. A police siren. I can't seem to move.

Something under the bed catches my eye; it's some way back, but it's blinking. Curious, I get down on my knees and reach out for it.

It's a phone. A pretty basic phone; in fact, it's the same as my 'holiday phone', but with a slightly different keypad, and the screen lights up when I press it, telling me it is working. It's not Syd's or Jamal's. Where did it come from? Has it been there all the time?

I stare at it. Hold it. To be honest, I'm glad of the distraction. I can hear Syd cleaning his teeth in the bathroom and then coughing and unlocking the door.

Then, for some reason, I tuck the phone under my pillow as Syd walks out into the bedroom.

'Better?' I ask him. 'I got you a fresh T-shirt. There.' I point at his things and walk into the bathroom to splash my face with cold water. But before I can turn the taps on, Syd is beginning to talk again.

'I'm going home, mate,' he tells me. 'I don't feel like having fun any more.'

Eloise

Your roots are showing, is the first thing I think when I look in the mirror. And it is true, there's at least four centimetres. Six months ago, hell, three weeks ago, I would have been speed-dialing Raj, chief stylist at the local salon to make an urgent appointment.

But today I am just staring at the mousey brown, noting it. I don't intend to do anything about it. What's the point?

What's the point in anything any more?

I shut my eyes, and do a Mind Wash. A Mind Wash is what I call the process of shaking out bad, negative thoughts. Thoughts that slow me down, that just aren't who I am. Or who everyone thinks I am.

See, my hair has always been my thing. Or one of my things. Let's face it, up until that Friday two weeks ago I had plenty of 'things'. There was my high-achieving academic mind. My slender but athletic physique. My knack of putting the oddest-seeming clothes combinations together and making the ensemble work. I'm the girl in the Street Style section of *Company* or *Grazia* magazine. The girl snapped out getting coffee on her way to meet friends, looking effortlessly pulled together, with messy blonde hair that curls just enough but not too much and never gets frizzy. Oh, and there's my generous, kind nature, my habit of putting lesser mortals at ease. Did you get the 'lesser mortals' snipe? Yeah, that's my internal code phrase for everyone who isn't me. Because I'm the girl every other girl wants to be. The girl who has everything. Including the perfect, shiny boyfriend who, just like me, gets everything right and never misses when he shoots to score.

Oh, right. That was until that Friday two weeks ago.

I'm wearing my pyjamas. I've been wearing the same ones for a fortnight, and they smell musty and sad, but – and this is going to sound really stupid – I can't wash them, because they haven't been washed since the Thursday before the Friday two weeks ago.

I am shutting my eyes again as what feels like a javelin tears through me, and I want to gasp. But I don't, I just hold on to the pain for a few seconds, and then I use my fading powers of Mind Washing to send it on its way.

And then I open my eyes again. And I blink. I twist my mouth into a smile, a really fake, ghoulish smile. I am taking a minute to memorize this smile. I doubt very much it will appear naturally again.

In fact, I simply can't imagine smiling ever again.

Outside it is blue skies and it feels hot for a September morning. My eyes drift to my bed and the clock on the table and I see that it is in fact a September afternoon. The house is quiet, and then I remember that it's a weekday and my parents are at work and my brother is at school and I am alone.

I used to be scared of being alone. From when I was very small up until . . . well, two weeks ago. I would panic at the thought of not being near people and hang around my mum, my friends, even my younger brother, to make sure I was always protected.

Protected. Now, what was all that about? Nothing and no one can protect you when something bad happens. It's a chilling thought, but even in the midst of what must be depression I can see that it is also a liberating thought.

Because I am not afraid of what could happen to me now. It has already happened. The very worst thing that in the back of your mind you know is possible, but so unlikely, has already happened.

I get back into bed. This also smells musty and sad. Pull the duvet over me and up to my chin, and huddle there. I can hear the birds chirping outside and it feels as though I am seven years old again, in bed before the sun goes down, awake and feeling outside of everything. But, this time, getting out of bed and tiptoeing downstairs to listen to the sounds of my parents opening a bottle of wine and chatting easily with each other is not going to take away the sense of isolation I have; the feeling that life is going on normally and leaving me up here, lost and alone.

'Huck,' I whisper finally, surprised at how normal his name sounds, unchanged, even though . . .

And then his face comes into my head, and though I try my hardest to do the Mind Wash thing and shoo it out again, it only becomes clearer. His brown curly hair, his green eyes, his smooth olive skin, the residue of childhood freckles fading on his nose, his smile.

Huckleberry Julio Rafael.

Lost and gone for ever.

Eloise

I was thirteen when I first laid eyes on Huckleberry Rafael. We'd all heard about him, of course – I mean, Huckleberry?

'So pretentious,' Jessica had said, wrinkling her nose and licking a blob of yoghurt off her spoon. It was a Tuesday lunchtime, and me and my beautiful posse had commandeered the top table in the canteen. Not that we had to. Everyone else knew that we were its rightful owners. We must have walked round like we owned the world, I suppose.

'It's from the book, I guess,' I'd replied, still turning the pages of the French textbook. I had been trying to cram for the test after lunch. I didn't really need to cram, of course – I knew my past, future and future imperfect tenses like I knew the colour-coded contents of my wardrobe – but you can never be too prepared. I had my reputation as the cleverest girl in Year Nine to uphold, after all.

'Well, yeah, obvs,' Jessica said drily, dropping her spoon into the empty carton and rolling her pretty brown eyes. 'Like I said, pre-tent-ious.' She yawned. 'I have to admit, though, Brazilian boys are usually easy on the eye.'

'Yeah, I wonder what he looks like,' I said vaguely, before scribbling down an example of pluperfect use to quickly memorize in the girls' toilets in the five minutes before class began. 'I bet he's one of those hippy kids. Long hair and bad hygiene.'

There was a collective titter from the girls around me. Jessica, my official best friend but also my nearest rival, with her poker-straight black-brown hair and sharp blunt fringe, which few can carry off unless they happen to be a gorgeous half-Malaysian, half-Swedish princess with a perfect little nose and wide full lips. Then there was Destiny Tallulah Okenendo – apparently a bona fide African princess whose mother has a thing for a certain late 1990s girl band, and a not too shabby gift for vocal harmonies herself. Next to Destiny was Laura, but pronounced Lowra on account of her impeccable Italian heritage. Laura is related to Sophia Loren, or so she claims, though Sophia hasn't yet turned up in the family albums . . . But still. Laura is our town's answer to *La Dolce Vita*. She works it, too. Laura arrived at school wearing her mum's vintage Gucci headscarf and shades to match.

'I think,' said Jessica slowly, 'that Huckleberry is among us.' She gestured with a sharp eye movement to her left.

'Don't all look at once,' she added through her teeth. 'We're not interested.'

I shook my head. I doubted very much anyone with a name like that would be my type, but I wasn't going to look anyway. Back then I didn't look for anyone – people tended to look for me.

'Interesting . . .' said Jessica, baiting me as I studiously looked at my nails. 'Seems that Huckleberry is really, in a scruffy not-my-type kind of way, really, actually quite hot.'

I sighed melodramatically but finally lifted my eyes. And there he was, a lone olive-skinned angel in a sea of spotty pubescent boys. Taller, a little broader, with mid-brown hair that was just long enough to curl becomingly at the nape of his neck. Unlike the others, his white shirt was a little creased but very nicely contrasted with his skin tone, his tie was loose and he was wearing black cords – not the hideous regulation polyester-mix black trousers the rest of the boys wore.

'Wow, make an effort, Huckleberry,' Jessica said sniffily, trying to bring down the unspoken and undeniable approval of the boy's style. 'He'll not get away with that get-up.' She ran a hand through her hair, as though dismissing him, but we all knew that the new boy was the most interesting and the prettiest thing to walk through the school gates since . . . well, since I had at eight forty-five that morning.

'If he looks like that now,' said Destiny, finally chipping

in. 'What in heaven's name is that boy gonna look like when we get to Year Thirteen?'

Nobody had an answer. We were all lost in our own private reveries. I was quite sure that Jessica, Laura and Destiny herself were silently, uneasily, wondering how they were going to get to know Huckleberry the best.

Me? Like I said. Back then, I didn't look for people, they looked for me.

I wasn't always an arrogant girl. Once upon a time I was normal. I knew I was smart and pretty, but I didn't let it go to my head. My mother, Valerie Campbell-Taylor, is to blame for that. I know it's a cop-out to blame the parents, but my mother was, and to some extent still is, eighty per cent beauty pageant mum and twenty per cent normal.

She got to the stage that a lot of mothers get to, I suppose, when she's had her kids, can't get back on track career wise (my mum was once a well-respected medical researcher, not that you'd guess that now) and lucky enough to have my father's very comfortable income to spend. On herself, on people she paid to keep our house the way she wanted it, on my younger brother Jake, and on me, her precious golden girl Eloise. Lois, or Lo, to those in my inner circle.

Mum started buying designer. Not just bits and pieces. I'm talking a constant scrutiny of *Vogue* and *W* magazine and a massive, environmentally shocking, draining of the world's fuel reserves in driving her petrol-consumptive Jaguar into the nearest city on a daily basis to raid every high-end designer stockist of the latest must-haves. That's a long, excessive sentence, but kind of appropriate. Because that's what she became: excessive.

If Dad wasn't a millionaire, having set up and then sold his software company for an eight-figure price a few years back, then he would be bankrupt. Mum filled her wardrobe and our house with priceless and beautiful things. When the allure of that began to fade just a little, she moved on to me.

I was enrolled in every kind of class imaginable. Ballet, fencing, extra maths, French, Spanish, Latin, junior science prep, piano, Little Book Group, athletics . . . And I excelled at them all. Because I always do my best, and I didn't want to let her down.

And then she bought in the big guns. A twice weekly stylist (I was eight years old), a speech therapist (to tone down the Estuary vowels), a yoga teacher and a housekeeper. Nothing was left to make its natural progression in the world as far as I was concerned. I was my bored mother's new project.

And then I came home after another Grade A tap class to find all my clothes replaced with new ones. All carefully grouped by colour and by fabric.

I had a moment then. A real moment of distress. Where was my beloved Snoopy dressing gown, my holey, way-too-small but beloved *Sesame Street* T-shirt? It felt like she'd chucked out my childhood. Let me rephrase that. She'd got someone else to chuck out my childhood.

25

'You threw out all my stuff?' I sounded ungrateful but I couldn't fake pleasure at a cupboard full of clothes I hadn't chosen and had no emotional attachment to.

Mum had waved her hand, dismissing my feelings. 'You were growing out of all those tatty old T-shirts,' she'd said. 'Don't you want to be the best you can?'

And there it was, the phrase that would echo in my head until it became a mantra I myself believed in. An eight-year-old doesn't have too much of an idea of who they are. Why not take on the character your mother chooses for you?

There was not much that Mum didn't decide on my behalf. Even my friends. Out went shy Sarah and slightly overweight Natalie. In came the daughter of a glamorous media CEO. That would be Jessica. Jessica and I practically lifted our tails and hissed like cats at each other when we first met – before we realized that the beautiful ones are best as allies. Then there was Destiny Talullah – our mums did salsa together every fortnight. And finally, Laura: glacial, contained, and a fine role model according to Mum.

'Men don't find animated girls attractive,' Mum had told me, when I had dared to suggest that Laura was ever so slightly frosty and dull. We were in my parents' bedroom, me on the bed watching as Mum changed into her latest von Furstenberg wrap and Prada heels. After satisfying herself that she did indeed look incredible for her age, Mum had come to perch carefully on the bed next to me.

'You'll thank me, darling. It was only a matter of time

before you left Sarah and Natalie behind. It's best for all of you.' She'd reached out and gently tugged at an errant lock of my hair. 'Nobody likes to hang around with someone more attractive than them.'

I had said nothing, of course, as I was already Mummy's little puppet, but inside an uneasy, sad feeling had crept through me. I liked Sarah. She was straightforward and kind. And Natalie . . . well, Natalie had that lack of vanity that is strangely inspiring. Natalie made me think of the important things in life – well, in my life then: eating jelly beans until we felt sick, laughing at the TV and knowing there was no other agenda than friendship between us.

Even as I accepted and adapted to having Jessica, Destiny and Laura as my new best friends, I missed my old friends. I missed knowing I was liked.

I carried on missing it, though I pushed it to a place far inside of me, so that it didn't feel so painful.

After a time, I forgot I was ever friends with Sarah and Natalie.

Daniel

Syd and Jamal have been gone for twenty-four hours, and it's weird without them. Weird not to have the constant hum of Syd's chatter, or watch Jam staring down at his Nintendo. But it's also a blessed relief.

When Syd made his announcement, at two in the morning on that fateful night, I'm slightly ashamed to admit that I felt relief. I mean, had I not been wishing that he and Jamal would just disappear? I have known them both most of my life, and over the years the three of us have guided each other through the battlefields of childhood and adolescence, united by the things we had in common which gave us our Beta status amongst our peers: the inability to enjoy sports, a discomfort with intensely male camaraderie – or, in fact, manly pursuits of any kind. Not one of us has really been more attractive than the other, not unless you count Syd's 'squint years', when Jamal and I had

28

a slight advantage. But we were eight years old at the time, so it hardly mattered. No, we were united against the world. Invisible, overlooked, happy to be the socially clumsy kids who girls never looked at twice.

But things seemed to change when we touched down in Athens airport – our first stop on the trip. Syd made it his mission to move closer to the stud he had clearly secretly always wanted to be. But his methods, unsubtle and often quite crass, had Greek and then, as the trip went on, French, German and finally Spanish girls moving away from us, rather than towards us. It became irritating to be associated with him. It was like he was making a virtue out of being a clown. Like a silly parody of a lovable loser. Even I know that this only really works if you're truly witty, or brilliant and, underneath the spots and the awkward hair, genuinely handsome. No one wants to go out with a fool. As for Jamal, he is absolutely no asset when it came to chatting them up. Girls, I mean. Not that I have a clue how to do that at the best of times.

So the friction that was growing between us became hard to ignore. It was as if each of us, in our different ways, was quietly biding his time . . . waiting for something to happen, but unable to confide in the others. I suppose hopes and dreams kicked in the moment I stared in wonder at the spectacular beauty around us. Rome – Paris – that tiny deserted Greek island that screamed romantic adventure. It is very hard to remain steadfastly a contented loser when you are surrounded by so much that glints and gleams and beckons to you. At least … this is what I was thinking. I can't speak for them.

I was beginning to dream.

I mean, pretty soon I'm going to uni – Bangor in Wales – to study engineering. Three years of hard work, and maybe if I'm lucky a few new social opportunities. But mostly it will be hard work. I want to get a First. Not a Second. And that meant heads down, no talking in class.

I couldn't help thinking that this – this time away from home, without my mum directing my every move, telling me what to do – this time was mine. And I had to make it count somehow.

It was obvious that was going to be difficult with Syd and Jamal at my side.

I wanted to reinvent myself. Just a bit.

So the day after Syd left I went and got my hair cut. When I say cut, I mean a Number One. As I watched my hair, dark and prone to a slight wave, drop to the floor of the barber's, leaving the shape of my head no longer open to interpretation, I felt this was step one in my plan. I looked up expecting to feel sick; instead I saw someone older, with cheekbones, and a slight tan, and the beginnings of stubble. I looked, if I closed my eyes slightly, just a bit like that guy off *Prison Break*.

I went down to the Lido just out of the centre of Madrid, and swam for an hour. As I rubbed myself dry with a towel on the little patch of grass by the pool, I sensed eyes on me. Turning, I saw a group of kids about my age observing me.

Apparently without amusement, but interest.

This will sound sad to those familiar with the thrill of acceptance. But I was quietly thrilled.

When your mum's constant refrain is that personality counts for more than good looks, you have to conclude that she means your personality will have to cut it because your face probably won't. It's a vicious circle, that kind of thought process and, as much as I love her, I see now that my mum's ambitions for my future are not mine.

I don't know how I am going to shake off the self-deprecating habits of a lifetime, but I want to try.

All at once it matters that I am attractive to the opposite sex. Just once. Fleetingly. Like Huck. If you put aside the shady use of narcotics and eventual death from what I would bet weren't entirely natural causes, Huck is the kind of kid any male under the age of eighteen secretly or not aspires to be. Charismatic and articulate and easy with life. No confidence issues with that kid. No self-doubt.

So here I am at the Lido, on the first day of the rest of my life, and I turn over on my stomach.

'Hey, you!' a husky female voice is calling to me. I turn slowly to see her, surrounded by her mates, grinning in a way I can't quite decipher.

I smile back, confidently but a little questioningly. Surely it can't be this easy? Lose your friends and get a haircut and suddenly you're in.

'Your shorts?' She points at my swimming trunks, causing the two girls either side of her to dissolve into laughter. I rub at my forehead self-consciously.

She is on her feet now, advancing towards me, stopping a few metres away.

'Your shorts,' she whispers dramatically. 'They are . . . how do you say? See through?'

'Oh, right.' I can feel the heat on my face. 'Thanks. Thanks very much.'

'Is no problem,' she says good-naturedly, then takes another step towards me and whispers again. 'Is nice, your bum.'

A mixed day, I muse, as I walk into the centre of town and back to the hostel. Yeah, I got laughed at, but that girl thought I had a nice bum, so it's a start.

I have no idea what I'll do with myself in the few weeks I have left before I start uni, but I kind of want to discover what I'm capable of without surplus baggage weighing me down.

Alone now, maybe I can finally be who I want to be. The guy who dares to dream. Out here in this beautiful country, where the pace carries you along with it, and people will smile and stop and talk to you if you let them, see you as someone like them. Why not?

Why not dare to dream?

5

Eloise

I must have fallen asleep because I'm woken up by the sound of my brother coming in from school. I lever myself up and look at the clock. Ten minutes to four. It doesn't mean much to me. My sense of time was shot since . . . since that Friday.

I don't bother to get up. I find conversation with Jake difficult at the best of times. He's going through a grunting phase as fifteen-year-olds often do. I know he finds it even more awkward to be around me lately.

What would I be doing now . . . normally . . . before? I take a breath; this was going to be hard. I would be with him. I would be hanging out at his dad's studio, drinking contraband beer and watching Carlo create another masterpiece, listening to records – mostly old-school rock – thinking that no one could look better in old jeans and a paint-splattered T-shirt than my Huck. Huck and his dad talked to each other like adults. Being with them was like being on another planet. Carlo had an easy-going attitude to parenting, but he thought the world of Huck. Maybe that was why Huck was so confident. So convinced that the world was at his disposal.

I breathe out; it helps me feel calm. It stops the tears. It has worked so far . . . I haven't cried once in two weeks. I know that once I start, I might not stop. And in this house, being out of control like that is simply not an option.

God forbid I should be 'animated', even at a time like this.

I turn on my side, as another memory threatens to smuggle itself into my thoughts. Huck holding my hand, leaning against me, and then the feel of his lips gently against my forehead.

Out! I kick my feet under the bedclothes in anger, trying desperately to Mind Wash. I drop my gaze down to the carpet by my bed and stare absently at my phone. It must be dead by now. I haven't charged it since the day of that last phone call. It's a Swarovski-encrusted iPhone. Another essential purchase by my mother on my behalf. Right now I hate it more than anything. I pick it up and start frantically gouging at a jewel on the case, which eventually plops satisfyingly on to the floor. I turn over the phone and frown, surprised to see it still on . . . though nearly out of gas. The phone is upside down, but my cover photo is unavoidable. Me and Huck at last year's Bestival. I'm wearing a straw hat over my tangled bleached hair that

Mum would have shrieked at if she'd known about it (which somehow she never did), with one of Huck's brown arms snaked around my shoulder, nuzzling his head against mine. We're both smiling – I can see it upside down – and the daggers start stabbing at my heart. We're smiling, we're happy. We didn't know.

I force myself to turn the phone the right way up.

I am squinting in the sun, or I must be, because my smile is lopsided, like I am actually grimacing. But all I remember is the sun and the music and Huck's gregarious, infectious charm. As I recall, we were surrounded by some new friends Huck had made. He made friends easily, wherever we went. But I didn't mind sharing, as long as I had the biggest piece of him. Huck is smiling at something – at someone? Maybe the one who took the picture? I give my head a little shake. I don't remember exactly. I linger on the photo for a few more seconds before I slide the bar to access my phone – stuffed with apps and games and videos. The garish colours make my eyes hurt as they roam and then locate the Contacts icon.

I'm not ready to call my friends. I can see on the Phone icon that I have a lot of missed calls. When I click through I see the usual suspects: Jessica, Destiny, my cousin Lou, Laura, my dad and then, Sarah . . . Natalie. I suck in my breath. Sarah and Nat. I haven't talked to them for years. It didn't end badly exactly; they knew the score. Or rather, they knew my mother. They knew what I was up against. But out of all the other names on that list, those two stop me short.

Why would Sarah and Nat still care about me?

For a second I have an urge to call them. They didn't know Huck, they won't talk about him. It will be safe to call them.

But really, what would I say? What could I say . . . after I just dumped them for better friends?

I breathe in now, hard. Another effective technique for dispersing feelings. But I am still holding on to the phone and then I can't help myself. I scroll down the numbers in my history until I find it. Huck's number. Or rather the number he has – had – been using since the end of July.

I stare at that number, wondering whether to delete it. Wondering but not doing anything. It's all I have to connect me with him.

Eleven harmless little digits.

You know those moments when you convince yourself of something, even though logic, and bare facts, tell you that it is impossible. You tell yourself that somehow it is true, that if you believe it, it will be true.

So I lightly touch that strip containing his number and, with the blood swirling and pumping noisily through my head, I hold the phone to my ear.

A lifetime goes by and my heart begins to sink before I hear the sound of the connection being made, and then the distinct, international ring tone . . .

I'm frightened now. Adrenalin is going mad inside my

veins. I feel exhilarated too. I feel wide awake, alive. Invincible.

Then a voice. Just as I'm about to faint, a voice cuts in. But it isn't Huck's. It's a recorded husky Spanish voice, a woman's, telling me . . .

'I know, I know,' I whisper out loud, as the voice repeats itself over and over.

I drop the phone on the floor and drag my knees up to my chin, in a kind of protective gesture.

'Stupid, stupid, stupid,' I berate myself, digging my nails into my legs. 'He'll never answer the phone. How can he answer the phone?'

Huck is dead.

Eloise

It took a while for me to actually meet the new kid at school. What with all my extra-curricular tuition, social engagements with the girls, not to mention an undoubted general air of stand-offishness, I didn't catch sight of Huckleberry Rafael for another three weeks.

Jessica had roped us all in to one of her ludicrous liquid diets and forbidden entry into the school canteen, so we took to eating our lunch underneath the giant cedar tree in the school grounds and distanced ourselves from the 'lesser mortals.'

Just for the record, that was a phrase initiated by Jessica and Laura, not me. Not that I didn't go along with it. A mini-me of my mother, I was well on my way to achieving her dream for her precious daughter: an aloof, impeccably stylish, super-studious little snob.

It feels good to admit that now. Even if it feels awful too.

'How much longer do we have to endure this disgusting slop?' said Laura, staring disdainfully at a LighterLife banana milkshake. 'I swear, I'm beginning to smell.'

Destiny snorted, bringing up a little too much milkshake through her straw. She removed it from her lips, dabbing at her mouth with a tissue. 'She's right, it's gross. Personally, I'd rather be fat.'

The three of us turned mechanically to stare at Destiny, as though she had just confessed to murder.

Jessica turned away first, sighing and then pouring the remainder of her shake into the grass.

'OK, OK, I know it's vile. But don't come running to me when you can't fit into those J Brand skinnies,' she said in a weary sing-song voice. 'We must suffer to be beautiful, you know.'

'We don't suffer,' I said, leaning back against the tree and smiling. 'Look at us, we are genetically programmed to be gorgeous.'

Believe me, I am cringing at that statement now. Cringing.

'Speaking of gorgeous,' Laura said, lifting her pretty chin and gazing through giant sunglasses at the school's main entrance. The rest of us followed her line of sight. A gaggle of lanky boys were exiting. There was Ollie (bright, but pock-marked skin from a hormonal acne situation), Nathan (think Jay from *The Inbetweeners*, but with an even sadder track record with girls), Seb (posh and pompous, with rugby thighs) and, bringing up the rear, taller, broader and distinctly more attractive than the rest, was new boy Huckleberry.

'So sad about his name,' murmured Jessica. 'I could never take him home to meet the parents.'

'You'd be better with a Justin, or a James,' I mused. 'Jessica and James. James and Jessica.'

'They're all morons,' Jessica sighed, shutting her eyes. 'Though I will admit Huck's got something.'

'Act indifferent,' Laura said quickly. 'They're coming past.'

We adopted a laconic, bored pose, chins in the air catching the rays, mouths set in sulky semi-pouts, the plastic LighterLife cartons shoved out of sight behind us.

I ignored the faint buzzing sound that was approaching my left ear, just squeezed my eyes shut and hoped the interloping bee would buzz off. My wish appeared to be granted as the noise stopped. I relaxed my shoulders a little bit, and was just leaning back on my elbows when—

'Excuse me?' A husky voice spoke into my ear. I snapped my eyes open.

Huckleberry Rafael was leaning cautiously into me.

'You . . . you have a little thing on your—' I dropped my gaze from his full, wide lips, somewhat regretfully, and directed it down to my shoulder.

I screamed.

'Getitoffmegetitoffmegetitoffme,' I carried on screeching repetitively. From the corner of my eye, I saw that my friends had disloyally scattered to the far corners of the well-kept school playing field. And I was left, hopping from one foot to the other, with Huckleberry standing calmly before me with a small and really quite gentle smile on his beautiful lips.

'OK, OK,' he said softly. 'Calm . . . Be calm. It will only react to your . . . noise.' He took a stealthy step closer to me, and to my shoulder, where the tenacious insect was still clinging to my soft grey cashmere cardigan.

'I like your . . . cardigan,' he said conversationally, as though we had met at the polo or something. 'It's a lovely colour . . . and so soft.'

'Thank you,' I said tautly. 'It's Brora.'

'It is even nicer than the one you wore yesterday,' he went on, one hand cupped to close over the insect. 'The midnight blue.'

I stared at him, confused yet vaguely flattered at his powers of observation. And the rare sartorial eye, the kind that I was pretty certain no other male in a five-mile vicinity would have possessed.

'Thank you,' I repeated, my eyes planted on his other hand closing round the bee. With a quick and skilled movement he captured the insect, swung his arms out and released it.

The bee thankfully scarpered, buzzing off to terrorize another pupil. Glancing round at my so-called friends loitering by the impeccably clipped giant box hedge, I couldn't help hoping that that pupil would be one of those three Jezebels. I narrowed my eyes at them briefly before turning back to my rescuer.

'Disaster averted,' said Huckleberry, his smile stretching up to his pretty green eyes. He put out his hand. 'My name is Huck.'

I hesitated. Years of my mother's misguided directions on how to treat the opposite sex told me I should coolly leave my hand where it was, hanging lamely by my side, and sniff, or something equally contemptuous. But – and for this rare moment of overwhelming instinct I am truly thankful – I lifted my arm and placed my hand in his. He had big hands for his age, I noticed, and strong.

'Eloise,' I replied, adding, 'But you can call me Lois.'

He nodded, almost comically, sweetly. 'A pretty name. It suits you.'

'Thank you,' I said for the third time in five minutes.

'Bees are usually just inquisitive,' he went on with endearing seriousness. 'In future, just pretend it is a boy kissing your shoulder.'

For some totally absurd reason, I then did something truly unprecedented.

I blushed.

'You mean to tell me . . .' Jessica said, very nearly becoming animated, I noticed, 'that you allowed yourself to be seduced by that – the oldest trick in the book?'

'I don't think it was, strictly speaking, a "trick",' I said carefully, looking down at my hands. 'He was actually rather nice. Chivalrous.'

Destiny did something that looked distinctly like eye-rolling.

'Seriously,' I protested – mildly, I couldn't let standards slip – 'He came to my rescue.' I narrowed my eyes. 'Which is more than can be said of the three of you. Where were you when the bee flew in for the kill? If it hadn't been for Huck—'

'Huck?' came the unanimous chorus. 'Huck, is it?'

'I believe that's his name.' I stared them out. No mean feat. Those girls are pretty intimidating when they put their minds to it.

Jessica held my gaze, before her shoulders dropped a little and she sighed. A disappointed, Jessica kind of sigh.

'Well,' she said, shrugging for good measure. 'I'll let this one go. On this occasion.' She smiled then. 'But from this point on, Eloise, you need to play it cool with this Huckleberry character. He sounds suspiciously smooth to me.'

Laura and Destiny nodded seriously. 'He does.'

'We'll see,' I said, irritated by this sisterly censoring, or by my own exposure, I wasn't quite sure. 'I'll see. Perhaps it's time we let our hair down a little for once. All work and no play and all that . . .' I trailed off. I seemed to be in a situation I was really quite unprepared for. Torn between the opinion of my three best friends, and the butterflies that were circling inside me.

There was a moment's silence before Laura elegantly

removed her hand-me-down Gucci shades and blew gently on the lenses. 'He does have nice eyes,' she said casually. 'This Huck boy. It wouldn't be so bad if he were an experiment . . .' She glanced at Jessica and Destiny, then replaced her shades, crossing her arms and lifting her chin. 'Would it be so very bad?'

I looked at the others. Waiting for the verdict.

Jessica sighed again, shaking her glossy head. 'I have a bad feeling about these two . . . Lois and Huckleberry. I think this girl might lose her head.'

7
Eloise

Dad made dinner tonight. His speciality: lasagne. Mum doesn't cook any more. She lost interest fairly soon after Jake started eating solids. After that our housekeeper supplied the food. Well, Mum paid for it, but Mrs DiLieto cooked it. It was a rare treat to have a parentally cooked dinner.

But as delicious as it looked, years of Valerie's disciplining and two weeks of sheer unadulterated hell had put paid to my appetite.

Mum wasn't bothered, naturally, but Dad frowned at me over his wine glass.

'Eloise, please eat something. You're looking far too thin for my liking.'

Jake instinctively snorted, before some shred of humanity – sensitivity – stopped him short. He recovered himself by putting another forkful of pasta into his mouth.

My mother, her tiny portion half eaten, shut her eyes as though rising above the situation. She's not one for emotion, my mother. Avoids it if possible. Even when someone has died. She just lets it all wash over her immaculate Yves Saint Laurent jumpsuit.

'You'll fit into that size six Miu Miu skirt I bought you now, I expect,' she said idly, before catching Dad's disapproving eye. 'I mean . . . that's the upside to this whole ghastly situation.' Aware that scrutiny was upon her, she attempted a rare warm smile. 'We must start thinking about everything you'll need for university,' she went on. 'Best to keep busy.'

'Yes, Mum,' I said, looking down at my plate. 'In a bit.'

The thought of having to front it out to a group of strangers when I start my degree in classics at UCL is like preparing to climb Everest.

Exhausting .

'Let's go shopping tomorrow,' she said. 'It's literally weeks till you start. There's so much to—'

'Mum,' I sighed, concentrating on not getting in any way emotional. 'Can we talk about this another time . . . *Please?*'

Though I couldn't see it, I knew her mouth was a little pinched now.

'Yes, Val,' Dad said. 'Let's just deal with one thing at a time, shall we? Lo is trying to come to terms with something . . .' Poor Dad, as clueless with feelings in his own way as Mum, hesitated, trying to find the right words.

'Huck's dead,' Jake supplied simply. 'She's not going to want to go to uni now . . . is she?'

I looked up, both surprised at Jake's fluky emotional intelligence, and intrigued by the possibility of shelving uni for another year.'

'Oh, Jake,' Mum said wearily. 'Life goes on, sweetheart. It will do your sister good to reinvent herself with a whole new group of friends. And I hear there are some marvellous social activities for girls of her . . . background at University College London.' She dropped her napkin, revving up for some more tactless social climbing advice. 'Forget about halls. You don't want to live anywhere so squalid just now. We'll need to buy you a nice flat. Somewhere pretty and safe.'

Reinvent myself? Somewhere pretty and safe? Was this woman an alien?

'Valerie,' Dad cautioned. 'It's too soon. We haven't even had the funeral yet. Give the poor girl a chance.'

There was a clipped silence.

'Fine. Of course.' Mum rose from the table. As I lifted my head, I couldn't help noticing the perfect uncreased expanse of Yves Saint Laurent over her non-existent stomach. It depressed me. It made me want to scream.

Imagine – screaming, right now?

If I hadn't felt like sticking my fork in my eye, I would have laughed.

'Please,' I said, my head starting to rush. 'I can't . . . I can't think about that now. I just want to . . . sleep.'

I stood, coming face to face with my mother across the table.

To her credit, she didn't look away. Though the sight of me so . . . so unlike me must have repelled her.

'Lois . . .' she began uncomfortably. 'I do know . . . Your father and I are very sorry . . . for your distress. I just want to do the right thing. The sensible thing . . .' Her eyes flickered. She must be desperate to end this scene. It was everything she abhorred.

'I know,' I said, putting her out of her agony. 'I just need some time.'

As I walked up the staircase to the East Wing of our large Neo-Georgian mansion, I felt bad. Bad because my boyfriend's death had upset my mother's applecart, bad that my dad had no idea what to say or do to make it better for me and bad because, for the first time in a long time, I was on my own. Suddenly the things Valerie had crammed my life with as one giant distraction from real life were lying dead by the roadside, leaving me ill-equipped. I knew the best methods of revision for any exam you can name, I can tell a cheap pedicure a mile away, I can hold my own in a room full of people who don't care about me. I even have a passing knowledge of the stock exchange, know the right way to make a cup of tea (milk in afterwards, never before) and the correct hemline (to the millimetre) for this season. What I don't know how to do is deal with misfortune, with tragedy, with unhappiness. With being a victim. With death.

With losing the only thing I ever really cared about.

I pick at the cold meat and cheese on my breakfast plate. Mrs Diaz, who runs the hostel, passes by my table with fresh coffee and glances down at my untouched food.

'You not hungry?' She shakes her head but gives me a friendly smile. 'Is all bad news about this poor boy who dies. He was friend of yours?'

It's my turn to shake my head. 'Not exactly . . . I met him a couple of times, but . . .'

Mrs Diaz makes a clucking sound in the roof of her mouth. 'These boys,' she says wearily. 'They always take the drugs too far . . .'

'Well, I don't know if it was drugs—' I begin, holding out my cup for a refill.

'Is always that.' She puts down her coffee pot and parks her derrière on the seat opposite me. 'Listen, I have these boys staying here. And this one, this one that has passed, I

knew the type. He so alive . . . so alive it is not quite right.'
She stares at me, her really quite nice brown eyes penetrating
mine like a cobra.

'Alive . . .' I say slowly, not exactly sure what she's
getting at.

'I have three boys,' she says, straightening up proudly.
'Good boys. But let me tell you . . . when they are teenage,
they asleep. All the time. I can't get them to move!'

I am laughing now. 'True. We do like our sleep. But I
thought that Huck was just naturally . . . exuberant.'

She knits her eyebrows together at this word, but shrugs.
'I am just saying. Is not normal. And you know . . .' She
leans forward. 'I did not like the behaviour with the girls.'
Mrs Diaz sniffs. 'Is not respectful.'

I have a mouthful of coffee, which I swallow quickly.
'What girls?'

'Every night a different *chica* – drinking and dancing
and smoking . . . and all sorts.'

'Boys will be boys,' I reply evenly.

'Heh?' She is definitely confused by that one, and rises,
clutching her coffee pot. 'I not wish death on another.' She
crosses herself one-handed. 'But some boys should learn to
keep in the trousers and respect a woman. Is all I'm
saying . . . You seem like a good boy. Very good boy. Your
mother pleased with you, I think.'

I am smiling at her as she moves off to attend to a couple
sitting across the room, but frankly the notion that my
mother is pleased with me does not fill me with as much

comfort as it does Mrs D. In fact, I can't help believing that good boys finish last. And that a touch of the bad boy would do me no harm at all.

As I finish my drink and pick up my small rucksack, I remind myself of my vow to try and get a life now that Syd and Jamal have gone back home. Maybe get a job somewhere. I'll meet new people. Become 'alive'. Just until I have to get serious with my studies in a few weeks' time.

As I head out into the bright Spanish sunshine, I catch sight of a bus heading for out of town. Maybe it will take me somewhere further down the coast where I can ask around for work. Maybe I will just lie on the beach and work on my tan. I pick up speed as the bus slows to a stop and let an old lady with a giant shopper on wheels climb aboard. Catching up with her, I automatically reach out, pick up her shopper and heft it up the short staircase and on board.

The old woman shuffles to sit on the front seat, and as the bus door slides shut, reaches out one tiny brown hand and squeezes my cheek.

'Good boy,' she says, giving me a gummy smile. 'Very good boy.'

9

Eloise

'Adorable fascinator,' whispers Jessica as she leans in closer for a better look. 'It's so cute, it actually looks like a real orchid.'

'It is a real orchid,' I say absently.

Jessica frowns. 'Real? One you picked yourself?'

'One my mother ordered from the local McQ,' I answer, unable to keep the sigh out of my voice. I cast my gaze around the churchyard and see lots of people I don't recognize. Except for Carlo and his estranged wife, Helena. Huck's mum and dad.

'Oh, look at Carlo.' Jessica puts a little wobble into her tone. 'He looks so . . . so . . . .'

'Numb?' I close my eyes. 'I can hardly bring myself to talk to him. He must be devastated. He and Huck were so close.'

Typically insensitive, Jessica ignores this remark. 'The

old man's not bad looking, is he?' she says, sounding distinctly less wobbly. 'Like George Clooney. I see where Huck got his looks from.'

I say nothing, but my eyes are rolling as I turn away from her. All of a sudden Jessica's perfume smells overpowering. Predatory.

The service has been pretty much as expected. Mostly formal, endless Catholic hymns on the insistence of Isabella, Huck's formidable grandmother and the boss of the Rafael family. There had been moments of heart-wrenching sadness. Like when Huck's younger sister Elena walked behind his coffin holding a bouquet of sharply crimson bougainvilleas. At ten years old, she is shaping up to be as physically beautiful as her brother, her long crinkly brown hair falling prettily down her back, her plain white cotton dress contrasting becomingly with her dusky skin. And Helena, her head bent in silent sobbing. Carlo, his head lifted high, but his eyes without their sparkle. As the coffin passes by, I see him close those eyes, a look of sheer pain cross his face; he runs his strong artist's hands through his wild brown hair, already flecked with grey.

The Rafael family have come across continents, from all corners of the world, to pay respects to the prodigal boy, the shining jewel in their crown.

Huck is . . . was . . . certainly beloved, I reflect. Beloved by all.

Not for the first time I feel the weight of his popularity, of all those who clamour for a piece of him. And this time

I feel as though I have surrendered for good the one piece of him that belonged to me.

To say I feel insignificant is woefully understating it.

My spirits dip lower as I spot my mother heading towards me, ostentatiously clad in black Prada and a pair of eight-hundred-pound patent Louboutins, stamping across the springy grass.

I read somewhere that graveyards and cemeteries always have the springiest grass. Watching Mum's loudspeaker shoes march in my direction, I have a vision of her sinking, further and further, into the earth. Until she disappears.

'Are you OK, sweetheart?' She takes my arm, nods at Jessica and pulls me, just a bit too forcefully, to one side.

'Awesome.' The sarcasm – a new interactive mode with my mother – is heavy.

Mum cocks her head to one side, her eyes drifting down, taking in my shockingly out-of-season Burberry Prorsum tea dress and my comfortable but frumpy French Sole ballet flats.

'I think you've made the right decision dressing low key,' she nods. 'I understand. It's respectful. You don't want to be the centre of attention. This is a family time.' Mum's eyes move around to watch as Carlo, Helena, Isabella and Elena walk past in a daze.

'Just look at them,' she breathes. 'A walking Ralph Lauren advert.'

My heavy sigh is audible. Not just to my mum and to Jessica, but possibly to the whole of the parish.

Mum looks awkward. She has mistaken my loathing of her at this moment for the pain of loss. Don't get me wrong, that's in there too. In spades. But just at this particular time my emotional focus is all about my mother. I realize I have never fully taken in the depths of her shallowness. Clever she may be, but emotionally intelligent she is not.

A hand gently takes hold of my arm. I turn to see Helena at my side. Her pale English colouring only accents what she must be going through right now. As she lifts her head I see those eyes. Huck's green eyes, staring into mine.

'Mrs Rafael,' I say, stepping as far away from my mother as I can. 'How are you?'

She smiles wearily, and I see the shadows under her eyes.

'Not so good. I can't believe I am here . . . It seems so wrong.'

I nod, and slide my arm around her. She looks so small, like a pale, auburn-haired child. 'Let's sit.' I gesture at a bench over by the entrance to the churchyard.

Helena allows me to escort her over to the seat. She removes her hat and places it on her lap. She clasps her hands together, staring down at them, lost.

I decide not to speak. Sometimes there aren't really words. So I am surprised when it is Helena who turns to me first.

'You knew Huck well, didn't you?' she asks innocently.

I frown at her. She knows we'd been together for four

years; of course I knew Huck well. 'As well as you can know your boyfriend,' I reply emphatically.

Helena holds my gaze for a moment, before she takes a breath.

'He was a lovely boy. But he was . . . complicated.'

I smile, though I'm not sure I know what she means.

She registers my confusion; I can tell by the way she clears her throat, preparing to explain further.

'I mean . . . He is like his father. Curious, dynamic . . . restless.'

'Restless?' I feel a little tick in the corner of my eye. I recognize it as my response to insecurity.

'Yes. He experiments. He discovers . . .'

If I was confused before, I am bewildered now. But then Helena has just lost her beloved boy. Possibly she is confused herself. Shock does that, I've heard.

Out of the corner of my eye I see Carlo approaching. I am half relieved, half frustrated at his intrusion. I can see Helena is keen to say her piece.

'Don't listen to me,' she says, gripping my arm. 'I'm just thinking too much.' She stands, still holding my hand, and then suddenly her grip on it strengthens. And I think she's going to say something, but whatever it is, she glances quickly at Carlo who has arrived at her side and gives me a warm smile instead.

'He was so fond of you,' Carlo tells me. 'You were definitely one of his favourite people.'

I stare up at them, the September sun making me squint.

And I am glad of it, because I have no idea how to respond.

Fond of me? One of his favourite people? What does *that* mean?

But Carlo moves to block the sun and I manage to smile back. They're grieving; they're not going to be making much sense right now.

That's the most comfortable explanation anyway.

Still, I stay sitting on the bench as I watch them walk away, feeling more insignificant than ever. Helena's words tumble inside my head, and Carlo's parting remark . . . It sends a dull pain shooting through to the heart of me.

If Huck were here now he'd be holding my hand, kissing the tender part of my neck, just by my ear, telling me that of course he loved me more than anyone. That he and I were perfect together, that my eyes, my hair, my body were all he could think about when we were apart. That he could spend hours just staring at me, that no one else had made him feel this way.

Huck always knew what to say to make things better. He always seemed to have the answer. No one else could talk my anxieties away like Huck.

'Huck,' I whispered. 'I need you to tell me you love me.'

After the bee incident, I found myself loitering . . . staying just a little too long in the canteen, waiting . . . waiting to see Huck, walk past him with a cool smile, not caring one bit if he smiled back or not . . .

This was easier said than put into practice. For one

thing I could never shake off my entourage. Jessica, Destiny and Laura had their crush radar on red alert, and they seemed to be everywhere, at all times. Eyes darting along with mine, ready with a quick observation, ready to thwart any sign of moping.

'He's obviously a player,' Jessica had said one afternoon a couple of weeks after Bee-gate. 'Just look at him, lapping up those Year Eight twits and their silly plaited fringes.'

I glanced over at a couple of pretty girls in Jake's year – Ellie and Snow (yes, I know, Snow), wannabe bohemians, who managed to work festival chic into their regulation school uniforms. Huck was laughing at something Ellie was saying, but it looked friendly, not predatory. He was careful, I saw, never to stand too close, to keep his smile scattered equally between the two of them, laid-back, just friendly.

'If by lapping it up you mean not behaving like the rest of the jackass boys in this school, then yes, you have a point,' I said, feigning a yawn. 'Not that it has anything to do with us.'

'Of course not,' Jessica said with light sarcasm. 'Not us. Not me, Dest and Laura . . . But you . . .' She waved a forkful of goat's cheese salad in the air. 'You, I am not so sure.'

'Admit it, Lo,' Destiny chipped in, popping the last of her burger in her mouth. 'You luuuurve him.'

'Oh, seriously!' I rolled my eyes, perhaps a little too dramatically. 'I don't care if he has a foursome with those two and Miss Dobbs.' OK. That had been a ridiculous retort, and only provoked the three witches further.

'Can't kid a kidder,' Jessica told me, scrunching up her napkin. 'You've fallen for his Latino charms, Lois. Don't try and deny it.'

My mouth was open to unleash another over-the-top retort when I caught his eye and he smiled, a different smile, right at me.

'I knew it,' said Laura softly. 'You and him. There is something . . .'

I wanted to say, 'Shut up!' or 'As if!' or another exclamation along those lines, but I couldn't get the words out of my mouth. I mean, how often does this happen? That you have this kind of unspoken connection with someone. A connection that makes you know. Just know. That something is 'going on'. That syrupy, honey feeling that seeps through you, a sort of lazy butterfly, just taking its time to flutter around inside you, and rest on your heart. It's that intangible, that irrational, that delicious feeling of rightness. Ladies, when you feel it, just savour it, because it's the best feeling in the world.

But, for now, back to 1.45 in the canteen, and Huck is heading straight towards me.

'Lois,' Jessica says, full of warning. 'Watch yourself. That boy knows exactly what he's doing.'

I heard her words. On some level I filed them away, but on a whole other, primal level I tossed them aside as irrelevant.

'So do I,' I said softly, my eyes still locked on to Huck's. Before the royal entourage had time to speak, Huck was in front of me. If I were another girl, I would be coyly looking down at the canteen floor, flushed and nervous. But I'd learned my lesson from Bee-gate. To blush once is careless. To blush twice is . . . well, simply not how this was going to go.

Ignoring my friends, I rose, pushing aside the tray of barely edible canteen snacks and stood, my head level with his shoulders. I gazed up at him.

'You took your time,' I told him, giving my best impish smile. 'But you're here now, that's the main thing.'

It was a gamble. Huck could decide that a girl with such a blatant sense of self-entitlement was not what he wanted. He could have frowned and walked away. But it was like my mother always said ad nauseam: confidence is everything. Boys want to know you're willing to take a risk, and look like you couldn't care less if it backfires on you.

'My dad has a private view on Saturday,' Huck said huskily. 'He's showing his new collection of oils. Would you do me the honour of being my plus one?'

He smiled, relaxed and casual, turning his head ever so slightly to nod in acknowledgement of the girls behind me. I couldn't see Jessica's face, but I was willing to bet it had a new expression. Blindsided.

'I'll need to check,' I said slowly. 'But that could be an option. What sort of time and what's the dress code?'

'Eight,' said Huck, his eyes firmly back on mine. 'And it doesn't matter what you wear. As you well know.'

As I opened my mouth a little, very nearly blushing (God forbid!), Huck turned to go back to his friends, adding over his shoulder, 'See you Saturday at seven thirty. I'll pick you up on the bike.'

'OK.' I watched him go. Damn, falling at the last hurdle. I waited a beat before turning back to face my friends.

'Way to play it,' Jessica nodded. 'Though you messed up at the last minute.'

'Whatever.' I finally allowed myself to feel excitement. This just gets even better. His dad is an artist. Of course! Huck would never be the offspring of an accountant.

Huck collected me on his bike. Literally, his pushbike. I saw him coming from the window seat of the big bay window that looks over our drive. I rushed out so that my mother wouldn't see him.

And we rode all the way to Carlo's studio. Oh, I felt very Katharine Ross in *Butch Cassidy and the Sundance Kid*. And though Huck wasn't exactly my Paul Newman, he was pretty damn near it. Offbeat, carefree, exciting.

As we passed by Laura's mum putting money into a parking meter on the high street, I hid my face in Huck's back. I inhaled the scent of Huck. A hint of washing powder and paint. I would come to know this smell. Know it, and make it as necessary to me as the air I breathed every day.

'You'll like my pappy,' Huck said as he dismounted, and

his beautiful messy brown hair blew cinematically in the breeze. 'Every woman likes my pappy.'

So I went from a girl to a woman. I was hardly a woman. I was a fourteen-year-old ingénue (yes, I actually called myself that). But Huck had this way of making you older, more substantial, more significant than you knew, deep down, you really were.

Everything that had come before. All those things that had seemed so very important just faded away in that moment.

Huck's dad Carlo was – is – nothing like my father. He smiles a lot, he hugs, often, and his idea of parenting is just to leave his kids alone. Elena and Huck had that relaxed, innately confident air of kids who have never been told that they need to be better, smarter, prettier than they are already. When we walked in, Carlo handed us both a beer, as though it was lemonade. At home I was allowed wine – one glass only – on family occasions, though alcohol brought my mother out in hives. She was careful only ever to take a sip and only ever of white or translucent liquid, on account of the heinous calorie content. As her protégé, I had always followed suit. But walking into Carlo's informal private view was like walking into Narnia, or at least another, magical world. Things tasted different; I felt different. I relaxed.

Believe me when I say, this was the biggest revelation. That I could relax.

'So, Eloise.' Huck pulled me over to a long wooden sofa

thing, covered in comfortable bright cushions. 'What is with these friends of yours? They seem a little over-protective. Do you have fun with them?'

Instinctively I came to their defence. 'Of course, they're my best friends.' I hesitated, trying to think of a time when we had fun that wasn't at somebody else's expense. 'We have a lot in common.'

Huck raised an eyebrow. I tried not to quake a little at just how organically perfect he was. 'Like what?' he asked.

'Well, our mothers are friends, we like clothes, we . . .' I trailed off. I had pretty much run out of things that bonded me with Destiny, Laura and Jessica. I could have said, 'We enjoy feeling superior to all the other girls at school', but something told me that Huck wouldn't consider this a positive attribute. I shrugged instead, pulling my Marni sweater over my new Hoss capri pants. I could feel his eyes on me, trying to get the measure of me.

'You know, Eloise,' Huck reached out slowly and caught hold of a carefully GHDd blonde lock, tucking it behind my ear, 'I think you want to escape from these friends of yours. I think behind all this . . . this money and noses in the air thing –' He grinned at the startled look on my face. '– I think there is another, sweeter girl waiting to let go . . .'

'There is?' I stared at him. I had no idea what he was talking about. Another me? Let go? I had spent so long keeping a lid on my feelings and never looking and performing less than perfectly that the notion of letting go was not just strange, but terrifying.

Huck straightened up and then casually pulled me closer to him, wrapping his arm around my shoulders, his fingertips softly rubbing at my arm.

It was like stepping into a hot bath after being out in the cold. Warmth was spreading deliciously through every part of me, and a medley of small fireworks was sparking in my stomach.

Perhaps letting go wasn't so terrifying after all?

10
Eloise

After I urge my parents to leave the wake in Dad's Lexus so that I can make my own way home, Jessica and Destiny insist on walking me back to Chateau Campbell-Taylor claiming I 'shouldn't be alone at a time like this'. But I know they secretly want to see for themselves how much I have let myself go since Huck's death. Jessica had complimented me on my orchid earlier, sure, but I had seen the disapproval in her eyes at my Burberry failure. Jessica never wears anything more than six months old. Clothes make her itch once they're out of season.

'Are you coping?' she barks in a schoolmarm voice as she marches alongside me in sky-high Jimmy Choos. 'I don't think you're coping.'

'Jessica,' says Destiny in a warning tone. 'For heaven's sake, girl, she's just buried the love of her life.'

Jessica makes a noise that sounds like a snort, though

she quickly coughs to conceal it. 'Of course . . . But life does go on, you know, Lois. Huck wouldn't want you to start shopping at Primark now, would he?'

Huck wouldn't have cared less. At least, he always gave the impression that these things didn't matter to him. But I can't help remembering his vintage Rolex and the APC jeans he had at least five pairs of. Huck *looked* as though he couldn't care less about fashion, but nothing he owned was cheap. It was just cleverly disguised. Scruffy chic.

'Hmmm,' I grunt, irritated by this thought somehow. 'I suppose.'

Back at the house my mother is on the phone to the decorators in our large study. We're having a pool house built adjacent to our large twenty-metre swimming pool. Jake and I are competing to be the one to move in to that pool house when it's done. The further away from the parents the better as far as we're both concerned. Or I was. Now I hardly have the energy to fight Jake for it.

'It's the wrong colour,' Mum is saying, frowning at her Chanel fingernails. 'I quite clearly said oyster pink, not . . . peach.' She lifts her head and spots Jessica, Destiny and me wandering into the room. Jessica is already inspecting a new Missoni cushion. 'Darling.' Mum looks down at my ballet flats. 'Please take those ghastly shoes off. Hello, girls.' She gives Destiny her version of a friendly smile, though it is actually more like a skeleton's rictus grin. Scary.

'Your mother is back in business, I see,' Destiny whispers. 'Time nor Valerie stop for no funeral.'

I raise a smile at this, looking sideways at my friend. Destiny can almost be perceptive at times.

'Yup,' I say, tired. 'She's a dynamo all right.'

My mother finally hangs up. 'Bloody builders.' She picks up a glass of what looks like gin and tonic, but, knowing my mother, is probably top-of-the-range sparkling mineral water. She takes a sip, leaning carefully back against her new Swedish-design sofa. 'What a day. I can't bear those long Catholic funerals. So intense.' She shuts her eyes for a thirty-second Valerie nap.

Even Jessica looks vaguely shocked at this insensitivity. Destiny gives my hand a brief squeeze. When Mum opens her eyes again, she finds the three of us just staring at her like three curious crows.

She frowns, her selfishness possibly dawning on her.

'How are you feeling, sweetheart?' she asks unconvincingly. 'Horrid day for you.' She sits up. 'I must say, Helena Rafael is a strange woman. All that sobbing. I know it's a terribly sad thing, burying your son, but that kind of public display . . .'

I suddenly feel acutely embarrassed about my mum. This has gone beyond self-contained. It's practically sociopathic.

I can't think of anything to say that isn't rude and confrontational, so I content myself with nodding, pursed-lipped, at a space just above her head.

The silence that follows tells me that Jessica and Destiny are pretty shocked too.

'Shall we go hang out in your bedroom?' Jessica says in a high-pitched, fake-breezy voice. 'Listen to CDs or something?' She looks at me with almost circular eyes.

'Sure.' It has to be better than this situation, at least I think. I cast my mother my best angry look, positively animated for me. As usual, Valerie is thinking of something else already and she barely registers it.

'Have fun,' she murmurs inappropriately.

Upstairs Jessica closes my bedroom door before she and Destiny take a minute to look around.

'God alive!' Jessica breathes. 'It's a pigsty, Lo!' She moves towards the bed, tugging at the grubby duvet heaped in the centre of the bed. 'Have the cleaners resigned or something? I can't believe Lady Penelope would allow this to happen.'

Destiny holds her breath, but she can't help the snigger that escapes her mouth at these words, and following Jessica's horrified gaze around the rest of the mess, I can't help the hysteria that is shaking the top half of my body. Before I know it I let out a shriek of laughter.

'I know,' I manage to say, trying to get a breath. 'Lady Penelope would have a stroke if she saw it.' I look from Jessica to Destiny. 'Luckily, she hasn't been allowed in here for nearly three weeks. I lock it every time I leave.'

'Why?' Jessica frowns. 'And why would you want to sleep in this crap?'

I stop laughing. They are staring at me, obviously

freaked out by the new Eloise they see before them.

'It matches my state of mind,' I say at last. 'You know, totally and utterly rubbish.' I kick at a bundle of tights on the floor. 'Just . . . nothing. I feel like nothing matters, and I am nothing, and this . . .' I stretch out my arms, as though to encompass the whole of my room, 'all this stuff, so much of it . . . it just doesn't mean anything.'

Destiny has a look of shock on her face, though I can see that she is intrigued. Jessica, however, is out-and-out horrified.

'Shall I get someone?' she says slowly, carefully. 'Lois . . . I don't think this is healthy.' I can see Destiny making some kind of eye code with her, but it doesn't bother me.

'I'm so tired.' I move to the bed and flop down on the heap of bedding. 'Just so tired I can't think.'

'You want to rest, honey.' It's Destiny. Softer, more maternal than Jessica. I look up and see her pretty features, anxious. She perches by my feet and attempts to pull the duvet out from under me. She half succeeds, in spite of the kind of rigor mortis effect my mood is having on my body, and manages to wrap enough of it over me. 'Sshhh, now. Maybe have a sleep. It will all be better when you wake up.'

I know this is unlikely to be the case, but Destiny is trying to be kind. Jessica, on the other hand, has never looked more awkward.

'It's OK, just leave me,' I tell them. 'I'm sorry.'

'I think we should let Valerie know,' says Jessica. 'This needs to be sorted out. You can't go on like this.'

'I'll be fine.' I look up at them through hazy eyes, and inch the duvet up to my chin. My legs are sticking out of the end, dangling over the bed, and I am pretty sure I'm still wearing those ballet flats. I am in what you might call a pretty undignified position.

'You look really quite romantic actually,' says Jessica, cocking her head to one side. 'Like a dying heroine.'

'Jessica,' hisses Destiny. '*So* not an appropriate description. Don't you ever take a rest from the aesthetics of a situation?'

I close my eyes. 'You may leave,' I say regally. 'I'll call you.'

'You'd better.' Destiny tugs at a toe. 'I'm worried about you, girl. I didn't realize how hard this has knocked you. We should have been here more these last two weeks.'

'I totally would have been here, but the dogs . . . what with my parents being away for a month, I can't leave Pixie and Clover for long, and what with your mother's allergies . . .' Jessica sighs.

Those hideous pugs of her parents' rule the household. But I am beginning to wonder whether in fact Jessica and I were swapped at birth, and Brenda has been raising the wrong child all these years. If it weren't for the Malay-Swedish thing I'd look into it further. Jessica seems so much more Valerie's child than I do right now.

Finally they're gone and I lie listening to the sound of the birds. It's becoming a familiar sound. I seem to have spent my life in my bedroom, pigsty that it is. I try and Mind Wash, but my ability to do this has dwindled increasingly over the weeks and it isn't working on this kind of stuff. Loss, emptiness, loathing . . .

A spear of intense feeling shoots through me and I sit up in bed. Pain, but anger too. At my family . . . my so-called best friends. I now understand the meaning of the term 'wretched'.

My phone beeps, signalling a message. I take my time to view it, thinking it can only be Laura or possibly one of the girls who've just left, checking that I haven't killed myself yet.

But the name popping up on the screen jolts me wider awake.

Natalie.

Hey Lola, long time. My mum says she saw the funeral procession going past our house this morning. So sorry for your loss. Thinking of you. If you need to talk, call me. Love Nat.

The simplicity, the kindness in her message, and her using my childhood name, Lola, seems to unleash something that has been lurking inside of me for a long time. Two fat tears roll down my cheeks. And suddenly the reality of my future dawns on me, bright and clear. I stare at Natalie's words. I desperately want to talk to someone who cares. Someone who hasn't got one eye on my appearance and the other wary eye on an escape. I think of Natalie's sweet rounded face, her awkward, mismatched dress sense. Her cheap Forever 21 jeans. I smile.

But I can't reply. That would be totally using her. She deserves better than a friend like me.

Instead I go back through my phone and find Huck's number again.

Before I know it I am touching the New Message icon and starting to type.

What are you doing? Missing me? I wish you were here.
Love always, Lo.

Daniel

Back at the hostel I review the day's events. The first day of the rest of my life.

I took a train first thing in the morning to the nearest coastal village I could find on the map, a small stretch of nearly uncorrupted beach about a hundred and fifty miles from Madrid. I found myself a spot to sit and consider things and to achieve the first on my list of things I have never attempted. Get a real tan. The truth is I just stared into the sea, removed my trainers and my T-shirt, and lay back, the sun beating down on my face. It was still a novelty for me to be here alone, without Syd talking a mile a minute, pointing out every fit girl who passed, or Jamal's draining habit of analysing everything – from the origins of sand to the average hourly wage of a local bar worker.

It felt good not to talk, or think . . . though I couldn't help running bits of Mrs Diaz's conversation through my sleepy head. I know I can't help being innately polite and chivalrous. It is something that my karate-kicking mother terrorized into me from an early age. Mrs Levenson had no time for cool kids, or smart-arse boys. She wanted her boy to be the boy a girl would be proud to take home to her mother. She refuses to acknowledge that this renders that boy utterly undesirable to most girls in the twenty-first century. My mum is a 1950s housewife with a black belt.

I realized that years of ingrained training would be difficult to undo, and I didn't want a personality overhaul, I just wanted to be . . . less nice.

Having had my think for the day, I was drifting off when I felt a hand shaking my shoulder. I opened one eye. A tall guy in his thirties wearing a faded wife-beater and covered in tattoos was looming over me.

I sat up quickly, reaching for my T-shirt.

'You can't be here,' he said in heavily accented English.

'No?' Come to think of it, I was the only person on this beach. I got to my feet, hastily putting on my trainers.

'Is dangerous,' the man went on. 'The sea. Dangerous. The tides very strong. Not safe for a boy like you.'

A boy like me. Why did this make a little rebellion, finally, course through my veins? I think of Mrs Diaz's words earlier this morning. She, like everyone else in the world, assumes I am wetter than the Mediterranean Sea.

'You've been out there?' I turned to look at the admittedly aggressive waves.

The man's eyebrows shot up, and for a moment

he looked angry, but then his lips widened and he gave me a grin. His teeth were blindingly white against his dark skin.

'I have been out there.' He puffed out his chest a little. 'But I am a man, my friend. And a strong swimmer. I can handle this sea.' He nodded to reinforce this.

'I'll be fine,' I said evenly. 'I'm a strong swimmer too.' There is some truth in this. I was the under-fourteens champion at the 1000 metres at school. But that was in a heavily chlorinated swimming pool with the tidal strength of a puddle. But I can swim. I glanced quickly at my bare top, half noting that I have something resembling a muscular physique.

He flared his nostrils, digging his hands into his pockets. 'Kids,' he said wearily. 'You think you know it all, heh? You like taking the risks, heh?'

It dawned on me in that moment that I have never really taken a risk in my life. Not a proper one. Not an exciting risk. I had no wish to drown on a remote Spanish beach, far from my friends and family. But I really needed to do something about my clean-cut image.

'I'd kind of like to stay here,' I told him. 'For a bit. I need some time to think.' I didn't imagine he had any idea what I was talking about, but his expression softened, in a manly way, a bit of defensiveness evaporating.

'Up to you.' He threw out his hands, gave me long look and then turned to walk away.

For a second I felt like running after him. I didn't need

to swim a rough sea to prove myself. Not to him. Not to anyone.

But I didn't move. There's a mantra that life coaches use to strengthen the spirit: *Do something every day that scares you.* This always seemed quite idiotic advice. I mean, why? Why deliberately scare yourself? But now I was starting to get it.

'Bye then,' I said bravely to his retreating back. He didn't turn round. I just hoped he was going to some vantage point where he could come to my aid if I did actually start to drown.

I got as far as a large piece of beach wood when the not-so-gentle tide really began to kick in. I was trying to get my breath and swim at the same time, but the waves hitting me violently in the face were tough. After a minute, I plunged myself under; it was easier beneath the waves, you knew where you were with your breathing, and below the waterline I glimpsed, for a few seconds at least, some spectacular fish. It was like being in an aquarium, floating and observing the exotic and possibly highly dangerous marine life. I could feel my eyes stinging, and I knew I would have to swim up and confront the beast of the current again. I launched myself up and was hit squarely in the face by the biggest, fiercest wave yet. I swallowed a mouthful of salty, sour water. I was not enjoying myself at all. But I *was* scared. Mission accomplished. I honestly did not know how, or if, I could swim back to the shore. The sea felt like a pair of giant slippery hands, grabbing me, pulling me forward when I tried to go back.

I wondered briefly if the man in the vest was watching me. If so, I bet he was smirking to himself. I must have looked a proper fool.

Then something took hold of me. It was as though my entire reservoir of stamina clubbed together to pull me out of this hole. For ten seconds the waves retreated and I seized the chance to turn. I made it just as I felt a huge wall of water rolling up my back. It obscured my sight but I kept going, thrashing like a wild animal; my legs kicked into super-power mode and I scissored forwards, using my arms to shovel the sea to either side.

It seemed to take hours to move even a metre; my throat was sore and one ear was blocked. I felt possibly the most uncomfortable I had ever felt in my life. I kept myself going by imagining the sun, the dry clothes waiting for me. My bed back at the hostel. Dry land.

Eventually, breathing so loudly I felt like I'd run a marathon, my feet touched the sea bed and I waded forward, closer and closer to the beach.

When I reached it I collapsed in on myself, my head upside down level with my chest, and I swear I could see my heart jumping through my skin.

When I looked up again I saw four pairs of brown skinny legs in front of me. Lifting my head I came face to face with a line-up of ten-year-old local boys. I straightened up, rubbing at my wet hair, prepared for an onslaught of jeering. But instead they were grinning, and then one by one they started to clap, slowly, chanting something in Spanish I couldn't understand but which I chose to hear as a plaudit, and not the kind of insult football fans sing at the enemy team.

I took a moment to enjoy the novelty, and then I spotted the tattooed man behind them, holding something in his hand. He was looking at me, his expression difficult to read. He cuffed one of the boys lightly round the head.

'Get out of here,' he told them, shaking his head as they scarpered.

I guessed it was time for him to give me a dressing down. I didn't really care; I was just thankful to be alive.

'Very stupid,' he said gruffly. 'Very dangerous.' He took a step closer and chucked the thing he had been holding at me. It was a towel with a feminine flower pattern on it. He smirked as I rubbed my wet hair and wiped the last of the sea off my chest and stood up. Then he moved closer, reached out and tousled my hair.

'You are man now, heh?' he said, raising an eyebrow. 'But never do that again.' And with that, he took the towel off me, turned and strolled up the beach as though he were taking a leisurely walk through the English countryside.

It seems unreal now, as I sit on my hostel bed, putting on clean socks after an hour-long shower. But I think I can see the appeal of extreme sports after all. There is no satisfactory way to describe the feeling of escaping drowning by the skin of your teeth. The sheer happiness of landing on safe ground and allowing yourself to experience what you have just done, but without actually still doing it. I feel dazed, bone-tired, but grateful, and alive.

I lie back, preparing for a long sleep, when my phone beeps. But when I check it, there's no text, no missed call, no voicemail alert. I frown, wondering if my blocked ear is playing tricks on me. But then I hear it again, and realize it isn't coming from my phone.

I am just about to call Mrs Diaz for the number of a local doctor, when I remember. That phone, the one I found under the bed. I charged it up by mistake, thinking it was mine, then chucked it in my large suitcase when I realized it wasn't. Vaguely curious I get up and retrieve it. There's a message from someone called Lo.

I hesitate for a minute. The good boy in me is uncomfortable invading somebody's privacy. But the curious human in me is unable to resist. I click on to the text and stare down at the message on the screen:

What are you doing? Missing me? I wish you were here. Love always, Lo.

OK, so I have just invaded this person's – I am assuming it is a girl's – privacy. It's an intimate message, sent to someone who is probably at this minute missing this girl too. Except he doesn't know about this, heartfelt cry through cyberspace.

I am jealous. All of a sudden my brave act of derring-do in tempestuous seas seems pathetic and pointless. Actually, it was a really stupid thing to do, and I will never tell anyone about it.

What really matters is written in those two sentences from Lo. Love, and feelings.

I take a swig of water, which is unpleasantly warm, and put my feet up on the bed. I should really try and find the owner of this phone. He could be married to this Lo person, he could be an investigative journalist here to infiltrate a drug ring and she worries about him. On the other hand, he could be a total jerk, running around this place with a different girl every night. He strings Lo along. She's probably pretty, but she's too into him. He wants to shake her off. This text message will be the straw that broke the camel's back. And he won't care.

Or Lo is in fact not a girl, but a somewhat clingy man, and maybe if I were his intended recipient I would be alienated by this show of neediness. Well, I wouldn't be, because I would just be grateful that someone like Lo cared about me that much.

I really need to try and find the owner of this phone.

I go to Contacts and search for other numbers. Something to give me a clue. But the list is empty except for this one number. I frown. This must be just a temporary, travelling phone, like the one I have.

I'll ask Mrs Diaz if anyone has come looking for it. If she

says no, then I guess whoever's phone this is isn't that bothered about finding it. They probably have another one by now.

I should also not think so much about these things.

But it's funny, when you're miles from home, and your friends have gone, and you've just done something that is exactly the kind of thing you would never normally do and that scared you into being a slightly different person, well, it's funny – because it makes you feel like you want to share it. And then it makes you feel melancholy because you don't have that one person to share stuff like that with. Well, not someone who'll listen without taking the piss out of you. Or in my mum's case, whack you over the head.

When I get down to reception, instead of the usual deathly quiet at this time of the evening I can hear some kind of party going on. Peeking through the slightly ajar door of the breakfast room I can see a group of ladies Mrs Diaz's age, swaying their hips to a loud salsa track. I spot Mrs D herself, clasping the head of a man at least fifteen centimetres shorter than she is to her ample bosom. Her eyes are shut; she is lost in music.

I am just about to creep up the stairs again and call it a night when there is a loud scratching sound, followed by a collective disappointed jeer from the ladies, and the record stops.

Mrs Diaz is shouting something in Spanish and then suddenly the door to the living room swings open.

'You, Mr Daniel!' I turn and give Mrs D a smile that hopefully tells her I am in a hurry.

'You can fix the record machine?' She stands, hands on hips. She looks like she's wearing my grandmother's curtains.

'I . . . uh . . . I'm not really an expert—' I begin.

She beckons at me, looking not unlike my mother when she is not *asking* but *telling* me to do something. 'Please try. You're a good boy.'

Here we go.

I follow her into the room and immediately her friends flock round me. They're dressed very colourfully too, and their red-lipsticked smiles give the impression of exotic birds in a state of some excitement.

'This is Daniel; he will mend the music,' Mrs Diaz announces in English. Putting a strong arm around me she propels me to the table where the ancient-looking record player looks like it has given up.

I glance at it, not having a clue about these things. But then I spot the plug is pulled a little out of its socket and I bend down and push it back in. Then I carefully place the needle back on the record, and the piano starts up.

When I turn, Mrs Diaz is giving me the kind of smile my grandmother gives me when I have got something down from a high shelf for her.

'Silly women,' says Mrs Diaz, shaking her head. 'We don't think of this . . .' Her friends nod gratefully, their bodies already starting to move.

'Join us!' shrieks Mrs Diaz, buffing away her small male dance partner and reaching out for my hands. 'Make an old woman happy, heh?'

'I . . . can't really dance,' I say, my body language surely screaming out that I really don't want to. 'And I'm meeting somebody . . . you know. I'm a bit late.'

She puts her head on one side and pouts a little. 'Is a shame,' she sighs.

After a second's thought, I relax and walk closer to her. 'Did someone come looking for a lost phone, Mrs Diaz?' I shout over the revelling. 'Anyone?'

She looks at me, a little confused, then purses her lips in thought. 'I . . . eeh . . . ah . . .' She is thinking about it. 'Uh. No,' she says finally, shrugging. 'Nobody looking for phone.'

'OK.' I smile and nod. 'Well, I'll be off . . . have a good night.'

As I walk out of the vibrating breakfast room I can a feel a weight coming off my shoulders. I can't account for my happiness at Mrs Diaz's response. Just how sad am I that I want to hold on to something that belongs to somebody else. Just because it makes me feel less lonely.

Pretty sad, huh?

12

Eloise

'Is this all there is?' My mother twitches the lace curtain at the window to one side. I can see her frown at the sight of three dumpsters and a mangy-looking cat asleep on the wall. She turns back to me and my dad. 'Just a room?'

'It's pretty standard, I think.' I sit down on the mattress and bounce up and down a little. 'Students don't need a lot of space. They're too busy having sex and taking drugs to bother about their living arrangements.'

My mother's face darkens and she looks at my dad, aghast.

'I'm joking, Mum.' I shake my head. We've been here ten minutes and the truth is that I know this room will make me want to jump out of the window. But my parents are making threatening noises about looking at property in nearby Marylebone. Metaphorical suffocation by elders is a worse prospect than death by bed bugs at this point.

'Reminds me of that song,' Dad says, scratching his head. '"Common People".'

I look up, caught between admiration that my dad has some hip left in him, and deeper shame that I am the living embodiment of the posh girl who wants to rough it for a while.

'It's not that bad,' I tell them. 'Really. I mean, I have to learn to stand on my own two feet. I've got to fit in here.'

'But you can fit in just as well in Paddington,' Mum says. 'Think of the grateful person who will occupy this . . . place . . . instead. Rather like private healthcare versus the NHS.'

'Valerie . . .' Dad starts. 'Part of the point of university is independence. I can see what Eloise means. She wants to feel she can survive by herself.'

Mum throws back her head and laughs. 'Don't be ridiculous, darling. We'll be paying two thousand pounds a month into her bank account. I don't see her protesting about that.'

'Well, actually—' I interject, but from the warning expression on her face I can see my mum isn't going to countenance a last-minute objection. '. . . Actually, that's really kind of you, Mum,' I finish lamely. 'I'm very grateful.'

'No need,' she says briskly, buttoning up her Donna Karan jacket. 'We have money and we will spend it on our children. I won't be able to sleep at night if you have to resort to a part-time job in some disgusting Soho bar.'

'No,' I say submissively. 'Of course you won't.'

'That's decided then.' Mum throws her Mulberry Bayswater over her shoulder. 'I did like that adorable little maisonette behind the station . . .'

But I can't go along with this. It will be social death. I have to make a stand.

'If I come to this university, then I want to live near the friends I won't make if I live in a bijou apartment a mile away.' I finally take a breath, my eyes boldly meeting those of my parents. 'See?'

Valerie looks murderous. Just when she'd nearly got her way. My dad on the other hand is giving me a proud smile.

There is a silence, as Dad gauges the level of fury in the room, before he speaks.

'I understand,' he says, turning cautiously to Mum. 'Honey, she does make a good point. I for one don't want my little princess to be lonely. Especially not after what she's been through.'

My father's emotional trump card has done the trick at last. Valerie lets out a long, melodramatic sigh.

'Fine. But I'm going to insist we have an industrial cleaner in here before you move in. It's filthy, and hideous. At least let me get a decorator to give it a makeover.'

I can't help laughing in her face. I think it might make the news. *Designer living for Students: Valerie Campbell-Taylor campaigns for change!*

'Good luck with that,' I say smiling. 'I'm pretty sure it's unheard of for student accommodation to be done out in Farrow & Ball.'

But then again, knowing my mother, she'll somehow make it happen.

Mum nods. 'Now that's settled,' she says, 'let's go and have lunch at Nobu. I could murder some decent sushi.'

The truth is that going to uni seems unreal. I know everyone feels like that before they go. Because it is this new phase of life, right? It's Stage Three. It's the time you spread your wings, open yourself up to experience. And in those three years, stuff goes on that no one else will ever know about. Like that film Brad Pitt made when he was young and kind of hot, only I secretly fancied the other guy, Edward Norton, and didn't admit it to my geek-averse friends.

But I am not ready. I am not ready for Stage Three. I wasn't done with Stage Two. I want it back. And come to think of it, I don't just want Stage Two back, I want a good part of Stage One back too.

After trailing Bond Street with my mother, I beg off shopping to be alone for a while. I've got to admit, she took it pretty well. She handed me a wad of cash, then gave me a loving air kiss and sent me off to the station.

I settle down in first class with a book and out of the corner of my eye I can see a couple about my age, snogging voraciously in standard class. I am torn between a miserable voyeuristic compulsion and of panic. I immediately drag my eyes from this taunting sight, crack the spine of my book and start reading. For a minute I wonder if I have chosen badly: *The Perks of Being a Wallflower* – not exactly 'perky'. But I want to be dragged under and float around in fictional dysfunction for a while. I have lost all optimism. I figure that the narrator, Charlie, might just be further down the road in this regard than I am. My weird logic convinces me that this is helpful, rather than depressing.

'Lo?' A familiar voice is saying my name. I keep my eyes rooted to the page. I am not in the mood. But the owner of the voice is hovering, really not gauging the situation at all.

After a good long thirty seconds or so I can't sustain my bad manners. I may be a bit superior, but good manners are crucial at all times.

I put a winning smile on my face and lift my head to see short mid-brown curly hair, and a pair of familiar blue eyes.

'Natalie!' I jerk forward and my book tumbles to the floor.

'Hey, allow me.' She bends and retrieves it, handing it to me with a nervous smile. 'I thought it was you. I recognized the hair.' She fiddles awkwardly with her fake leather bag.

'It's so good to *see* you,' I say. I shove the book in my Louis Vuitton holdall and scoot across on the seat. 'Sit down. Tell me all about what's been happening since . . .' I flounder with the unspoken truth – *since we were eight and I mysteriously dropped you.*

Natalie kindly lets this go by. She flumps down heavily beside me, adjusting her polka-dot skirt self-consciously. 'I can only stay a minute.' She waves a ticket at me. 'I'm in standard class.'

'Oh . . .' I grimace, automatically reaching for my purse inside my holdall. 'Let me get you an upgrade—'

'No.' Natalie's tone takes on a steely quality. 'No. I'm fine in standard. There's no need. But thanks.'

I wave my hand in a gesture of de nada. But brief tension has passed between us and for some reason I am desperate to defuse it. This time, though, I can't make it better with a smart remark. I have no idea what to say.

Natalie rubs at her knees, feigning interest in the grubby antimacassar on the seat opposite for a few seconds before she turns back to me.

'I'm really sorry . . . about . . . about your boyfriend,' she says. I see her blue eyes are sincere. It touches me that she is so awkward and so genuine. It feels real.

'Thank you.' I meet her eyes. 'That means a lot to me.'

'Really?' The surprise in her voice sways me a little. I can hardly blame her. I have ignored her for nearly ten years.

'Natalie . . .' I begin, trying to find the words. But it's new to me, this frankness. I'm so used to avoiding difficult truths, I find myself utterly inadequate to express myself. And I thought I was so articulate.

She's staring at me, and I realize this is one of those famous emotional tipping-point situations. The one where the estranged friends hug, crying with relief at having found each other again. But I also realize that I am not that innocent little girl any more; too much has happened, too

90

many soft layers have been shaved off me.

'I'm fine,' I say eventually. 'Really. I'm coping well. Life goes on, as they say.' Bravo, Eloise, I think. A fine performance. You're still Mummy's little princess. Poised, barricaded by your own self-importance.

Natalie's eyes stay focused on mine for a while longer, before she gives up.

'Well . . . if you ever need to talk,' she says, looking down at her sad little ticket. 'I'll always listen.'

Well, wouldn't that be nice, I think sadly. Someone who will actually listen.

'I'll remember that.' I know my smile is tight. 'Thank you so much.'

Natalie's face, still bent over her hands, falls a little, and I can see I have disappointed her. Obviously not for the first time. For a minute I feel like grabbing hold of those fidgeting hands and holding them tight. Something about her sincerity has touched me. After Jessica, Laura, even Destiny, Natalie's presence is so comforting.

The ticket inspector is moving through the standard carriage, heading our way. Natalie grapples with her bag, rising from the comfortable first-class seat.

'I'd better go then,' she says brightly. 'Back to the cattle wagon.' She grins, and my heart flips with the memory of that guileless smile. She hesitates before putting a hand on my shoulder. I resist the instinct to flinch at her touch.

'You are OK, aren't you?' she asks, a note of pleading in her question. 'I mean, you're not just putting on a show?'

My smile is steady, emphatic.

'Of course I'm OK,' I tell her. 'Please don't concern yourself with me.'

Inwardly I cringe. I sound uncannily like Miss Marple or a similarly buttoned-up lady from another era. *Please don't concern yourself with me.*

Natalie gives me an odd look, her eyes narrowing ever so slightly at me.

'That's your fake voice,' she says evenly, but her mouth twitches. 'Some things never change, Eloise.' She raises an eyebrow before turning back to continue plodding to her standard seat.

A defensive rebuttal is on the tip of my tongue but I halt it. Instead I watch her as she finds a spare seat, plops her fake leather bag on her lap, and stares a little dreamily out of the window.

Natalie belongs to another stage in my life. That would be Stage One, the stage that was cut short. The stage where, long ago, I had real friends, and real feelings that I wasn't afraid to show. I miss that part of my life more than ever now. Without Huck, I seem to be bobbing like a lonely buoy out at sea. I ache to see him now, with an intensity that almost makes my heart shut down altogether.

I drag my eyes away from my old friend, sitting there contentedly all alone, and I grapple in my Louis Vuitton for my phone. At first I hover over Jessica's number, but I don't really want to speak to her – it's just habit. I continue scrolling until I find his name.

Today was a strange day. I saw Natalie. You never met her. She was kind. I wish you'd known her. She was a real friend to me. Are you out there? Are you thinking about me? I feel lost without you. Please come back.

I touch 'send' and let out a sigh. That feels good. I realize that not once when I was with Huck did I open up to him like I just did. I didn't need to. There was an unspoken thing between us. An understanding. Maybe, I think, irrationally now, that understanding still exists.

With tears tugging at my eyes, I shove the phone back into my bag, and rest my head on the grubby white antimacassar, holding out my ticket for the inspector like an automaton.

13

Daniel

I am sitting in an Internet cafe finishing off an email to Syd, filling him in on the amazing adventure I'm having without my two loyal compadres at my side. I'm about to begin a considerate email to my mother, updating her on my daily nutritional intake, when my phone beeps.

I fish around in my rucksack to retrieve it. But it isn't my phone, it's the 'other' phone. The one that doesn't belong to me. I screw up my nose, mildly torn as I see the notification on the screen. It's from her. Or him. Either way it's from one complete stranger to another, and I really should not be doing this, but . . .

I shut my eyes, like I used to do just before I had finished unwrapping a Christmas present, prolonging the anticipation.

When I open them again and actually view what is written on the screen, I feel terrible. It's another cry into the wilderness. And this time I am pretty sure it is a maiden's cry. Not many boys I know would wax on about a kind old friend named Natalie. And it's the way the message is structured. Feminine. Vulnerable. Exposed.

I feel lost without you.

Whoever, wherever, the intended recipient is, he clearly doesn't give a damn enough to put this poor kid out of her misery and find another way to contact her now that he's lost his phone.

This is not good. Not good for her. And definitely not good for me to be observing her pain.

I am so tempted to say something comforting. Seriously tempted to be part of this passionate one-sided exchange. But the chances are, texting her back would result in me losing the one intimate dialogue I have in my life. My mother's views on healthy bowel movements do not count as such. Even I, an emotional novice, recognize this.

I glance up at the computer screen and my half-written email to my mum. It feels even sadder, more pathetic, than it did while I was writing it. I cancel the email and log off.

In front of the cafe, the sun is bright. Hotter than hot. I tie my hooded sweatshirt round my waist and use a sleeve to dab at my damp forehead. All around me, life is happening. A pair of wizened old men are playing chess outside a liquor shop; two small boys are kicking a football at each other. A couple in their forties are kissing tenderly in the doorway of a pharmacy. Two ridiculously attractive girls are walking along, arms linked, sharing the headphones on an iPod.

Everyone has someone. Except for me.

For a second a picture of Syd, shaking his head at my sheer loserdom, pops into my head, and I give a little snort. The two little boys stare up at me, their football rolls slowly into the gutter.

'Hey.' I stick out a foot and loop it back to them. 'Eyes on the ball.' I smile down at them as they resume their pointless kicking back and forth. Insanely grateful to have been part of something, even as a forgettable interloper, I sigh and amble off past the old men, who are shouting at each other over the chessboard.

I really should move on from here, I think. A new place might shake the blues away. I am just unzipping my rucksack to see if my map is in there, when I feel the presence of others around me.

'Good morning, Daniel.' Mrs Diaz bumps her huge shopping bag against my thigh. She grins in that way older ladies do when they are attempting to flirt with a grandson substitute. To the other side of me, I recognize one of her friends from the salsa night.

'You remember this lady?' Mrs Diaz nods feverishly at her companion. 'Anna Ronaldo.'

'Uh . . . yes.' I stick my hand out and Anna grips it with

the strength of a wrestler.

'So pretty,' she coos over at Mrs D, as though I were invisible. 'So handsome . . .'

'Uh huh.' Mrs Diaz is nodding slowly. 'We just talking about you, Daniel. We have an idea for you.'

'Right . . .' I am looking at the two of them, absolutely dreading the words: 'You want to be DJ at salsa night?'

Instead, she says, 'Anna's cousin, Ronnie, he owns bar on the coast, about two hundred kilometres north. You have heard of San Sebastian? Ronnie's place is along from there. A quiet place . . . but pretty. Peaceful. You can take a bus, or the train . . .' Mrs Diaz is beaming as though she is describing heaven. It sounds to me suspiciously like the kind of place where geriatrics wearing knotted handkerchiefs sit playing dominoes all day before retiring to bed at 7 p.m.

On the other hand, I was planning to go to San Sebastian at some point. It's Spain's answer to the Cote D'Azur, apparently. I nod, waiting for Mrs D to continue.

'Poor Ronnie, he has broken his arm. He needs help in the bar. You know, serving the drinks, taking out rubbish . . . working with public.' At this last bit, she gives me a different look, probably assessing whether I am fit for the purpose, before adding, 'We thought you might be interested in this? If you have no other plans . . .' She turns to her friend with a look that says 'of course he has no plans. He is like every other listless teenage boy.' And she would be right, of course.

Anna is smiling like the proverbial Cheshire Cat.

My instinctive reaction is to pass. But then, I reason, don't I want to have an adventure? Surely taking out the rubbish by an idyllic coastal village in Spain is more of an adventure than doing the same thing on Canal Street. And probably safer.

'Let me think about it,' I say slowly, buying a bit more time.

The two ladies engulf me with a mutual look of impatience.

'I've thought about it,' I say brightly. 'And . . . OK. When do I start?'

'How about today?' Mrs Diaz shrugs and turns to Anna. 'Ronnie laid up on bed, yes?'

Anna shakes her head sympathetically. 'He needs help straight away. He desperate.'

'Thanks.' I try not to sound too dry. They're only wanting to do me a favour, even if the phrasing could be more flattering. 'So I guess I'd better go pack then?'

'Such a good boy,' says Mrs Diaz.

'Such a good boy,' echoes Anna. She gives my arm an extra squeeze.

So now I am on the train heading for a little beach town just outside San Sebastian. I am fantasizing about morphing into one of those lithe, six-packed Spanish boys who effortlessly kick a ball around the beach like David Beckham. I can't play football, and the truth is, I don't want to. It isn't me. But, as I stare out at the sun dropping a little in the sky, I have to admit that a bit of time not being me may be the kick-start into reinvention I need. Pun not intended.

By the time I get off the train, my legs really do feel as though I have just spent twenty-four hours in intense training for the World Cup. I'm knackered.

I throw all caution, and all my money on a taxi.

Inside, I get out the crude map that Anna has drawn. Directions to Ronnie's bar. I picture Ronnie as a jovial guy with dark skin, a moustache and a beer belly. He will slap me too hard on the shoulders, hand me a tea towel and tell me to get to work in his charming and rustic beach bar.

What I find when I emerge from the taxi is a big shack with a corrugated roof and a large sign in Spanish with a drawing of a beer bottle.

It looks a bit like our neighbour Mrs Terry's garden shed back home, but slightly bigger.

My fantasy evaporates.

Ronnie has a dog. An angry-looking Alsatian who sticks his snout out from a wire mesh cage at the side of the shack and bares his teeth.

I fight the overwhelming urge to get back in the cab and tell it to go forth to Madrid and spare no fuel. I am almost dewy-eyed at the thought of DJ'ing for Mrs Diaz's salsa group.

Why have I come here?

The door of the shack creaks open and a vision appears.

A petite, dusky-skinned, brown-eyed maiden with her hair tied loosely in a plait is looking questioningly at me.

'Is you,' she says in halting English. 'Danielle.'

'Daniel. Dan,' I correct her. 'I'm looking for Ronnie?'

'Yes, yes.' She smiles broadly and her teeth are ubiquitously white, though endearingly a little crooked. Up close she looks young. My cousin Rachel's age. About thirteen, fourteen at a pinch.

Totally off limits.

'My name is Cristina,' she tells me. 'Ronnie is my father.' She giggles a bit. 'He is inside.' She beckons to me. 'Come on.'

Eloise

'Ugh, my rooms at Cambridge are far too small,' says Laura, dipping a hand into a large bag of jelly babies. Laura is the only one of the four of us whose hourglass figure, her calling card, gives her free rein in the candy shop.

The rest of us eye the handful of sweets she throws elegantly into her mouth. If I were to look over at Destiny, I know her mouth will be watering.

Jessica distracts us from the torture by faking a massive yawn.

'I couldn't be more relieved not to have to go through the student grunge period,' she says. 'I'll be sunning myself on the roof terrace of the Eagans' brownstone.'

'Aren't you supposed to be looking after their kids?' Destiny asks, a bit smugly. 'I mean, you are the au pair, aren't you?'

Jessica is deferring uni for a year to be an au pair on the

Upper West Side of Manhattan. Strictly speaking, that just means she'll be lazing around in her mum's friends' elegant brownstone, popping down to Fifth Avenue whenever she feels like it.

'Well, obviously I'll check on them from time to time. I'll just give them some of Mr Eagan's whisky if they get noisy. That's what *my* au pair used to do. Didn't do me any harm.' Jessica yawns again, while the rest of us regard her wide-eyed.

'You'd get the children drunk?' breathes Laura. 'That is not right.'

'She's kidding,' Destiny snorts. 'Jessica's not actually going to see those children. Ever. She's on a free pass to shopping central is what she is.'

Everyone laughs. Except Jessica.

'Just because the rest of you are spending three years trapped in what amounts to council accommodation and pretending to study doesn't give you the right to judge,' she says stonily. She frowns, the cogs of her brain turning ever so slightly, before touching my arm.

'Not you though, sweets,' she says softly. 'I know it won't be the same for you.'

'I'll be fine,' I say, though I'm not sure if I mean it. I am still feeling like my head has been hit by a breeze block. A little bit out of it and in a fair amount of pain.

'Of course she'll be fine,' Destiny cries. 'She has us!' She moves to hug me, but before I can stop myself I flinch.

'What?' Destiny's large brown eyes say wounded.

'Oh, nothing . . .' I get to my feet and put on a waterfall cardigan that my mother has left on one of the loungers by the pool. 'I just don't want to be touched right now.'

'Not even by your best friends?' Jessica adopts a silly, little-girl voice. 'Your bestest friends in the whole wide world?'

'Jessica.' Destiny's tone is warning.

'I'm just trying to cheer Lo up,' protests Jessica, shooting a venomous look at Destiny. 'Lighten things up a little.'

'Thanks,' I say, trying hard not to sound sarcastic, or ungrateful. I'm getting a little tired of this 'evading the real issue' thing that Jessica has going on. Funny, because up until recently I had that kind of behaviour totally down pat. These days, it makes me feel empty and depressed.

There is a new uneasiness between me and my friends. I can tell by the lack of sassy comebacks, the eerie silence by the pool.

'Well,' says Destiny uncomfortably after a bit. 'I should really get back. I have to get ready for a dinner thing my parents are having.'

'And I need to persuade Pappy to pay my rent on that little house I want near Pembroke College,' Laura puts in, already up and wriggling into her Herve Leger bodycon dress.

'Yeah . . .' As usual, Jessica is the last to catch on. 'I guess I'd better go and play with the pugs. Brenda and Tony are still in Barbados.'

'Jeez. Will you stop calling your folks that?' Destiny

rolls her eyes at Jessica. She is catching my eye, trying to retrieve some of our old camaraderie. I offer up a little smile.

'Those are their names, Destiny,' Jessica says wearily. 'Really, "Mum and Dad" is so provincial.'

This makes me chuckle at least.

'So, I'll see you guys . . . sometime,' I offer, in lieu of wanting to actually arrange anything with them.

They are staring at me. I know they're battling with confusion and the desire to be sensitive.

I wrap my mum's cardigan a little more tightly around me and catch a faint whiff of Chanel No. 19. It makes me want to cry. Mum has worn this perfume ever since I can remember.

I watch my friends as they link arms and stroll out of my back garden, and as they pass through the bowered exit, I shiver. It really is getting autumnal now. A cold breeze brushes me and I sink down on to a lounger.

What is wrong with me? Only a month ago we would have hung out until midnight, moving inside to the kitchen and a post-pool snack of edamame beans and fresh tuna chatting about nothing, making jokes about our peers at school.

It feels as though an era has ended. And I know that the Eloise of a month ago is disappearing. Tonight I was bored. And restless. And lonely. All at once.

I need to pause. Just deal with the crap that is rotating inside my head. All these feelings, where do they go?

I sit out by the pool for another hour. I am really cold now, but in a way I am getting off on the discomfort. It feels closer to where I am than constantly moving, or talking about something – anything – else in order not to rest on the one thing that threatens to overwhelm me.

Huck's dad is the kind of person that shuts you up. By that I mean that he fills a room with his six-foot-two solid physique and his dark-brown hair (like Huck's), with flecks of grey. He usually wears faded, paint-splattered jeans and white T-shirts with interesting logos on them. He has strong tanned arms and his house – the house that Huck shared with him and Elena – was one of those beautiful modern builds, right on the edge of town, with acres of windows and a long patch of land, like a meadow, reaching down to a brook. The grass was wild and romantic, and in the summer evenings we would sit – the three of us – listening to Carlo talking about his youth. Growing up in Brazil, hanging out with arty kids, going with the flow. Carlo comes from money; his family makes and exports a very famous brand of Brazilian coffee. Not that Carlo wanted in on that business. But the security came in handy when he wanted to pursue his dream. To paint, and live an untethered life, doing something he enjoyed.

Huck's mum, Helena, the unlikely interloper, is the one who threw the proverbial spanner in the works. She is as pale and delicate as Carlo is swarthy and strong. They'd met when Helena spent a summer in Brazil as a teenager.

Carlo told us he had never met anyone like her. Growing up with dusky-skinned, gregarious women, Helena was like something out of a Henry James novel. Classy and intelligent, beautiful and orderly. They say opposites attract. Well, it seemed that way for a while. Helena and Carlo separated when Huck was eight years old. They remained friends. Huck had lived with Helena until she got a job teaching abroad and then he and Elena had moved in with their dad.

Apart from the separation bit, I liked to think – to dream – that Huck and I were a similar pairing. Only *we* wouldn't split up. We were like coffee and cream. Meant to be together. I could see how much Carlo still thought of his ex-wife. And I suppose I tried not to think about what had driven them apart.

'Other women, in the end,' Huck had told me, uncomfortably, when I had asked the question. We were lying in his dad's garden. 'Dad just couldn't resist them.' He'd shrugged, picking at a piece of grass. 'And Mum just couldn't turn a blind eye any more.'

'But Carlo seems so nice. So . . . loyal.'

'He is. But he can't be tied down like that, I guess.' Huck had looked away then, not meeting my eyes. 'He found it really hard to be monogamous.'

'Poor Helena,' I'd sighed. 'I don't know what I would do if my parents split up. I mean, my mother is insanely controlling at times, but I know Dad couldn't do without her.'

Huck had looked back at me then and said the strangest

thing. 'Maybe he doesn't know how to be without her. Maybe he doesn't know any other way.'

The sun had been in my eyes, I remember that. It meant that Huck couldn't see the unsettled look on my face. He made it sound like Dad was putting up with my mother because he was cowardly. I knew Huck couldn't have meant it like that.

Remembering that conversation now, though, I do recall the little flutter of fear that passed through me.

At any rate, the discomfort was fleeting, because Huck had pulled me towards him then, nestling my head against his chest, stroking my hair tenderly, and I had shut my eyes, like a cat being adored.

'I'm glad you're not like that, though,' I'd said sleepily. 'I know you wouldn't do that to me.' I'd basked in Huck's arms, allowing happiness to push away the conversation. So I guess I hadn't noticed that he didn't respond. I guess I was just too deep in my dream to notice.

'Eloise!' My mother is coming through the gate to the pool. She's wearing an exquisite peach silk wrap dress and silver peep-toe Louboutins. Still she manages to glide towards me. Years of heels and painstaking good posture practice have done this. She reaches me and frowns down at what must be a somewhat bedraggled picture.

'I was just coming in,' I tell her wearily. 'Are you going out?'

'In a bit. You have a visitor,' she tells me. The look on

her face is signalling that whoever it is has not passed muster with her. Valerie would do a security check on all my acquaintances if she could.

I look at my watch. It's 8 p.m. 'Now?'

'Yes.' Valerie brushes a non-existent piece of fluff from the front of her dress. 'So hurry up and deal with it. Your dad and I are going to be late.'

I sigh and do as I am told, passing my father adjusting his sports jacket in front of the hallway mirror. He smiles at me.

'Your visitor is in the study,' he says. 'It's rather nice to see her again. I always liked her.'

I raise an eyebrow. So no one is willing to tell me who my visitor is, it seems.

'Your mother, of course, is not keen on people just dropping in. You know her.' He kisses me lightly on my forehead.

Thank goodness for my father.

Walking into the study, my breath catches in my throat as I recognize the small, dark-haired girl examining the ornaments on the mantelpiece.

'Sarah?'

She turns, looking nervous, and no longer the mousey little thing she'd been when we were friends. She is, in fact, quite beautiful. Like a young Rachel Weisz.

'You're so pretty,' I blurt out. 'I mean, you always were pretty, but—' I stop, realizing that her looks might be irrelevant at this point. Natalie and I had always teased her about her seriousness. She no doubt thinks I am utterly shallow.

'I'm sorry to just turn up like this,' she says calmly, her soft voice a nice contrast to those of my three best friends'. 'Only I'm spending the last few weeks before I leave for uni working at that care home on Elm Avenue. I remembered you live just around the corner. I thought I'd chance it.'

'No.' I shake my head vigorously. 'I mean, I'm glad. How are you?'

I am overdoing it.

Sarah's eyes flicker over my bare legs and my mother's ill-fitting cardigan.

'I've come at a bad time,' she says.

'No!' I reach out and touch her arm, and, just for a second, I am sure she flinches, before she recovers and smiles. 'I was just out by the pool,' I finish lamely.

Sarah's look is impassive, but I wonder if she's thinking what a spoilt cow I am. Doing nothing with my time but lazing around in my big fancy house, while she's spent all day looking after the elderly in the Elm Avenue old people's home.

'I just wanted to see you because . . . because of your loss,' she says earnestly. 'I was so sorry to hear that your boyfriend died. My mother is very sad for you. She sends her love.'

Hearing her words, I feel a sudden lump in my throat. Just like Natalie, Sarah has simply acknowledged my pain.

I can't help but think of the difference between them and my mum – and my so-called friends.

'I saw Natalie,' I say quickly to stop myself from blubbing there and then. 'It was so good to bump into her again.'

There is an awkward silence. The huge elephant appears in the study, roaming precariously. One of us has to say something. I have just decided it's going to be me, when Natalie starts speaking.

'It doesn't matter about the past,' she says gently. 'It's not important. What's important is that you are coping OK.' She pauses, her pretty, hazel-coloured eyes locking on to mine. 'Are you coping?'

See, this is the thing about proper friends. They know who you really are. They know when you're faking it. Even after all these years, both Natalie and Sarah are on to me, within minutes.

Sheer habit makes me want to produce that blindingly confident smile I have perfected. But this is my moment to put things right. To be honest.

I sink down on to the leather chesterfield behind me, and I realize my legs are shaking.

'I'm not so good,' I begin. 'And I seem to be coming apart more every day. It's getting worse.' I look up at her. 'It's so hard to explain how it feels.'

Sarah's face is full of concern but she doesn't speak. She is waiting for me to go on.

But I can hear the sound of Mum's heels coming down

the hall. Any minute she'll come in, and she can't see me like this.

I get up quickly. 'I'm sorry, I didn't mean to offload that on you. It isn't fair. You and Nat . . . I didn't treat you well. I haven't been there for you.' I lift my head and meet her eyes. 'This is something I just have to get through by myself.'

'But you shouldn't have to.' Sarah's voice is firmer. 'You shouldn't have to hide your feelings like this.'

The study door handle is being rattled. Any second now my mother will stick her impatient, flawlessly made-up face into the room and make it clear that visiting time is over.

'You'd better go,' I tell Sarah. 'My mother—'

Sarah nods. 'Yes. I know. Your mother.'

We smile at each other then and I realize that, for the first time in . . . well, actually in a very long time, I really don't feel alone with my feelings.

15

Daniel

I have hefted what felt like my nine-hundredth beer crate out into Ronnie's backyard, very much avoiding eye contact with Rubi the temperamental Alsatian, and am back in the bar ready to clean the counter, when I realize I am being watched.

Cristina and her friend Rosa are perched up on the other end of the bar sucking on Chupa Chups lollipops, swinging their legs like proverbial Lolitas.

Not that attention from a pretty young lady wouldn't usually be flattering (not to mention a small miracle), but when that young lady and her friend are more of the little sister than the little siren variety, the novelty wears off immediately. Cristina and Rosa seem to be stalking me. Everywhere I turn, they are there, grinning, asking if I have a girlfriend, or if I know Robert Pattinson personally. I must admit, I am pretty impressed with their command of the English language. I have been in this country six weeks and I have barely spoken a word of Spanish.

No to both, I have told them, perhaps unwisely in regard to my relationship status. I have an awful feeling Cristina thinks we will have something going on soon.

'Shouldn't you have homework to do?' I ask them now, loading glasses into the dishwasher.

They stare at me, uncomprehending.

'You know . . . schoolwork? Studies?'

Cristina rolls her eyes, removing the lollipop from her mouth. 'Is holidays, stupid,' she says in halting English. 'You don't have the studies also.'

'Well, no.' I close the dishwasher door and turn on the wash cycle. 'Not now. But soon I'll have more homework than I have ever had in my life.'

'College?' pipes up Rosa. 'My brother Tio, he is going to college too. He studies in America. In California.'

I nod. 'That sounds cool. I'm going to Bangor. It's very similar to California.'

I turn away, running a cloth over the bottles of spirits on the back counter, wondering what on earth induced me to apply to Bangor University. Possibly because of the distance it will put between me and my mother. It wasn't for the endless sunshine and glamorous accent, that's for sure.

'Is nice, this Banging university?' asks Cristina, jumping down from the counter and coming to perch on a bar stool.

'Bang-or,' I correct her, before I see the smile twitching

on her face. 'Funny,' I say drily. 'You're funny.'

'Thank you,' says Cristina, more seriously. 'You think boys don't like funny girls? Boys only like the girls who pout.' She sticks her lips out comically. 'Like this.'

Rosa giggles and jumps down from her seat to sit down next to her friend.

I stop what I am doing and give Cristina what I hope is a kind of paternal, or older-brotherly, look. 'Boys like funny girls,' I tell her. 'Where did you get that idea, *90210*?'

The girls both shriek. 'We love that show!'

'What a surprise.' I smile at them. 'You know, you shouldn't let what you see on that show influence you. It's rubbish. I mean, those kids don't actually look real anyway. No one is that attractive when they're eighteen.'

Cristina focuses her brown eyes on me. 'You are,' she says seriously. 'You are very handsome.'

Bloody brilliant. My first real ego-boost is from a thirteen-year-old.

'Well, thanks, Cristina,' I tell her with equal seriousness. 'And you're a very pretty little girl.'

At this her face darkens a little and I almost feel guilty. She and Rosa exchange a mutual look of disappointment.

'And you're going to be a beautiful young woman,' I add, possibly unwisely, because Cristina is getting a renewed flush in her cheeks. 'You're going to find a nice boyfriend, of your own age, who will love your cracking sense of humour.'

I realize that the language barrier may have made this

come across as slightly more encouraging than it was meant to be, because the two of them are giggling and whispering to each other in delight.

To my relief, a shadow crosses the doorway to the bar and Ronnie appears. Ronnie is small, and muscular, and very brown. He looks hard. Like a little boxer, but he seems friendly enough, and he is paying me over the odds.

He gives a fake lion's roar at the two girls.

'You nuisance,' he growls at them in English. 'You leave this poor boy alone. He very busy.' Ronnie adjusts the cast a little on his arm. 'You lucky I have broken arm or I throw you out of here.'

Cristina sighs. 'Pappy, we are so bored. Daniel is helping us with English.' She widens her eyes at him, swinging her legs childishly.

'OK, but just this once, chiquita,' he says gruffly. 'The boy not want to talk to little girls.'

The two of them look huffy at that, but Ronnie is smiling. He turns to me. 'They are a handful. With my wife visiting her mother, I can't keep up with the brats.' He grins. 'I just going to see my brother for a bit. You will be OK here with these two nuisance?'

'Sure,' I say, through slightly gritted teeth. 'I'll be fine.'

Ronnie waves his non-broken arm, roars again at the girls and leaves us to it.

As soon as he is gone, the girls resume their giggling and whispering, casting secretive looks at me.

I decide to give up on the conversation just as my phone

beeps with a text message. I fish it out of my pocket and realize, again, that it is the wrong phone. I have unashamedly been charging the anonymous phone as well as my own. Almost anxiously awaiting the next message from Lo. For she seems to be the only one who texts him. This is a bit odd when I think about it.

And sure enough there is a text, from a now familiar girl. I hesitate, deciding to save it for later.

But it's too late. Before I can blink, Cristina's small hand has reached out and grabbed the phone out of my hand.

'Hey!' I hold out my hand. 'Give it back.'

Cristina smiles coquettishly, then gives her head a little shake.

'Cristina,' I say warningly. 'Give me my phone back.'

She and Rosa huddle over the small screen.

'Ooh. You have a text . . .' says Cristina. She looks up. 'Who is Lo?'

Very good question, Cristina, I think. An excellent question, in fact.

'Just someone . . .' I say instead, only fuelling the fire of curiosity further because, good Lord, I am colouring up. 'Just a friend.'

Cristina's eyes narrow slightly. 'So is a girl. Is your girlfriend. You tell me you don't have a girlfriend.'

'I . . . I don't,' I say. 'Not that it's any of your business.'

'So why don't you see what she says, your friend?' Rosa puts in, and she rests her cheek against the cool bar top. I for one am thankful for the mugginess in the bar.

It might explain the strange colour I am pretty sure my face is right now.

I look at the two of them, trying to find a reason not to open that message. But the more time I spend thinking about it, the bigger deal it will become. I sigh.

'Fine.' I hold out my hand to Cristina. 'If you'll just give me my phone back.'

With the offending object in my hand, I click on the message:

I sat out by our pool today and thought about how you used to make me feel. Like there was no other girl in the world for you. And the way you stroked my hair back off my face, and kissed me, just where I liked to be kissed.

The message is broken into two. I click on the next text without even pausing to consider what I'm doing.

But I also remember that I never seemed to have the whole of you. You were never all mine. I wish you could tell me that I am remembering it all wrong. That everything is going to be OK. That you'll never leave me alone again.

I am staring down at this message, and I am thinking what a bad person I am for reading it. I am also thinking that whoever should be reading it is some kind of arsehole for not giving Lo an explanation. One thing's for sure, he isn't thinking about her right now. If he was, he would have got in touch.

A little cough jumps me out of my thoughts and I look up to see Cristina and Rosa craning over the bar top.

'Well?' breathes Cristina.

I am about to tell her again that it is none of her business, but then I remember that it is actually none of my business either. And that I have double standards. And that I am a liar.

'It's private,' I say firmly. 'You know what that means?'

She makes an impatient whistling sound through her teeth. 'OK. Is fine.' She wrinkles her nose. 'I understand.'

'Good.' I am about to put the phone back in my pocket when an insane thought occurs to me. I chew my lip a bit and study Cristina's face. I know she's a kid, but she reads the magazines, she watches the shows – she might have some advice. And maybe, just maybe, she'll stop with the uncomfortable flirting if she has a mystery to get to the bottom of. Maybe she'll tell me what I should do. OK, I run the risk of her blabbing to Ronnie that I am harbouring the pain of a stranger in my pocket. But if I treat her like more of a grown-up, maybe she'll act like one.

It's a gamble, but what Lo doesn't know can't hurt her. Not any more than she already is.

'OK.' I put the phone down on the bar and slide it over to her. 'If I tell you something, you have to swear that you won't tell anyone else. This is very important, Cristina.' I lean forward and give her a stern look.

Both girls are rapt, paying close attention.

'We promise not to tell,' they say earnestly, together.
'We promise.'

I take a deep breath, and start talking.

'Is so romantic,' Cristina says, swivelling excitedly on her
stool. 'Is like *90120!*'

I roll my eyes, regretting what I have just told them.

'You call that romantic?' I shake my head. 'It's sad, is
what it is.'

'Why you not give the phone back?' asks Rosa. 'To her
boyfriend.'

'He just told us,' Cristina says wearily. 'He don't know
where the boyfriend is.'

I am nodding slowly in agreement, but the fact is I
haven't really tried very hard to find Lo's boyfriend. Or her
husband. Or her girlfriend, for heaven's sake. Perhaps I
have had this all wrong. It's just my pathetic inexperience
that has made me put things together the way I want them.

'You know, you should tell her.' Cristina purses her lips
in a Poirot-esque way. 'You should say you have this phone
and that you need to know who you should give it back to.'

Rosa is nodding. 'Yes. My God! I would be so
embarrassed!'

'Exactly.' I stick my hands in my pockets. 'It will only
embarrass her more if I tell her, surely?'

They think about it. 'Maybe.'

'Maybe I should just throw the phone away,' I say.
'Problem solved.'

But I know I really, really don't want to do that.

'No, no, no.' Cristina is emphatic. 'Then you won't hear the rest of the story.'

I frown. 'The story?'

'Yes. The story she is telling.' Cristina has the knowing air of someone who has watched too many crappy rom-coms. 'You don't want to know her story?'

'I never thought about it like that,' I say, considering this. 'I suppose it is like being read bits of a story.'

'Yes, and is so romantic,' Cristina says, her brown eyes serious. 'Is a broken heart.'

'A broken heart,' I repeat softly. 'My first broken heart.'

Then Cristina says something wise beyond her years.

'Your first broken heart should never be thrown away. Is something you hold inside all your life. You need to know.'

I smile at her. 'You make a good point there, my friend.'

16

Eloise

I have two weeks to get my act together. Mum has already been on to the student accommodation people, 'informing' them of her plans to give my room a makeover even though this is completely unheard of and against university regulations. I heard her on the phone, barking orders like how I imagine Genghis Khan addressed his army. I challenge anyone to defy my mother when she is in full throttle.

In a way I'm relieved that she has taken over. Because I am unable to fold a jumper, let alone organize my facilities at uni.

I stare despondently at the clothes I have laid out to take with me on my bed. Running my eyes over ten grand's worth of garments, all I feel is exhausted. I pick up a pale-pink Brora sweater and sigh. I never was a pale-pink kind of person, however much my mum insists it brings out my

English Rose complexion. I stuff it into a drawer.

A black All Saints mohair sweater seems much more me. I put it to the 'keep' side of the bed. Along with two pairs of black skinny jeans, a leather skirt and my cream angora cardigan with the snowflake pattern around the neck. Next are three pairs of Converse: white, off white and black-and-white, a grey marl sweatshirt, a white Prada shirt, a darker-grey Acne vest and a dark denim dress.

There's a bit of a theme going on here, I see. Muted. Dark. Depressed, perhaps? Just like me.

I am just wondering whether to throw in a curveball and include the Myla underwear that I got from Huck for my last birthday when there is a decidedly courteous knock on my bedroom door. It can't possibly be my mum. She doesn't bother to knock, she generally just barges in, to hell with the consequences.

'Come in,' I say warily. I watch the door cautiously opening.

Jake appears. I must look startled. I can't remember the last time Jake encroached on my side of the top floor we share. His 'quarters' are similarly alien to me. There's only so much Radiohead I can take. And Jake is most certainly in the Radiohead phase.

We stare at each other like a couple of wary meerkats.

'Jake?' I prompt him. 'What do you want?'

He scratches his head. 'Mum says do you want the duck-egg blue or the . . . the pea green?' he asks somewhat uncertainly.

'Excuse me?'

'Paint,' he says. 'You know, the stuff you put on walls?'

'Yes, I know what paint is.' I think about it for half a second. 'I don't really care.'

'OK.' Jake shrugs good-naturedly and turns to leave.

Poor old Jake, still mesmerized by my mother's commands. Like a field mouse caught in the gaze of a deadly snake.

'Wait,' I say quickly. Jake turns, looking confused and suspicious.

'Wait?' he raises an eyebrow.

'Come in,' I say brightly. 'Sit down. Shoot the breeze.' I gesture at the bed, which is still heaped with clothes.

Jake looks as though he is being tortured.

'Come on,' I say. 'We haven't talked in . . . ages, have we?'

Jake is well aware that in fact we have never talked. I can't say I blame his confusion. He's my little brother and I hardly know him. Pretty soon I will be gone and we will have had no relationship. This seems to matter all of a sudden.

Jake shuffles further inside my bedroom. His jeans are so low down I can see the tops of his underpants. Calvin Klein, purchased by Mum, of course.

His eyes flicker to the large mounted photograph of me and Huck, all dressed up for the school prom two years ago.

'I'm not going to the prom this year,' he says. 'Proms are

an outmoded American import.' He chews his lip seriously.

I am fairly sure he has overheard this, or read it in one of his mate's skater magazines.

'You're probably right.' I look up at the photograph. 'But it was a good night.'

It had been the night Huck had said he loved me. For the first time. Looking at my face in the photo – glowing, my eyes wide and a little stunned – I frown. I look as though I am a bit out of it. Sort of vacant.

I look away quickly.

'He was all right,' says Jake suddenly. 'Huck.'

I let out a long breath. 'Yes. He was all right.'

'You must feel like crap,' Jake adds. He rubs at his nose with his sleeve. 'I mean, you were serious with him, yeah?'

I nod. 'I think so, yes.'

Jake looks up at me. 'He made me feel kind of inadequate. He was, like, the ultimate guy, wasn't he? Never put a foot wrong.'

I eye my brother. 'What do you mean by that?'

Jake shrugs. 'Nothing. I don't mean anything by it.'

I sit down on the bed. 'No. You said it in a weird way.'

Jake looks more uncomfortable than ever. 'No, I never—'

'It's OK,' I tell him. 'I think Huck made a lot of people feel like that.'

'Yeah?' Jake is looking at me, a rare expression of curiosity on his face.

'Yeah, I mean, he was the "perfect" guy, wasn't he?

Good-looking, clever, charming.' Jake is still looking at me. I frown. 'I mean, I adored Huck, I didn't mean—'

'He wasn't that perfect,' he says clearly, and I blink. Now it's my turn to be curious.

'What do you mean?'

'Nothing.' Jake shrugs. 'Just sometimes he upset you. I saw it, Lois. I saw you that night he—'

A flash of memory comes into my head, and I want it gone. I can't deal with a change in script . . . not now.

'Well, that's what love does,' I said. 'Sometimes it hurts you.'

Even I know that sounded like a line from a bad chick flick. I wince and look away from my brother.

'Yeah, I suppose. I don't know anything about romance,' Jake mutters awkwardly. 'I don't really know what I'm talking about.'

I am pulling a little too strenuously at a thread in my mohair jumper. Still not looking at Jake.

'I'd better get on with sorting this lot out,' I say, looking over the clothes on the bed. 'Tell Mum that if I have to choose I'll go with the green. The paint . . .'

'Uh, OK.' I can hear Jake moving towards the door and I feel bad. But I need to be alone for a minute.

As the door closes behind Jake, I stare at a pair of silk French knickers as though they hold the key to the universe. But I am retracing my steps, going back. Back to a time I don't really want to remember.

* * *

125

Huck and I had been together two years. Two years and it felt like we'd known each other all our lives. Carlo's house was my *casa*. I knew my way around it blindfold. I didn't even get invited to Carlo's parties any more; it was just assumed I would be there. Like part of the furniture.

In a good way, of course.

Carlo threw a party one Saturday night to celebrate his latest sale for a seven-figure sum. The cream of the London art world were there, along with their glamorous other halves and the party rocked to the sounds of Carlo's favourite band, the Rolling Stones. It had been rumoured that Mick Jagger himself was coming, though I never saw him that night. Still, it sealed the enthusiasm of my three BFFs. Jessica had been planning her outfit for weeks.

'Jade Jagger could be there,' she said. 'Or Kate Moss.'

I sighed, adjusting the vintage 50s dress I had bought the weekend before in Beyond Retro. 'I doubt it. I mean, Carlos is influential in the arty crowd. But I hardly think Kate Moss will bother to turn up.'

'Oh well.' Jessica got out her compact and inspected her face. 'There's bound to be someone to write home about. Do I look OK?'

'Of course,' I said robotically. 'Have you never looked not-OK?'

'True.' Jessica snapped her compact shut. 'Seriously though, Lo. This could be my ticket on to the A-list. I've

126

always seen myself with an older man. An art dealer maybe? Or an investor.' She wrinkled her little nose. 'Probably more my type. I don't really know how to talk to hipsters.'

'Is there a way of talking to hipsters?' Laura had murmured, busy giving her fingernails a last-minute coat of Chanel Rouge Noir. 'I am so ignorant of these things.'

Destiny, in her Herve Leger ensemble, pulled a face. 'Man, who cares. There'll be music and good-looking people. I don't plan on seeing any of them again in my life. I'm just coming for the party!'

I smiled at her. 'Why not,' I said. 'I mean, we'll be about twenty years younger than everyone else. Everyone will assume that we're Carlo's love children.'

'Except for you, darling. You're with the heir to the throne,' Jessica remarked. 'You have special status.'

'I don't know.' I fiddled with my clutch bag. Carlo's parties usually meant that I didn't see much of Huck. Which meant he didn't often get round to introducing me as his girlfriend. I didn't mind. I just soaked up the atmosphere.

But Jessica's words had provoked a strange feeling in me. A kind of annoying neediness. I needed to knock that on the head immediately. The thought of being a 'clinger' was hideous.

Carlo's large glass-panelled sitting room was already crowded when the four of us walked in. Expensive but dressed-down designer everywhere you looked. Over by the bookcase I saw the man himself, Carlo, holding court, a trio of women in their thirties hanging on his every word. Beyond him, in the large kitchen-diner, I saw Huck deep in conversation with a female of some description. Huck was sixteen but, from this distance, his height and his general ease with himself made him look older. He was holding a bottle of beer, running his hands through his hair, smiling at his companion.

I didn't mean to keep looking, but I couldn't help it. I was intrigued; I stood on tiptoe and craned to see better. Whoever she was, she turned and I caught sight of her perfect straight nose, her glossy auburn hair, coiled effortlessly into a loose chignon. Even from where I was I could see the glow in her cheeks. She was beautiful. And she didn't look much older than me. I was just accepting the thud that landed in my heart when a hand touched me gently on the arm.

'Eloise,' said Helena softly when I turned to look. 'So good to see you. Have you just arrived?'

I was doing what I thought was good work keeping my composure, but Helena's large green eyes fastened on to mine, and I felt she could see right inside me.

'Are you OK?' she asked. A couple of centimetres taller than me, it was easy for her gaze to flicker over to the kitchen-diner. She turned quickly back to me.

'He's just like his father,' she said, smiling reassuringly at me. 'Ever the host. Wanting to please.'

I smiled back, but I couldn't help but see a subtext in her last statement.

'It's a gift,' I said brightly. 'Keeping everyone happy.'

Helena nodded, but it felt sombre – awkward even.

'Yes, I suppose it is,' she said. She looked at my empty hands. 'We must get you a drink, darling. That will take the edge off this thing.' She squeezed my elbow and sailed elegantly through the crowd.

I took a deep breath. I didn't really want a drink. What I wanted was to know what Huck was doing. I waved breezily at Jessica, who was pretending to laugh at someone's joke, and then pushed my way past people to the kitchen-diner.

Once I got there, I realized that it was pretty empty. In fact, Huck and his lady friend were the only two people there. She was leaning up against the counter now, and I got a proper look at her. Long legs, creamy skin, a waft of expensive perfume. I breathed in – Chanel No 5.

The scent of the siren.

'Eloise.' Huck's tone was friendly, but he didn't move towards me; he stayed where he was, his attention still mostly on this supermodel version of Florence Welch.

'Gosh, it's hot,' I said, in a good imitation of a 1940s debutante. 'Don't you think it's hot?'

Florence smiled a generic, slightly catty smile. 'I'm fine,' she purred. 'Perhaps we can get you some water?'

'It's OK,' I told her tautly. 'I can help myself.' I walked knowingly to the fridge and took out a bottle of San Pellegrino.

'Seriously, you should come along sometime,' she was

saying as my back was turned. 'We exhibit all the contemporary stuff.'

'My dad never stops talking about your gallery,' Huck replied smoothly. 'Or your boss. Savannah, is it?'

Florence giggled. 'She's such an inspiration. We're like sisters really. She's given me so much responsibility.'

I walked robotically to the shelf where Carlo kept his glasses and poured myself some sparkling water. I felt electrified, as though one touch would make me explode. It was childish, I knew that. But wasn't Huck going to introduce me?

I gulped a large drink of water, then turned to them.

'My name's Eloise.' I looked at Huck then back at her. 'Huck's girlfriend.'

'Oh.' For a second I saw the Notting Hill poise falter. 'I didn't know you had a girlfriend.' She prodded him teasingly, and too intimately for my liking. 'I thought you were single.'

Huck's face didn't betray any emotion whatsoever. 'Eloise lives in the area,' he said by way of answer. 'She's great.' He offered me what looked like a warm, but slightly pleading smile. 'She feels like part of the family.'

I stared at him, my mouth open.

Florence let out an annoying tinkle of a laugh. 'How lovely.' She flashed me a slightly triumphant smile.

'And you are?' I asked her. 'I didn't catch your name?'

'Seraphina,' she replied, but she was very much looking at Huck when she pulled a card out of her admittedly gorgeous vintage Fendi clutch. She handed it to him. 'Seph, to my friends. Next time you're in London, we should have lunch.'

Huck tucked the card in his jeans pocket. 'I'd really like that, Seph,' he said, giving her his best, most winning smile.

In that moment I recognized the flirtatious, perfectly mannered response. It was the same one he had used on me when we'd first met.

Another thud hit my heart.

'Seph! Seraphina?' A woman in her mid-fifties tore into our cosy threesome, grabbing Seph by the arm, a little roughly. The spite in me couldn't help hoping that she had snapped Seph's twig-like arm in two.

'We've got to go if we're going to be at Mahiki for Georgio's birthday,' said the woman. She glanced quickly at me. 'Nice to meet you. I'm Savannah. Beautiful dress. Vintage?'

I nodded, startled at the sheer speed of her question. This woman was like my mother on Speed – Valerie: the Club Mix version. Must be Seph's boss. Nightmare. But I felt no sympathy. Tough luck, Seraphina.

Seraphina smiled a frustrated kind of smile at her boss.

'Well, see you at the polo next month maybe?' she said to Huck, her gaze passing over me. 'It'll be a laugh. It always is.'

'Look forward to it.' Huck raised his beer bottle at her, giving her that irresistible Huck look again.

As Savannah practically dragged Seph out through the milling guests, I tried very hard not to round on my boyfriend. Instead I put down my glass of water and casually poured myself a glass of Prosecco.

'Having fun?' said Huck silkily. He reached out and smoothed a stray lock of hair behind my ear. It was a typically tender Huck gesture but I shrank subtly away from him, sipping my drink, which could have been liquid gas for all I cared.

'Polo?' I said, failing to keep the edge out of my question.

Huck's deep-brown eyes opened wider. 'I've been roped in to some boys' outing my dad has organized,' he said innocently. 'It'll be very dull. Especially as you won't be there.'

I hesitated, before taking another sip, then said, 'Won't I?'

'It's a lads' thing,' he said sheepishly. 'You'll hate it. Lots of blokes drinking and talking to the hoorays.'

I couldn't help digging in to my bottom lip with my teeth. A very unattractive sight, I have no doubt. But when you feel a bit wretched all vanity shoots right out of the door.

'But Seph will be there,' I said, in what could have been a whine. 'It won't all be blokes.'

Huck had been about to take another swig of beer, but he lowered his bottle. 'Babe, I doubt I'll bump into her. She'll be off with all her Notting Hillbillie fashionista friends. Dad and I are in special enclosure, I think . . .' He

132

trailed off, which was just as well as I may have been paranoid but he sounded very unconvincing to me.

'You never said,' I told him. 'About the polo. You didn't mention it to me. But you mentioned it to her. That Seraphina phoney.'

'Lo.' Huck was staring at me as though I were unhinged. 'Don't overreact. I was going to tell you. I just didn't think it was that important.'

A couple of sips of sparkling wine and I seemed to be drunk. I could feel the rational part of my brain closing down, leaving the irrational, emotional, entirely jealous side of my brain standing alone and unable to be OK with secrets.

'Don't patronize me,' I whispered, the prick of tears threatening my eyes. 'We tell each other everything. And maybe I would have wanted to come. If you had bothered to ask.' I turned to look at Carlo's party in full swing and saw Helena talking avidly to a woman with a severe bob and deathly white skin. 'Is your mum going?'

Huck sighed. 'I don't know. Why don't you ask her?'

When I turned to look at him, all the softness had left his expression. He just looked pissed off. Impatient.

I put down my glass and dabbed at the corner of my eyes with my fingertips.

'I don't feel very well,' I said stiffly. 'I think I'm going to head off. Say thank you to your parents for me.'

And with that I left Huck standing, beer still in his hands, very much not coming after me.

133

17
Daniel

'Any news, Danielle?' Cristina folds a bar napkin into a pretty good origami bird of some kind.

'Daniel,' I correct her. 'Danielle is a girl's name.'

Cristina shrugs, an impish smile on her lips. 'Sorree.' She lifts her face like a sunflower turning up to the sky. A move she will no doubt use to great effect when she is a little older. 'So, what is happening?' she persists. 'What is the next chapter of the story?'

I shake my head, opening the till to check the evening float is in there. For a clueless Manc nerd, I don't think I'm too bad at this bar job. 'Nada,' I say wearily. 'Zip. Nothing.'

Cristina frowns. 'She's given up? Oh no, this is terrible.' She screws up the napkin, agitated. 'She's just thinking about it. What she will tell you next.'

'She's not telling me anything,' I say. 'Is she?'

'Of course she is.' Cristina studies me. 'Is like a book, you see? Is just written down. She is telling you her story.'

'Maybe. But I want more than just a story.' For a minute I forget that I am conversing with a thirteen-year-old kid. 'It has to be the saddest ever case of waiting around for someone to call.'

'So, you call her?' Cristina leans forward eagerly. 'You are part of the story then?'

She's got a point, but it is not an option. For every reason you can think of, it's a bad, sad idea.

'I need to find my own romance. I need to start doing something.' I start energetically rubbing at the counter with a cloth.

'Here?' Cristina frowns. 'The girls in this place are not right for you.' She shakes her head. 'You need someone like you.'

'What does that mean?' I stop rubbing. 'That I'm not good-looking enough?'

'No. You are . . .' Cristina searches for the word. 'Cute. You're cute, but the girls around here, they just play sports and drink beer and kiss their boyfriend.'

'Sounds OK to me,' I mutter.

'Is not for you. You want the conversation.' Cristina puts her face in her hands and gazes at me. 'You want better girls.'

'Better, eh?' I smile at her. 'Is that a compliment then?'

'Believe me, this girl, this Lo, she sounds like your type.'

135

Cristina nods, wriggling a bit on her bar stool. 'She has emotions.'

How has this child somehow tapped into my innermost feelings, I wonder? She looks like she doesn't know squat. But. Out of the mouths of babes, I guess.

'OK, then. What's the plan?'

'You wait. Unless she died, or got a new boy, she will text.' She nods, like Yoda, and slips off her stool. 'I have to go. I need to make a costume for Rosa's party.' She grins. 'I am going as Bella from *Twilight*.'

'Good luck,' I call as she scurries out of the bar. I look down at the counter, then check my watch. Five o'clock. It's nearly opening time. I decide to have a rest before the mob comes in. When I say mob, I mean about three people. Ronnie's bar isn't exactly the most popular venue in town. Mostly I am bored, and watch the huge LCD screen attached to the wall. I am beginning to understand the appeal of football after all.

I click on the remote and move to the other side of the counter. I am just doing a channel flick when my phone beeps. By now I am on alert for Lo's messages, as opposed to a pointless text from my mum about how *Coronation Street* ended tonight. Or what she and Dad had for tea.

I count to ten and fish both phones from a pocket each. Then breathe out slowly when I see which one is alight.

'You took your time,' I murmur, opening up the text. 'Like to keep a boy waiting, don't you?'

But the words on the screen are not exactly what I expected. In fact, they come as a bit of a shock.

I hate you. I hate you for all the stuff you did and never told me about.

This is a new and unsettling development. Lo has got fed up with being ignored. I don't blame her. She must feel like she is crying out into the ether. To someone she thought cared enough about her to give a damn that she's hurting. It's frustrating, though; I want to know what stuff she is talking about. This guy, whoever he is, sounds like one shady piece of work. I know guys like that. At school there were a few of them. Charismatic but shallow, stringing multiple girls along, not giving a crap if any of them found out about the others. In all honesty, I wanted to know what it must be like to be so totally callous and selfish. Just for a day, I wanted to experience that power. But I feel bewildered by it. Why would anyone treat a girl like that?

There has been no further text and I've been staring at the phone for a few minutes now.

A slight panic grips me. Maybe this is her last message. A final statement.

I am still staring at the phone when I hear footsteps and realize I have to get my act together. The regular customers are coming in. Santos and Bobby, both around Ronnie's age. They usually park themselves at the bar and stare up at whatever sport is on the TV. Pretty low maintenance. All

I have to do is pass opened beer bottles over the counter.

Quite boring, as it goes.

But this evening Santos is in chatty mode. He slaps me on the shoulder, quite hard, before he sits down.

'You are doing good, boy,' he tells me and grins, showing a few stained teeth. He leans forward. 'We can't understand what you say for a long time, but now . . . we start to get the accent. Where you from? From London?'

'Manchester,' I say. 'It's in the north of England.'

'Is cold?' He raises an eyebrow. 'I hear is cold in the north.'

'It's not so bad,' I tell him. 'It rains a lot, though.'

Santos turns to Bobby and says something I can't decipher. I am not progressing too well with the native language. I can't make out a single word.

'Bobby says you talk funny,' explains Santos, and he drinks half his bottle of beer in one gulp. 'But you doing OK. You doing OK.'

'Thanks,' I say uncertainly. 'I'm just helping out. I'll be gone soon.'

'You don't like it at Ronnie's?' Santos enquires. 'Is not "happening" enough for you?'

I laugh a bit louder than I mean to at the irony in this. 'No. It isn't that. I have to go back home to start university. College?'

'Uh huh.' Santos slides his now empty bottle towards me and I dutifully hand him another. 'You got a lady waiting at home for you?'

'Only my mother,' I say in all seriousness.

Santos and Bobby find this hilariously funny. It's like watching those two old guys from *The Muppets* in a rare moment of harmony. I am smiling at the sight of them, but inside I fall a couple of rungs further down the sad ladder.

I am eighteen years old and I have never had a girlfriend. Not unless you count Donna Goldsmith from primary school. And that was only because she wanted to copy my maths homework.

'Plenty of time for the ladies,' Santos says once he has recovered. 'Boy your age should be having fun, be a bit of the player with the ladies.'

I wish he would stop referring to them as ladies. It's a word I would use to describe females of my mum's age. And right now it feels like by the time I get a girlfriend, she probably *will* be a 'lady'. Because we will both be middle-aged.

I shrug. 'Maybe. I am not sure I am such a player. I don't know how to do all that. Flirting and chatting up girls . . .'

Santos and Bobby regard me more seriously.

'Sensitive, huh?' Santos nods. 'This is good too.' Then he shakes his head. 'Not so good around here, though. The girls here, they are . . . very forward. They eat you for breakfast.'

If Cristina is anything to go by, then I believe him. Give her a couple of years and she will have boys quaking in their shoes.

I am so lost in self-pity that I don't feel the vibration coming from my jeans pocket.

'Danny. Danny . . .' Santos is talking to me. 'I think is your phone. This loud buzzing sound.'

'Oh, right, thanks.' I turn away from the two of them while I get the phone out. My spirits lift when I see there is another message from Lo.

> *I don't want to think about bad stuff. I want to remember how amazing everything was. But you're not here, and you can't tell me it was all in my head. So my memory is putting things together. If you were here, I know you would make it all right. I keep hoping I will hear from you. That's pathetic. Really sad.*

The way I am feeling right now I am fighting really hard not to make contact with this girl. I am so, so close to tapping out a message, when something else pings into the inbox.

It's a picture. A photograph. I maximize it and my breath literally catches in my throat for a second. It's a photo of a girl. A really beautiful girl with blonde hair pulled back and though I can see faint shadows under her sad eyes, she is a vision. Better than I could have imagined. Pretty but not all made-up and intimidating.

Underneath the picture she has written: *I know, I look terrible. This is what I am like without you. Plain and sad.*

You're beautiful, I tell her, but inside my head, as I know

Santos and Bobbi are boring holes into my back with their eyes. *I think you look lovely.*

She deserves to know this, I think. She is worth more than the arsehole she is moping for. She's way too good for him.

I put the phone away. I have to catch up with Cristina after her fancy-dress sleepover. I need her advice.

And yes, I am aware of how tragic that sounds.

Eloise

The thing about having a dialogue with a dead person is that it is one-sided. There's no one to bat one back at you, telling you not to be stupid, or that you're loved, or that you were just imagining that hurtful thing they said or did so long ago that they can hardly remember.

Because you remember. And all you have is a memory – of a feeling. And that feeling sucked. It really did.

Being with Huck was like a drug. It kind of infused a feeling of dependency in me. I was hooked on his charm, on his solid sense of himself, on his confidence, his intelligence and sharp wits. On his cute brown curls and his athletic body. I was carried away by his glamorous, artsy family, his dad's amazingly stylish yet understated house. I wanted to be in on all of that. I was addicted.

But now, maybe I was coming down. I had the space to come down.

'This is ridiculous,' I murmur to myself as I wade through the hundreds of photos I have saved on my MacBook Air. Photos of a couple deeply in love, with the world at their feet.

It had always felt like Huck and I were the golden ones. Like royalty. And if I am being honest, sometimes it felt pretty fragile. It was just too good to be true.

It was as though I was waiting for something to burst. Like a bubble.

The landline phone by my bed rings. I drag my eyes away from a picture of the two of us in Paris six months ago, and pick up.

'Babe, where are you?' Jessica's voice seems so shrill I have to hold the phone away from my ear. 'We had a girls' night planned. Don't you remember?'

'Uh . . .' I look back at my face on screen, my cheek pressed against his, and his arm around me, holding me tight. 'I totally forgot, Jess. I think I might bail . . .'

'Oh no you don't!' she shrieks. 'We got in the Robert Redford collection. You know, *The Way We Were*, *Barefoot in the Park*?'

Good choice, Jessica. Tactful. I sigh inwardly and log off my computer.

'Sounds fun, but I'm not really in the mood for romantic nostalgia.' I wait a beat for the penny to drop but, as ever, Jessica is oblivious to feelings other than her own.

'Eloise,' she says petulantly. 'I ordered in some delicious sushi too. You adore sushi.'

Come to think of it, I really don't. My mother adores sushi. So does Jess. Me? I've always thought it tasted like sticky wet cardboard.

'I know,' I lie. 'But I just have all this stuff to get ready for uni. And I think we're having a family takeaway tonight.'

'Fine.' Jessica sounds piqued. 'But you need to get your mojo back, girl. You're going to end up a sad little wallflower if you don't kick this miserable jag you're on soon.'

As my mouth drops open, I can hear Destiny's raised voice in the background. 'Jess, that is way harsh!' She is practically yelling. 'Girl, you need to wise up to humanity . . .'

There is a muffled kerfuffle taking place on the other end of the phone. No doubt Jess is giving as good as she got. I am seriously tempted to hang up. The petty squabbling of the three vapidos is not my concern right now.

I give it another thirty seconds and then I do it. I hang up.

But given that it was a lie about the family meal, and that I have nothing else to do tonight except listen to crying music, such as Coldplay or Belle & Sebastian, I will have to do something to pass the time.

I stare at my iPhone and, knowing it is a bad idea, read through my texts to Huck. I wince when I see them. They're so raw.

He was my best friend. I don't know how to be without him. And yet . . . something about the way I am now feels more real. Feels more like the me I used to be.

'Eloise?' I hear a tentative knock at the door. It's Dad. I am still lying with my phone in my hand. I shove it under the duvet and grunt something in response.

'Natalie and Sarah are at the door,' he says brightly. 'They've come to cheer you up, sweetheart. Are you decent?'

I struggle to sit up.

'They're downstairs?'

'Yes. I said I thought you had no plans tonight. But perhaps I should send them away—'

'No!' I swing my legs over the bed. 'It's fine. Tell them I'll be right down.'

I switch on the overhead light to see myself properly. I am a long way from my usual groomed standard. My hair is all over the place, and my jeans – a little baggy from where I lost weight – are no longer so much 'skinny' as 'too big for skinny me'. I wrestle my drawers open for a clean T-shirt, pulling out an expensive Jil Sander that is beyond creased. I am not in the mood for bothering right now. I pull it on and smooth it down to very little effect.

I shrug at my reflection. Who cares? Nat and Sarah certainly won't.

Downstairs the two of them are perched on the study sofa. Sarah is looking rather Left Bank in her close-fitting trench coat, tights and plimsolls, while Natalie is as casually dressed as me. Loose jeans and a navy-blue hoodie.

'We took a chance. Natalie's been walking her neighbour's dog and I came along for the ride,' says Sarah. 'When we walked past your gates, we thought we'd see if you want to come over to the old recreation ground, for old times' sake.'

I smile, remembering how once, long ago, we seemed to spend every waking moment in that park, swinging on the swings. I remembered Mum's face at my muddy trainers and grass-covered coat when I'd come home. That was no doubt the start of her plans for my metamorphosis. It was simple fun, no worries, none of us really caring what we looked like.

'I'd love that,' I say, my eyes sweeping the room. 'But where's the dog?'

'I had to leave him tied to the gates outside,' Natalie replied. She lowered her voice a little when she added, 'I don't think he's the type of dog your mum approves of.'

'He's a Staffordshire,' explains Sarah. 'But a real sweetie.'

But what my mother would refer to as a 'chav animal', of course.

'Let's go,' I tell them decisively. 'Let's get out of here.'

'I saw your friends in town the other day,' Natalie says, rubbing Bunchy the dog's ears. We are on a swing each. They feel a lot smaller than they did ten years ago. Even with my reduced BMI. 'They were getting their nails done in that fancy beauty place.' She picks up a bit of twig from the ground and hurls into the grass. We all watch as Bunchy trots after it. Staffies don't bound, they trot, apparently. Quite refined, really.

'They're in there most days,' I say. 'Needlessly. I mean,

how often do you need to get your toenails clipped?'

I can feel Sarah and Natalie looking at me curiously.

'Go on, say it.' My voice is clear and direct. 'You must be dying to let me know how shallow I've been the past ten years.'

'You were never shallow,' says Sarah quietly. 'But maybe a little easily led . . .'

I have never thought about myself that way. I've always felt totally in control. It always felt like *I* led the way.

'Actually, I don't really think you ever stood a chance,' says Natalie. 'Your mum used to terrify me.'

'She still does terrify me,' I say, laughing. 'I mean, she thinks she's got my best interests at heart, but really, they're *her* best interests.' I look down at my dirty Converse. 'You know, it's years since I haven't bothered to dress up. Even just stepping outside our house. It's like the run-up to Fashion Week condensed into twenty minutes, every single day. She has very strict rules about appearance.'

Natalie and Sarah exchange a look.

'How did your mum get on with your boyfriend, Huckleberry?' asks Sarah softly. 'Did he come up to her standards?'

I laugh wryly. 'Not straight off. She didn't really get him – or his family – at first. But then she caught sight of his Oakley sunglasses and his vintage Rolex and she had a change of heart. Nothing my mother admires more than money. And Huck's family are rich.'

'I know.' Natalie is cuddling Bunchy. 'My mum used to

clean his dad's house.'

I hold a breath and feel a flush creeping across my cheeks. 'I didn't know that,' I say quietly. 'I never saw Sandra there.'

'She only went three days a week, and only for a couple of hours.' Natalie shrugged. 'I guess you must have just missed her.'

There seems something weirdly serendipitous about this.

'Did she have any good gossip to report?' I ask casually. 'Anything I might not have known about?' I can't help the slightly desperate note in my voice. I am hoping Natalie hasn't caught it, but when she looks up at me there is something guarded about her expression.

'What kind of gossip?'

I can see Sarah looking between the two of us, curiously.

'Oh, nothing,' I smile. 'Just . . . I was there a lot . . . But I always kind of felt I only got the top layer, the exuberance and the laid-back thing.'

Natalie laughs shortly. 'Huck's dad had a laid-back attitude towards parenting, I think. My mum was shocked at how he let those two do what they liked.'

'He wasn't exactly Victorian Dad,' I say, trying to sound light. 'That's for sure.'

There is a kind of different awkwardness between us now. I can't put my finger on why or how, but it feels like Natalie is holding something back. She has turned away from me, stroking the dog's flanks.

'I mean, it opened my eyes to just being free,' I go on. 'Not being confined to the kinds of rules that exist in my family. Huck was just so go-with-the-flow. He was the same with everyone.'

Natalie makes a noise, like she is sucking in a breath, or a response. I don't want to hear it for some reason, so I witter on.

'He made me realize how uptight I can be. Huck never examined anything too closely. I think he was better off for it. Nothing was a big deal.' As I say the last sentence I realize I am not buying into it. Not now. I want to, but it just feels like I am making excuses. 'He wasn't perfect,' I say finally. 'I know he wasn't perfect.'

'That's not what makes us fall in love,' Sarah says at last. 'Perfection. It's what we crave from someone that makes us attach to them.'

For a minute I am confused by what she's just said. But as I take in her words, I feel a rush of nausea coming up from my stomach. I feel as though I'm going to be sick.

'Lois?' Sarah touches my arm. 'Are you OK?'

'I'm fine. Fine . . .' I say, but I am brittle and I feel like another layer of me and Huck has peeled away, and I don't like what's underneath it.

I shiver. 'I'd better get back,' I say. 'But thanks for coming over. And thanks for talking to me.'

They look a little startled.

'That's what friends are for,' says Nat, reaching over and squeezing my arm.

'Thank you,' I say again. My eyes are cloudy with tears. All these weird new feelings are too much. I wrestle myself out of the swing.

'Don't be a stranger,' says Sarah. 'We're always here.'

I nod and turn to go home, quickening my pace as I walk. If I stop still for a moment, I think I might just start sobbing.

19

Daniel

I'm trying desperately hard not to look over at the group of girls hanging out further along the beach here in San Sebastian. They are all so way out of my league that I might as well have landed on another planet. Planet Attractive.

I am wishing I could put something over my head – actually over my whole body – so that my pale, English form was invisible.

Why does everyone in this country have to be gorgeous? It's weird. At least back in Manchester I can sometimes feel almost superior. I mean, not if you put me next to an Indie hipster, but down our road I am considered quite exotic. Even stylish. I should qualify that with the fact that most of our road is overy fifty. Apart from the ginger boy at number eighteen who has an unfortunate skin condition. He's my age, but so shy that no one has ever spoken to him. He also wears what even I recognize as bad clothes. Not that I'm an

151

expert. I'm not much good with fashion. I tend to find a pair of jeans I like and wear them non-stop, just switching T-shirts to mix it up, until the jeans disintegrate and I buy an identical pair. Don't even get me started on hair products and man moisturizer. All that stuff just baffles me.

I am ashamed to say that I even let my mum buy me clothes from time to time. I figure what's the point of trying to catch up with the cool kids when you're starting at such a disadvantage.

OK. Maybe I am taking the self-deprecation thing too far. I'm not that bad. I suppose I just lack confidence.

'What you need is a nice girl to boost you up,' my mother is known to say. 'Mrs Cohen's daughter Tamara is single. You should ask her to the cinema.'

Perhaps you begin to see what I mean by 'disadvantaged'. My mum's heart is in the right place, but seriously, Tamara Cohen? She has those thick *Ugly Betty* braces and frizzy hair, and she is halfway through elocution lessons, which makes it very difficult to understand anything she says. Other than that, and the way she spits her saliva out at you when she does start talking, she's a really nice girl.

Just not a girl I would ever want to take to the cinema.

I'd take Lo to the cinema though. I'd even let her eat popcorn or nachos all the way through the movie, something that usually sets my teeth on edge. But a girl who looks like Lo would never come within a million miles of me.

I am probably much better off with the Tamara Cohens

of this world. And it would make my mother so happy.

I just want to know what it's like to hold a girl's hand, and like it. And kiss her, and make her happy. But the girls I want are just out of my reach.

One day I will settle for someone, and my dreams will be dashed but I will be so broken by loneliness that I won't care any more.

I need to stop this self-destructive thinking, and rub factor 50 into my not-quite-so-white skin.

A ball lands next to me, along with two very pretty brown feet.

'Sorry.' The owner of the feet dazzles me with her blinding smile. That and the sun are totally doing my head in. But even so I can see that she could be around my age, maybe a little younger.

'No problem,' I manage to reply reasonably normally.

'You are working at Ronnie's place, yeah? Daniel?' She holds out her hand. 'I am Paula. Cristina is my cousin. She tells me to look out for you today. I guess it was you.' Her eyes travel over my pale skin. 'Why you putting so much cream on to you?'

'I burn and blister in the sun.' I flip the top of the suncream down. 'I'm like a vampire in that respect.' As I squint up at her, I know I have just shamelessly used the only hook I have at my disposal as bait. The V word does seem to get the girls going.

But Paula isn't taking the bait. She stares down at me, bemused, while I avert my eyes from her tanned cleavage.

153

'You want to play football with us?' she asks good-naturedly. 'We just about to start a game.'

I am about to shake my head and protest that I am useless at all ball-games, when I realize that maybe I am not actually useless. I've just never made that much of an effort before. There never seemed to be a point.

Which, clearly, there most certainly is now.

'OK,' I say casually. 'But I've got an old injury that plays up from time to time, so I probably won't be on top form.'

Paula giggles. 'We are rubbish! We're only a bunch of girls.'

This doesn't make any difference as far as I'm concerned, but I shrug as though it does.

The phrase 'Fake it till you make it' has never been more appropriate. I have a chance to engage with a girl who is actually in close physical proximity. The least I can do is make a total fool of myself trying to make something happen. In real time. Here in this paradise.

If the girls are bad at the game, I really don't notice. I'm too busy trying to look like I know what I am doing. But this does seem to be more of a knockabout than a serious game, and after a few minutes I relax a bit, and have a chance to check them out.

As I said, they are undeniably hot. All different shapes and sizes, but each of them has that physical ease that you see in those who spend a lot of time outdoors with not many clothes on because the weather designs it that way.

154

They don't have that tribal insecurity that girls back home have. There is no fear behind the eyes, wondering if they look thin enough, or tanned enough, or dressed up enough, and this relaxed attitude seems to extend to those around them.

No one has yet laughed at what my mum calls Uncle Ray's legs – quite thin and with no muscular definition to speak of. But the funny thing is, when I look down at them, I realize they really aren't so bad. In fact, they seem browner and less skinny. I would hardly compare them to David Beckham's but I may have just escaped the curse of Uncle Ray.

Paula kicks the ball towards me, and by sheer fluke my foot catches it and I volley it back. Encouraged, I smile at her. She kicks it to a blonde girl wearing a tiny bikini and then jogs over to me.

It's pretty hard not to stare at the contents of her bikini top jiggling as she moves but I have an admirable stab at it, forcing myself to look directly into her bright brown eyes.

'We are going to a cafe in town soon,' she tells me, a little breathlessly. 'You want to come too?'

'Me?' Out of sheer habit, I look confused. A common reaction when a pretty girl deigns to talk to me. 'Uh, well, I have to be back at Ronnie's at seven. He gave me the afternoon off now that his cast is off.' I check my watch. 'But I could come for an hour, I guess.'

'Cool.' Her smile broadens and her eyes drift very slightly over my body.

Am I imagining this, or is Paula actually flirting with me?

She holds out her hand and grabs my elbow. Her touch feels strange, soft and nice.

'Cristina is always talking about you,' Paula tells me as we follow her friends off the beach. 'I think she has a crush. To her you are like the boy from *Twilight*.'

I nod sagely. 'Robert Pattinson has single-handedly elevated the socially retarded pale geek to stud status. For that, at least, we should all be thankful to him.'

Paula laughs. 'You're witty.' And she smiles a bit shyly at me.

'Thanks,' I say, inwardly chuffed. 'And you're nice.'

Why didn't I say she was pretty? Which she is. Very. What's wrong with me?

But Paula knocks my elbow gently with hers. 'Thanks.'

I clear my throat. Better to change the flirting vibe between us before it inevitably disappears. 'Cristina's cute,' I reply guardedly. 'But she's just a kid.'

Paula looks amused. 'She is a clever one, though. She is a real romantic too.'

'I suppose she is.' All of a sudden, I am thinking of Cristina and her belief in Lo's 'story', and of course this makes me think of Lo. Far away. Lonely . . . angry, confused. It feels irrationally disloyal to be strolling around with someone else.

'What's wrong?' Paula drops her hand away from my arm. 'You have gone quiet.'

'I was just thinking,' I say. 'About girls.' Before I can register what I've just said, Paula swats me lightly on the shoulder.

'And I thought you were different,' she exclaims, though her eyes are shining at me as I turn to look at her.

I think for a split second before I come back.

'Nah,' I say, shrugging. 'I'm just like all the others, deep down.'

'I don't believe you.' Paula gives me a sidelong look. 'You are nice. I can tell. Believe me, growing up here, any boy who is not a . . . well, who is not out for his own needs . . . he stands out. I am so tired of all the macho men.' She sighs, a little too world-wearily for one so young. 'They are so boring.'

'Do you have a boyfriend, Paula?' I ask her.

She flushes slightly. 'Kind of. I mean, I don't really know if I am his girl. He has a few girls he likes.'

I raise an eyebrow. 'Oh.'

'See? This is what I am saying. They are all at it.'

'But I'm selfish too,' I say, and I realize it's true. 'I'm just selfish about different things. And the fact is, if I could actually find a girl who'd agree to go out with me, then maybe after a bit I would take her for granted too.' OK, that last bit I am not so sure about. I cannot imagine any scenario in which I would take a girl for granted. Chance would be a fine thing.

'No.' Paula shakes her head, echoing what's in my mind. 'You would not. I can just tell. And as for finding a girl

157

– well, maybe you are not looking in the right places?' And then she looks up at me, her eyes widening, vulnerable and I think, what is stopping me from just kissing her? She wants me to kiss her.

But, because I am not used to kissing girls, I don't know. And because I am a nice boy, I respectfully don't.

Paula gives me a slow smile, teasing me, and I smile back. And then, very respectfully, I take her hand in mine.

20
Eloise

Mum is sitting at the kitchen table, holding a pen and staring down at a long list she's making. It's 11 a.m. and after a sleepless night, I have slept in. She looks up as I take a carton of orange juice out of the fridge. Feeling her eyes on me I am tempted to skip the glass and drink straight out of the container. But the potential fall-out from this act makes it too much effort. I grab a glass from the counter and pour myself a large one.

Mum won't be happy about that, either. She's obsessed with portion control.

'You need a haircut,' she tells me absently. 'Your split ends are a disgrace, darling.'

I grunt and pull out a chair. 'I'll go into town later,' I say cooperatively, my eyes flickering to her list. 'What's that?'

'We're having a big barbecue on Saturday.' She sounds bored. 'It'll be the last this year. I'm trying to decide on the menu. I don't trust these catering companies. Everything's so loaded with fat.'

'Oh yeah,' I say, taking a glug of juice. 'Not to mention the evil carbs. Can you imagine the horror if a batch of sausage rolls were to turn up?' I didn't intend to sound facetious, but now that I have, I feel satisfaction at the sight of her nose wrinkling.

'Don't be silly,' she says, irritated. 'Now, who do you want to invite?'

'Nobody.' I drain my glass.

Valerie ignores my response. 'Of course Jessica, Laura and Destiny will come. And what about that nice boy across the road. Mrs Jeffries' son, Alex.'

'Who?'

'He's studying medicine, you know. And he's very dishy.'

A bubble of laughter gets stuck in my throat, along with some residual orange juice. I cough. 'He's what? He's *dishy*? Honestly, Mother. It's not 1975 any more.'

She stares at me. And though her face says disapproval, her thoughts are clearly already elsewhere.

'Well, he's a very nice boy,' she murmurs. 'And he's ambitious. Solid.' She taps her pen on her pad. 'You could do much worse.'

'Oh, is it that time already?' I look at my watch. 'Is it time to get a new boyfriend? Only I'm not really done being upset about the old one.' I stare at her. 'You know, the one who died?'

'Eloise, what has got into you?' Mum finally puts down her pen and glares at me. 'There is no need for this sarcasm. It's not like you.'

A strange feeling comes over me as I return her glare. A feeling like I have just ripped off a tenacious plaster. Or got the stubborn lid off a bottle of ketchup. A feeling of satisfaction. Relief. And strength.

'Maybe it *is* like me,' I tell her. 'But I never wanted you to know about it. I always behaved as you wanted me to behave.'

'What on earth are you talking about?' She looks genuinely confused.

'Maybe you're not the only one around here with a sharp tongue, that's all.' I eye her, waiting for Vesuvius to erupt, but I can see that her confusion merely deepens. Her artificially smooth forehead is very nearly wrinkling.

'I really haven't got time for this,' she says at last, wearily.

I let out a large sigh. What's the point? Seriously. Trying to communicate with my mother is like talking to a foreign-exchange student.

Her eyes linger on me for a few seconds more, before she picks up her pen again and stares down at her precious list.

'Actually, I do have some people I want to invite,' I say, running my finger around the rim of my empty glass. 'Natalie and Sarah.'

She's still bent over her list, but I see her hand twitch.

'I don't think so, darling,' she says airily. 'They're not

really going to fit in. Literally, in fact. I think we have too many people as it is.'

'Not if we don't invite Jess and the others,' I say. 'I'd rather Nat and Sarah came.'

That merits solid eye contact. 'Lois. I am worried about you. You're acting very strangely. Those girls are your closest friends. Have you fallen out?'

'Not really. I just . . . I'm not connecting with them any more. Ever since Huck died—'

Valerie sharply breathes in. 'It's difficult to know what to say, darling. For all of us. We're all just trying to jolly you along.'

'But I don't want to be jollied along, Mum. I just want you to listen to me.' I watch her face, waiting, hoping for the penny to drop, but she looks as nonplussed as ever. 'Sarah and Natalie . . . They're good listeners.'

'I see.' Her lips are pinching. 'I do my best, Eloise. Granted, I am not one of those touchy-feely mothers. You know that. But I do care about you. I care that you're sad.' And then her forehead actually wrinkles, defying science; it actually moves into little lines. I have to say, I am very nearly touched.

'I know,' I say softly. 'But maybe you can understand that my priorities have changed. I mean, all the Kooples jackets in the world can't fill this . . .' I trail off as I see the look of discomfort on her face.

'Yes, I see what you're getting at.' She sighs. 'But it isn't good to dwell on tragedy, darling. All this wallowing—'

'Wallowing?' My eyes widen at her. 'Mum. Huck died. He died. He is no more. Never coming back. Forgive me if I take a moment to absorb that. I mean, we were serious. We—'

'You were teenagers in love,' she says flintily. 'In five years' time do you think you would have still been together?' She shuts her eyes, possibly already regretting her insensitivity, and when she speaks again she has put a softer note into her voice. 'You and Huck. It was sweet. And he was a lovely boy. And his family. So charming and bohemian. But they were a little flaky, Eloise.' She puts her elbows on the table and pins me with her eyes. 'You have to admit. Carlo's gallivanting about without a care in the world? And you know, the apple never falls so far from the tree.' She stops then, leaving me to ingest that particularly comforting nugget.

'Well, thanks, Mother. Don't try and sugar-coat it,' I mutter, pushing my chair back from the table. Behind me I sense another presence in the room. When I turn, I almost fall into my dad's arms. He is eyeing the two of us.

'Something going on?' he says warily.

'Eloise is a little overwrought, that's all.' Mum is brisk, adding somewhat inappropriately, 'I got some nice steak for dinner.'

Dad, bless him, ignores this. Instead he puts a hand awkwardly on my shoulder. 'Are you all right, kid?'

I force a smile. 'Fine. Just my usual theatrics,' I tell him, sarcasm seeping into every word. 'Mum's sorted it.'

I push past him. It would be too much to ask that Dad would stick up for me with Mum. This whole family is seriously messed up. And I include myself in that.

But as I climb the stairs up to my floor, I think I hear the sound of my dad raising his voice. And when I peek over the bannister, he is shutting the kitchen door behind him.

Maybe he'll surprise me, after all.

Up in my bedroom, I sweep a pile of clothes off the bed and thump down on it. I have no clue what to do with myself. I simply have no idea how to deal with feelings. I am not so different to my mother, after all, I think. I am trying, but confronting reality is as alien to me as it is to her. It makes me feel naked and ugly and defenceless. I feel so alone. I need someone I feel comfortable enough to talk to. Someone who will just listen.

I sit up. Maybe there is someone. Even if that person isn't really there. Does it matter? Not if I tell myself they can hear me.

I reach for my phone in my bag and scroll to the now familiar number.

I hate my life right now. I want someone to tell me that everything is going to be all right. I want you to tell me that that you're coming home. That you'll take care of me.

I send the message. Then I sit back, relief mixed with sadness in my heart. I'm sad because something of what

164

my mother said down in the kitchen has struck a nerve. Did I ever feel safe with Huck? Am I asking something of him now that he never really offered me while he was alive?

It's almost as if I am not really talking to Huck at all. I am talking to the boy I want him to be.

Just over a year ago we were at Bestival. Huck and I had travelled down on the back of his Piaggio scooter. An experience I had enjoyed solely because my arms were wrapped around him for hours on end. The roughing-it element at the end of the journey, I was less excited by. But through a friend of her dad's Jessica had snagged a VIP room so we were all spared the indignity of dressing without a full-length mirror in the morning, and had access to a private shower. It was still roughing it. I was used to my en suite, as were my girls. And the less than a hundred per cent cotton sheets were not ideal, but it wasn't a tent. And that was the main thing.

My mother viewed music festivals as though they were the seventh circle of Hell. She hadn't bothered to conceal her disapproval.

'But it's all so dirty,' she'd said, wrinkling her nose. 'Doesn't everyone wear wellington boots?'

'Only as a fashion statement,' I told her, holding up a Ralph Lauren cagoule before stuffing it in my Vuitton holdall. I pondered how my luggage would fit on the back of Huck's scooter.

'And the toilets,' she went on in a ridiculous

melodramatic whisper. 'I just can't see the appeal of these things.'

'You mean to say you never let your hair down in your youth?' I said, zipping up my bag. 'You must have done.'

For a moment, my mother's expression was wistful. 'Your father and I did spend a lot of evenings at Kenwood House in Hampstead,' she said, the hint of a smile on her lips. 'But that was a very different thing. Civilized. I'd get dressed up, and your father would collect me from Granny's house in St John's Wood. He had one of those awful little Ford Fiestas. At the time I thought it was the height of sophistication . . .' She trailed off. 'We did have fun. We always ended the evenings at John and Deborah's rented flat in Parliament Hill Fields.'

She stopped talking then. A different expression came over her face. I wasn't used to emotion in her eyes, but I think at that moment I came close to seeing it.

'So Dad courted you at Kenwood?' I said, turning to her, wanting to keep the conversation going. 'I bet he made sure you drank only the best champagne.'

'Sparkling wine, actually,' she said quickly. 'We couldn't afford champagne in those days, but your father had lofty ambitions even then, so it was prosecco. He was such an adult.' She lifted her chin and a little bloom came into her cheeks. It was an almost excruciating moment. Like seeing a rare and beautiful animal stand still in front of you. I wanted to hold on to it. But the buzzer to the gates sounded, and Mum leapt into action. She grabbed a cashmere pashmina from the back of a chair and thrust it at me.

'Please tell me you're going by taxi,' she said, pressing a button next to the phone on the wall. Through the small TV screen next to it, we saw Huck, looking effortlessly gorgeous in chinos and a leather jacket, next to his Piaggio.

'It'll be fine,' I told Mum. 'Seriously.'

And it had been. Kind of. We'd arrived at our B&B intact, and after a quick inspection in Huck's rear mirror I allowed myself to relax.

Jess and Destiny were already shrieking in the room we were going to be sharing. Laura was in Lake Como, barbecuing with George Clooney, and no doubt totally gutted that she couldn't spend the weekend ankle deep in mud and old roaches.

'Oh God, look at you. Only you could look gorgeous after three hours on a scooter,' said Jessica, already stripped down to her La Perla underwear.

'Girl, you look like you need a cocktail,' countered Destiny, fully clothed and wearing so much bling I was amazed she didn't topple over.

'A cocktail sounds like heaven,' I sighed. 'But how about the local pub for an alternative?' I eyed the two of them. 'Huck's meeting some friends in there tonight.'

'Oh God. Another bunch of arty public schoolboys,' groaned Jess. 'What's the betting we'll be buying our own drinks all night?'

'Jessica, this is the twenty-first century,' I said wearily. 'I always buy my own drinks. It's empowering.'

'She's right,' said Destiny. 'Once they start paying, you start owing. You know what I mean?'

'Oh, I suppose so,' Jess sniffed, pulling some skin-tight Hudson jeans up her legs. 'And you never know, maybe the local squire's son will be enjoying a half pint of cider there too. I quite fancy myself as a country wife.'

Destiny and I bit our lips at the same time in an effort not to laugh.

'You are unbelievable,' Destiny murmured, putting one hand affectionately on Jess's shoulder.

Jess, Destiny and I all slept together in the same room. As I recall it was one of the few times we had real fun. It's hard to be a princess when you're sleeping on a blow-up mattress on a hideous carpet in a room that smells overpoweringly of lavender air freshener. That was me, by the way. It was decided that since I was the one with a boyfriend, I could forfeit the debatably comfortable double divan.

The next day brought a whole different kind of fun. I use the word loosely. While Jess and Destiny spent most of their time in the sun drinking sparkling water and refusing to touch any of the food on offer, I wandered the festival trying to keep up with Huck and his band of merry men.

The thing about being around Huck was that his magnetism kind of overwhelmed you. To the point where you didn't fully notice that he couldn't keep still, and was forever letting go of your hand to talk to an old friend we'd run into, or hustle to the front of the crowd when we watched a band playing. Quite often I was left on my own staring around me, bobbing up and down trying to catch sight of him.

It was around 11 p.m. I had long since lost contact with the girls and was standing at the back of a not-large-enough sweaty tent watching an obscure emo band. I say watching – I couldn't actually see anything. I'd had two beers and my head was thumping. I am such a lightweight. I was just looking around half-heartedly for a sign of my boyfriend, or one of his mates, when someone crashed into me from the side.

I held in a breath, determined not to show the full extent of my annoyance. Festivals are meant to chill you out; they just make me feel tetchy. And all wrong.

'Hey, sorry.' A girl with a short pixie crop wearing a vest and tiny denim shorts gave me a small smile. She pushed a hand through what little hair she had, and I noticed the joint in her other hand. She gave me a sidelong look.

'Want some?' She held out the joint.

'Uh . . . no thanks,' I said, sounding curiously like Princess Anne.

'Sure?' She took a long drag, held her mouth shut while she inhaled and then blew out a perfect smoke ring.

'I'm good.' The smell of her joint was making my nose itch. Another allergy I have, apparently – drugs of all classes.

Uptight. Square. And posh. That's me.

'I love your skirt.' Pixie Girl pointed her joint at my leather mini. 'Topshop?'

'Um, Malene Birger,' I said in a vague I-really-don't-think-about-clothes-that-much manner.

Pixie Girl looked blank, then her eyebrows moved towards each other in a ponderous kind of way. 'You're with Huck, aren't you?' she asked. 'I'm sure I saw you guys hanging out by the beer tent.'

'You know Huck?'

She smiled in a way I didn't much like. It was a conspiratorial kind of smile. Knowing. Cryptic.

'For a long time,' she said.

'Oh.' I looked at her questioningly.

'Yeah, I feel as if I've known him for ever. My mum went to art school with Carlo. I used to hang out at their house all the time.' And then Pixie Girl yawned, a really fake yawn.

'OK. I didn't know.' I held out my hand, wondering when she and Huck were so tight, and why I'd never heard him speak of her. 'I'm Eloise. Lo.'

Pixie Girl took my hand awkwardly, swaying a little. 'Angelica,' she said, hesitating for a few seconds before she added. 'So, he's gone AWOL, I bet? Huck?'

Having taken a short break, the band on stage were launching into another song. I had to shout my answer over the drums. 'What?' I shook my head, too forcefully. 'No. He's just doing his own thing at the front.'

Angelica gave me a strange look then. She dropped her

170

joint on the floor and squished it dead with her foot. She gestured to the tent exit. 'Come outside for a minute?'

I found myself following her. Curious, but with a horrible feeling in the pit of my stomach. My head was seriously pounding now.

Outside it was drizzling. To add to the already less-than-perfect scenario. My hair would soon resemble a feather duster. For once I wasn't bothered.

'I don't think Huck's around at the moment,' she said, looking down at the sodden grass as though it were utterly fascinating. 'I kind of saw him heading out in a car about half an hour ago.' She looked up at me then. 'I mean, he probably went to get cigarettes or something . . .'

'Huck doesn't smoke,' I said immediately. 'Why would he go off in a car? He has his scooter.'

Angelica shrugged. 'I dunno, hon. I'm sure he'll be back soon. You know what he's like. He gets bored easily.'

'Does he?' I said faintly.

Angelica put her hand on my shoulder. 'You OK? You look upset?'

'When did you two hang out?' I said, ignoring her question. Even though it wasn't cold I was shivering.

'A few years ago,' she said carefully. 'I suppose Huck and I were pushed together by our parents. And we had some stuff in common.'

'Like what?' There was a jealous edge to my voice. I couldn't help it.

'Like art and music and books . . . stuff like that.'

'Not anything important then,' I said, hugging myself. Did Huck and I ever talk properly about that stuff? All I could think of were his soft brown eyes as he leaned in to kiss me. His arms around me as we lay on Carlo's sofa watching box-sets. Huck did notice when I was wearing something nice. He knew his designers. I'd never thought that odd before, but maybe it was a little. It felt increasingly as though there was no depth to our relationship. Every time I asked Huck about Carlo's art, or started telling him about the plot of the book I was reading, there was always some way in which he switched the subject or got distracted.

'Look, I'm sure he'll be back soon. Like I told you, Huck gets bored. He doesn't mean to. But I suppose his childhood wasn't conventional. There was always something going on. Some other country to be in. Some party to go to. He's like his dad. Nomadic. Restless.'

The crowd inside the tent were shouting for an encore. Suddenly I wanted to go home. Not back to the B&B, but home home.

I made a bold decision.

'Well, thanks for the chat,' I told Angelica. 'It was very informative. If you see Huck around, tell him I'll see him later.'

'Sure,' she said uncomfortably. 'Of course. I'll tell him.'

I walked out of the festival gates with nothing on me but my small Miu Miu pouch, a pair of rubber Westwood ankle boots and no coat. But I was sure I'd find a lift, or get a cab.

Someone must be heading out of this hellhole.

I walked for a long time, until finally I saw a small van heading towards me. I put out a hand and the van pulled up. A man wearing overalls and smoking a cigarette stuck his head out of the driving-seat window.

'Want a lift?' he asked. His eyes travelled down me. Taking in my leather mini and my boots.

It was a stupid thing to even think about doing. But I wasn't in my right mind at that moment.

I was just getting into the passenger seat when a car pulled up next to the van. Actually it braked suddenly next to the van.

'Oi!' The van driver roared, and I paused. One foot inside the car.

'Lo?' I turned to see Huck halfway out of the window. 'What's going on?'

'I'm going home,' I told him coldly. 'You don't mind, do you? Or is that a terrible bore?'

He looked confused. He got out of the car and grabbed my arm, pulling me into him.

'Oh, baby, I am so sorry. We had to take Mitch to the local A&E. He cut his arm on a broken beer bottle. I tried to find you, but there was no time.' He put his arms around me. And as I took in his explanation I felt that blessed relief flood through me. Like waking up from a bad dream.

'Lo, Lo, Lo,' he murmured. 'I didn't think. I just didn't think.'

I tried to put up some resistance, but the feel of him

holding me was just too good. Too much what I needed right then.

'So, you want a lift or not?' came a voice behind me. The van driver was already starting his engine loudly. 'You kids think you own the world,' he said nastily.

As he pulled away I turned to Huck, pushing him gently on his chest.

'I met your friend Angelica,' I told him softly. 'She was very informative about your relationship.' I lifted my chin and stared into his eyes.

There was a split second's hesitation before Huck chuckled in response. 'Angelica . . . How is she? She just got out of rehab. I should really call her.'

'Rehab?' I frowned. 'But she . . .' I didn't finish my sentence. Rehab had clearly been a waste of time as Angelica was certainly back on the drugs again. That seemed to explain a few things. Another rush of relief hit me.

'She seems . . . fine,' I told Huck and wrapped my arms around his chest, leaning my head against him. 'Can we just go home now?'

'Of course, baby. Whatever you want.'

21

Daniel

So I blew it with Paula. Just when I was finally within reach of a living, breathing, attractive girl, I break the first rule.

I check my phone in front of her.

OK. It wasn't the checking of the phone so much as the thing that I was checking. Paula happened to peer over my shoulder and see the very unambiguous words:

> *I have a feeling you told me a lot of lies. Things are coming back to me now. I feel like a fool.*

Paula's intake of breath is sharp and also unambiguous.

'Daniel,' she whispers harshly, 'what is this?'

I am about to explain, when I realize that the truth will sound even worse. So I open my mouth, and leave it open for what seems like hours, my eyes doing a mild panic dance.

'It's not what you think,' I manage at last. 'Really. It's not.'

But Paula has stood up from her seat in the cafe, causing her posse to turn, narrow-eyed in our direction.

'I am such a fool, too,' Paula says, and to my horror I think I can see the glimpse of tears in those pretty eyes. 'I thought you were a different boy to the others. But all the time you have a girl. And you are not a nice boy!'

'I don't—' I sigh heavily, frustrated. I want to clear my name, set the record straight, but I am going to look like a weird loser if I do. Right now I look like a cheat. A player. And this is not satisfying. It doesn't make me feel powerful and in control. It makes me feel like crap. But it's easier than the truth.

At this moment a group of boys who look distinctly as if they do enjoy this kind of reputation pour through the cafe door. It becomes like a small reunion as Paula's friends clearly know these boys. For a moment my heinous behaviour is forgotten as loud greetings ring out all round. Until one boy, about my height, but infinitely more muscular, spots Paula's distress and puts one arm manfully around her shoulders.

He says something to her in Spanish. Something crooning and concerned. Paula's head rests her head sadly on his shoulder, her mouth set in a nice pout. Her comforter fixes his flinty eyes on me.

Before he can say a word, I am out of my seat, pulling my sweatshirt over my head and avoiding all eye contact.

The crowds part, and when I reach the door and glance back, I see Paula in Mr Man's arms.

I realize. This must be the on–off boyfriend. Playing the good-guy card for all he's worth. I guess there's nothing more guaranteed to make a boy feel like a hero than a maiden in distress. Pity I didn't think of that.

So now it is the morning after, and I am crating up empty bottles in the backyard and studiedly ignoring Rubi the killer Alsatian.

'Hey!' hisses a voice behind me, nearly causing me to upturn the crate of empty bottles I am holding on to the ground.

Recovering it, at the painful expense of my upper arms, I turn breathlessly to see Cristina standing in the back door entrance, idly watching.

'Shhh,' I tell her. 'The dog!'

Cristina shrugs. 'So you upset my cousin Paula,' she says, a hint of feminine disapproval in her voice. 'Why didn't you tell her the truth?'

I put the crate down and push it over to the wall with one foot before brushing my hands off on my jeans, and finally answering. 'Oh, I don't know. Because it would have looked weird.' I raise an eyebrow. 'I mean, come on. It is weird. A little.'

'Oh, Daniel.' Cristina sighs. 'You don't understand women, do you?'

I open my mouth in a display of amused outrage, but

Cristina is maintaining steady eye contact.

'Maybe not.' I put my hands on my hips. My turn to sigh. 'But it just seemed like an excruciating situation whichever way I turned. How could I explain that I am voyeuristically experiencing a stranger's pain like some kind of sad stalker? I mean, what am I doing?' I take the phone out of my pocket. 'I should get rid of this. And start getting on with real life. Don't you think, Cristina?'

She considers for a few seconds. 'Perhaps you need to solve the mystery before you do this.' She looks at the phone. 'Then you will know and it will be closed. And then, maybe, you could start a new thing with a girl.'

'And exactly how do I "solve the mystery"?' I ask. I start heading for the back door, but Cristina places one small brown arm across it.

'Daniel. Don't be mad,' she says softly. 'I am trying to help.'

I smile at her. 'I know. But it's time to stop this. It's getting silly.'

'Something about this girl is in your heart,' she says quickly, to stop me going inside. 'I think she talks to you.'

'Well, she talks to someone,' I say wearily. 'But it isn't really me.'

'But it is.' Cristina's hand moves to catch my elbow. 'She just doesn't know it yet.'

I give her a smile then. Suddenly I'm aware that this child-woman may be a whole lot more emotionally astute than I am.

'You're sweet,' I tell her. 'And quite smart.'

Cristina's cheeks flush, and she breathes in a satisfied kind of sigh, patting my arm in a sisterly gesture.

'Stick with me, Daniel. I know how romance works.'

'I'll bet you do,' I say. 'And I'm grateful. Because I don't have a clue.'

'Daniel!' Ronnie's voice roars cheerfully from somewhere upstairs. 'You finished with the crating? I need to let the dog out for her walkies now.'

Cristina giggles. 'You'd better hurry,' she whispers. "Cause Rubi gets very hungry round about now.'

I hotfoot it down to the bar, casting a wary look behind me.

My pockets are heavy with cellular technology. It's something I've got used to over the past couple of weeks. It's comforting, in a way. I park myself on a bar stool, checking the clock, and fish both phones out, placing them on the table in front of me.

One – my actual phone – contains communication from my friends back home and from my mother. The other is my hotline to the stars.

I am just pondering this when there is a beep. Incoming text. It's the right phone. The phone I am most inclined to.

I take a breath and check it. I am expecting another lashing from Lo. But still, I want to know how she's feeling. What new twist this story will take.

I'm sorry. I just miss you, OK. I just miss you.

No you don't I think. You really don't. You're just tired. And feeling nostalgic. He's a jerk. He's not missing you.

I have an intense urge to tell her this. I have to stick my hands in my pockets to stop myself.

But this is agonizing. It's like witnessing a wounded animal.

I sit back on a bar stool, just staring at the phone lying on the counter. How does she not know what an arse this guy is? But what do I know. I couldn't even sort out the misunderstanding in the cafe with Paula yesterday. I am clueless. I suppose I see things a bit too simply.

In fact, the world is populated by complicated, irrational human beings.

No. I don't want to join the ranks. I know for a fact that Tamara Cohen would be blissfully content with an uncomplicated, rational human being such as myself. I could ask Tamara out and get exactly what I want.

Only I wouldn't. Because I don't want the Tamaras of this world.

I am sighing inwardly. I have just contradicted myself. It seems I am not so straightforward after all. I too hanker for something that flips my stomach over. Or someone. I don't just want a girlfriend. I want to fall in love.

22

Eloise

Today we had a home-cooked Sunday lunch. For the first time in a long time. I realized today that was why I had spent so much time at Huck's at weekends; Carlo loved to cook. And if it wasn't exactly traditional English cuisine, it was made with gusto and love. The weekend was when he would cook his most delicious, extravagant meals. The whole family came, including Helena, and always a few of Carlo's friends. All of us sitting round the table, talking, eating for the sheer pleasure of it. We wouldn't get up and leave the table until it was nearly dark outside.

That must have been why I put on seven pounds over the time we were seeing each other. Mum had not even tried to hide her annoyance. Mum equates weight gain with failure, with lack of self-control, lack of self-respect. She very unsubtly hired a personal trainer to come over at the crack of dawn three times a week. She cleared the cupboards of all carbohydrates and stood over me while I ate grilled fish and steamed vegetables, and absolutely no dessert.

'You'll thank me in time,' she'd said crisply. 'As you get older, it's a nightmare to shift the extra weight.'

Dad had frowned while pretending to read the paper, but he knew better than to chip in.

I was taken shopping for new clothes. All size six and all naturally expensive. The rationale being that I would think twice before rendering them unwearable by eating more than 1500 calories a day.

I'd gone along with it, because I thought Mum knew what was best. She was easily the most glamorous woman in town. She was whip smart, whip thin, immaculately dressed . . . and she always got what she wanted.

A role model *toujours*. *N'est pas?*

Of course, I still dined at Carlo's, I just became a little more neurotic when the potatoes were passed around. I ignored my stomach's cry of longing at the sight of his special crispy fried chicken, and shook my head at the creamed spinach and custard tarts and the honey cheesecake. I denied myself all of it, pouring a healthy volume of sparkling water into my wine, and then finally just stuck with pure water.

But come to think of it, I did become just a little bit boring, too. I was succumbing to the Valerie Order, and it would have taken a coma victim not to notice.

'I love it when girls eat,' Huck told me. 'Are you off your

food? Because you usually dig in like it's your last meal.'

I had mastered the art of the laid-back shrug. 'I'm detoxing.' Or, 'I think I ate something a bit off at home last night.' Or, and I feel shame when I think about it now, 'I think I've developed an allergy to fatty food.'

And yes, I did say that with a straight face. And apparently without a hint of self-awareness. It became second nature to refuse things.

And I suspect it became second nature to turn into a giant blonde bore. Or, in my case, a shrinking blonde bore.

No wonder Huck's attention started to wander.

Because, now, every day, I think of something new that hurt me.

Angelica I let go. She was a recovering drug addict. I couldn't have trusted what she said. But there were others. There were daughters of Carlo's friends. There were Huck's many female cousins. All young, impossibly naturally athletic, dark-skinned and perfect-lipped, or coolly blonde and utterly poised. Or just plain bubbly and unselfconscious. While I distracted myself from my hunger with books and deep, intense conversations about 'us', Huck couldn't wait to get out there and have fun.

'I'm meeting some boys and their girls for a pizza later,' he told me one Saturday night, stroking my arm absently. 'You're welcome to come. I think we're heading for a party later.'

Pizza. One of the seven deadly sins. I yawned, giving him a sleepy-eyed look. 'I'm a little tired . . . maybe I'll have a nap and meet up with you guys later.'

I noticed the slightly impatient look he gave me, even though his voice was as calm as ever. 'I'm not sure, baby. It might be complicated to hook up . . . Why don't you just come along for the meal, then you'll be right there when we move on. Otherwise I'd have to phone, and wait for you . . .' He trailed off, his fingers still stroking my arm. A deceptively tender gesture. He was trying to shake me off. I'd blown it because I wouldn't let some dough and melted cheese pass my lips.

'You go. Have fun,' I said brightly. Inside I hated myself. I was ruining things.

But Huck never once asked about my eating habits. I realize now what that meant. That he just didn't care enough to bring it up. To him it was an annoyance, but he wasn't about to help me out of this hole I was in. That was clearly up to me.

Jess, Laura and Destiny, however, were totally on to me.

'OK.' Jess had flopped on to my bed and given me her serious face. 'You're just about bordering on Ana territory, Lo. I mean, right now a size four is normal, but you drop below and you're heading for Nicole Ritchie pre-baby number one.' She studied me hard. 'And that, my friend, is emaciated.'

'Are you eating *anything*?' Destiny put in while brushing a tiny amount of Moroccan oil through her straightened 'fro. "Cause the only thing I've seen you put in your mouth lately is one grape. Two days ago.'

'It's your eyes.' Laura coiled her hair into an elegant bun and stuck a chopstick through it. 'They are popping out of your face.'

'I mean, I don't think you've mastered the art of denial correctly.' Jessica rested her face on her elbow, her slightly too-big gold watch sliding down her long slender arm. 'You eat half of what you're given. You don't refuse food altogether. You eat half, remove any extraneous fat from what you do eat, then push the rest of your food artfully around your plate.'

'This way you don't arouse suspicion,' said Laura knowingly. 'And you just lose a little.' She looked me up and down. 'It is a complicated equation at first, but you never want to attract attention. This defeats the object. You see?'

It suddenly seemed like there was a whole etiquette involved in pulling off an eating disorder. My stomach had growled in agreement, and with it the sensible part of my brain. 'I don't want to belong to that club,' I said firmly. 'The Eating Disorder Society. I just want to get my mum off my case.'

Jess sighed deeply. 'Your mother has a point, Eloise. These are the years to nip eating in the bud. It only gets harder as one ages.'

'Hang on . . . Are you actually my mother?' I craned forward comically, sizing Jessica up.

I was fighting a losing battle. I couldn't deny that I didn't get a faintly self-satisfied feeling when a size four fit with room to spare. But that had been overridden lately by the lethargy, the dizziness when I got up, the mood swings and the sheer exhaustion of having to think about how I could avoid eating. I was so focused on it that I had nothing interesting to say to Huck. And this new, slightly more neurotic me did not have him paying me any more attention. What the diet gurus don't tell you is that developing an obsession with calorie consumption turns you into total bore. Who cares if you can fit into that dress, or that your waist is twenty-four inches? When you lose your sense of humour, and your personality becomes one-dimensional you are no fun. And boys don't want to spend time with you.

As the only one of us with a boyfriend, I felt obliged to point this out to *mes amies*.

'Huck is going off me,' I said quickly. 'I am becoming a cardboard cut-out of myself. A paper-thin cardboard cut-out.' I blinked at them sadly. 'And who wants to be with a cardboard cut-out?'

For a second, Jessica's iron-fast logic was shaken. Not ever having emotionally attached herself to another human being (Jess preferred the intimate relationship she enjoyed with her mum's credit card) she was without words.

'Pah!' said Laura dismissively. 'He would soon be complaining if you were a heifer.'

'But would I be a heifer?' I asked her weakly. 'I mean, maybe it would be fine if I just ate normally. Then I would be just . . . normal.'

This had the effect of stunned silence in the room. We are not normal. We are anything but 'normal'.

So why did the prospect of 'normal' feel good right then? Just to disappear into the crowd. Be acceptable looking, wear nice, high-street-bought clothes, be academically average. Not have Grade 6 piano. Have a mother who actually bothers to turn up to PTA meetings rather than send the home help to 'report back'.

But back then I was still under the spell of an illusory life. One where everything shone golden and sparkly and privilege was a given. Despite the fact that I could see Huck slipping away from me, my loyalty to the cause was stronger.

What if I had been brave enough to stand up to my mother, or defy my friends' polarized view of life?

Maybe then Huck would have paid me more attention.

Not that he would ever have dumped me. Huck knew that having a satellite like me on his arm gave him kudos. It gave him proper status as an alpha male. He carried on calling, he went through the motions.

And then he decided it was time. Time to move us on to a new level.

I wasn't sure I was ready for that. But the truth was I had to do something to keep him interested in me. That's how I felt. So when Carlo announced he would be out of the country for a month, it seemed like it was now or never.

23

Daniel

I haven't heard from Lo in two days. I wish I could say I am happy for her. Her errant boyfriend must have finally got in touch. Explained away the whole deeply unsatisfactory situation. They're probably on the phone with each other right now, and he's telling her how sorry he is, how he lost his phone and has been up a remote and dangerous Spanish mountain with no other way to get in contact.

But I am not happy for her. I am ashamed to say I am resentful. I have another two weeks here before I head home to the reality of uni, where I'll have to try and make friends, and stare at all the beautiful popular girls I can never get near. I have been a foolish dreamer. Imagining that this whole 'misunderstanding' would somehow result in . . . what? A romance? I seriously need to get a life when I get back. I need to participate, not just observe.

I am staring despondently at my bare feet while I take a

break from cleaning the bar and sit outside for a bit in the sun. I sigh deeply and shut my eyes when I feel a small, cool hand on my shoulder.

'Not now, Cristina,' I say wearily. 'I'm not in the mood for company.'

'Oh, I was hoping you will come for a walk, Daniel,' says a voice that is not Cristina's.

'Paula?' I open my eyes. I am wearing an oversized T-shirt and long combat shorts, yet I feel curiously naked. 'I thought you were Cristina. She can be a little demanding at times.'

Paula smiles down at me. From this angle she looks lovelier than ever. Her long, brown-blonde hair curling slightly at the ends, her fetching cotton dress erring on the right side of decent, just. Her flawless caramel tan twinkling a little in the glare of the sun. She studies me with her large brown eyes.

'We are demanding in this family,' she says, and lowers herself to perch, sharing Ronnie's shabby sun lounger with me. She is uncomfortably close. 'Cristina told me,' she says calmly. 'She explained.'

'Oh.' I concentrate on not flushing the colour of a ripe tomato. 'Right.'

'Why didn't you tell me?' She says it kindly. Pityingly, perhaps? I stop myself from going there. This is looking hopeful, after all.

Eventually I give a slight shrug, shifting a little on the lounger. Paula smells of suntan lotion and the sea. I feel a stirring, which is probably not appropriate right now.

I sit up straighter and sigh. 'It's nothing,' I say lamely. 'I mean, I found this phone and this girl starts texting . . . and, you know . . . I am a bit lonely. I guess it made me feel less alone to get her messages.' My eyes have drifted away from the girl next to me. I just can't look at her. I sound like such a loser.

'Yes,' she says softly. 'I can see you are lonely. I saw it on the beach.' She hesitates, then, 'I think it is what made me come and talk to you. You looked . . . lost. And nice. You looked like a boy I wanted to get to know.'

I am still not looking at her, but absorbing her words. Marvelling at her words. I would like to be enigmatic, as opposed to undignified. I really don't want to be the lonely boy that girls feel sorry for.

'Daniel. Look at me.' Paula's voice is gentle but firm. 'Please.'

Finally I turn and meet her gaze. I want to say something witty, something that distracts from the sudden intensity of the moment, but for once I am speechless. Along with looking A-list hot, she also looks kind and ever so slightly vulnerable. Her eyes wide and just the right amount of dewy . . . her bottom lip . . . It occurs to me that she wants me to kiss her. And I really want to kiss her. But if I've got the signals all wrong, which, given my lack of experience, could so easily be the case, then I'll make a complete fool of myself I do.

I shift a little forward and tentatively put my hand on

hers. Encouragingly, she doesn't whip it away in disgust. Instead she smiles shyly at me.

'Tell me about this girl,' she says then, diverting the moment. 'You have feelings for her?'

'No.' I am startled by the question. 'I mean . . . not real feelings. I guess I am just caught up in her unhappiness.' I sigh heavily. 'She doesn't know I exist.'

'It is safer then,' Paula says, her eyes never pulling away from mine, 'to be hidden.'

I am frowning, but I know what she's getting at. I am safe from rejection. Since Lo has no idea I exist, I can ride on a wave of false intimacy. Or something like that, anyway. But I don't want to talk about that right now. Right now, I have a real-life situation on my hands. I blew it last time with Paula on account of my imaginary girlfriend. I'm not making that mistake again.

'OK.' I look into her deep-brown eyes. 'I admit I kind of got sucked into her . . . her narrative . . . because I wanted to be. I wanted to feel close to someone.' At this point, it is really hard to carry on making eye contact. 'And I know you must think I am really tragic. Not to mention inexperienced. But . . .' I slow down, as I am not sure if I should really carry on. But what the hell – I am already in deep. What does a little more humiliation matter? 'But then I met you. And . . . you're real. And I realize I have totally ruined any chance of you thinking of me that way, but . . .'

'But, but, but,' Paula echoes me, teasingly. She slips her hand out from under mine and places one tanned finger on my lips. 'Don't talk any more, Daniel. Just . . .'

And, without engaging my brain, I circle her wrist with my fingers, and pull her gently towards me, and I kiss her. I kiss her soft, full lips and the sun seizes the moment to glow hotter in the sky. She doesn't wrench her mouth away from mine. She stays, and she kisses me back.

Paula stays all afternoon, just lying with me in the sun. And then she stays to help behind the bar. And then it is late and Paula looks at me when everyone has left and I've locked the door, and she pushes her hands through her streaked brown hair, and she looks so gorgeous I cannot believe she was kissing *me* hours before.

'I'll give you a lift home,' I tell her, not daring to touch her honey skin, even though I want to, really badly.

'You could . . .' she says, giving me a seductive look from under her lashes. 'Or I could stay?'

I blink. 'Stay?' She means, stay here, with me. In my bed. It won't come as any surprise to hear that my experience in the bedroom area is approximately none. The very thought of fumbling with Paula's bra strap, let alone what happens after that, is practically giving me a panic attack.

'I don't know.' I swallow. 'I mean, you know, Ronnie and Cristina are in the house. I don't think I'll feel comfortable being with . . .' I trail off. If Syd or Jamal could see me now, they would be throwing eggs or rotten tomatoes at my face. I am actually knocking back a beautiful

Spanish chick, who is nice and has the softest lips in the world . . . and who wants to sleep with me. I am actually doing that!

But I can't risk the potential humiliation that will result from my sheer inexperience.

'We don't have to do anything,' Paula says kindly, which makes the whole thing so much worse. Because I very definitely want to do something.

And then into my head pops up the memory of swimming in that crazy tide a few weeks before. My first daring act. The first of many, I had vowed then. So what if I mess up tonight? In a short time I'll be back home in England and will never have to face Paula again.

And then my mother's voice chimes in with: 'Your first time with a girl should be special, Daniel. You should take it seriously. One-night stands are not what nice young men do.'

That does it. I sigh, biting my lip, and pull Paula's body towards me, circling her waist with my hands. I breathe in her salty sweet smell and kiss her smooth tanned forehead, then her small freckled nose, and finally her slightly parted lips.

When I pull away, minutes later, I reach down and take her hand.

'Come on,' I say huskily. 'Let's go and do something.'

24

Eloise

For all our It girl bravado, my three best friends and I were innocents underneath. Innocent in that we looked at boys, we admired boys, we dreamt about boys, we imagined doing stuff with boys, but none of us had a clue about sex.

'It's all a bit messy, isn't it?' Jess had said, as she and I stood by the goal during an interminable hockey match.

'It doesn't have to be, I suppose,' I said cautiously. 'I mean there are things you can—'

Jess tossed her hair out of her face. 'But it's such hard work, all that positioning your body so you don't look fat, and having someone paw at you. I just can't see the appeal.'

'Jessica,' I said, laughing. 'You wouldn't mind being pawed if you were in love with the pawer in question. And it's nice to be touched, you know. At least you know someone really wants you.'

She snorted. 'Boys would have sex with a rock if it let

them know it was available,' she said, as if she had any experience whatsoever. She frowned at Miss Benson, our head of PE, who was yelling at a group of divergent players on the opposite team.

'Take her, for example,' Jess said. 'Miss Benson. I bet she'd be fair game if she stopped terrifying the male species with her shapeless shell suit and that hockey stick she has welded to her hand. Men are simple creatures; they'll go where the flesh is willing.'

I laughed. 'I'm not sure Miss Benson is into the gentlemen. I'm sure there was a rumour about her and Miss De Courcey. Anyway, you'd better move away from me – I think we're supposed to be playing hockey, not just standing here gossiping.'

'Speak for yourself.' Jess cast an irritated look up at the sky; true to form it was spitting dirty rain on us. She turned to me.

'So are you planning on doing it with Huck?' she asked. 'Is that the reason for all this sex talk?'

I shrugged. 'He wants to. I'm just not sure . . . I mean, it seems like a kind of pressure, even though he's not pushing me. He just . . .'

'He just what?'

'Well, I think something has to change . . . you know, "develop" in our relationship. To move it on to the next level.' I looked away from her, pretending to be interested in Claudia Harrison's ugly sports socks that were wrinkling like elephant's feet around her ankles.

'Oh, I see,' Jess replied in a pointed kind of way.

I turned back to her. 'I mean, I have to do it some time. And why not with Huck? We're in love, and . . .' I stopped talking, aware that my words sounded just a bit hollow, both out loud to Jessica and inside, to me.

There was a small silence. It seemed Jess had run dry of smart-arse remarks. But she was just thinking.

'Well, you sound thoroughly convinced,' she said at last. 'Seriously. It doesn't sound like you really want to.' She gripped my shoulder a little theatrically. 'And doing it because you're scared won't work. You'll just feel even worse.'

It was one of those rare times when Jess spoke some actual sense. I didn't like hearing it, but she was right.

If I gave in to what Huck wanted, I would lose all respect for myself. I'd trade in my last card for his affection, his interest, his love.

I sighed heavily, and, as if to end the subject, Miss Benson blew heartily on her whistle. At last the hideous match was over.

'Thank you, sweet Jesus,' murmured Jess, pulling the hood of her sweatshirt over her head. 'Come on, this is last period. Let's go and hang at Gianni's in town and get some skinny hot chocolate.'

'Sounds good, but I think I'll head straight home,' I told her. 'My aunt is staying and Mum's organized a boring dinner. I need to get my maths homework done before it all kicks off.'

'As you wish,' Jess said. 'I'm glad we had a little talk. Glad I could help.'

I realized Jessica was proud of herself for being a sensible friend for once. So it made what I was really going to do that evening weigh just a little bit more heavily on my heart.

Huck had been playing tennis with his dad when I called round at 8 p.m. They arrived in Carlo's beat-up old MG just as I was ringing the doorbell.

And they weren't alone. Huck's mum uncoiled herself from the back of the car, followed by a petite dark-haired girl who looked depressingly like Alexa Chung.

All the oomph decompressed inside me. I suddenly felt ridiculous in my new, tight, dark denim skinnies, Louboutin scrapers and the Prada top that made my boobs look bigger than they actually were. Totally overdressed and try-hard. I rarely feel like that. Funny how all your confidence is shaken when you want everything to be OK just a bit too much.

'Lo?' Huck climbed out of the passenger door of the sports car, looking casually gorgeous in his faded tennis whites. 'Did we have a date tonight?' He was smiling at me, but it was the kind of smile that didn't quite reach his lovely eyes. I got a chill then, in my stomach.

'No . . . I just thought I'd surprise you.' I turned and attempted to look cool yet provocative, but I could see Alexa Chung properly now that she had arrived to stand behind Huck, and let me tell you, she would have made Kate Moss feel cheap and unattractive. She had a gorgeous, heart-shaped face, with full lips that may have been just, gorgeously, a little too large for her face, and enormous brown eyes. Her skin was free of make-up and flawless, just two adorable rosy patches on her cheeks. She had the kind of haircut, a tousled pageboy with a small cute fringe, that only the truly genetically blessed can carry off. I looked from her to Huck and saw how perfectly matched they were in the looks department. I tried not to let the panic show in my insipid blue eyes.

Way too late, Huck darted towards me and gave me a noisy but chaste kiss on the side of my face. His free arm lightly touched mine, as though we had just met.

'Cool,' he said, turning back to Alexa. 'Hey, this is Valentina . . . A friend from home. Brazil, I mean. She's staying for a couple of weeks. V, this is Eloise.'

'Lo,' I corrected him, giving her the biggest smile I could manage under the circumstances. 'Nice to meet you.'

'Hi.' She didn't smile back, but her nose twitched and there was a kind of satisfied smirk on her lips.

I turned to Huck. 'Did you tell me your friend was coming?'

The passive aggression in that question was tangible. Huck's eyes narrowed for a split second before he gave me another one of his smiles. 'No . . . I . . . It was all a bit last minute. I must have forgotten. But it's cool, right?' He shot

198

a laser-like look of warning at me. Or at least that's what I interpreted.

'Sure, of course.' I laughed, hating myself just a little bit more. 'So what are you guys up to tonight?'

Carlo guided his ex-wife past us and unlocked the front door, before turning back to the three of us.

'We're all having one of my special dinners tonight . . . and that includes you, sweetheart.' He smiled kindly at me. 'You are guest of honour.'

I waited for Huck to follow his dad's example. Put his arm around me. Or something. Anything. Eventually he squeezed my arm. 'Isn't she always,' he says smoothly.

I really *really* wanted to go home. If I wasn't in the mood before, I was even less in the mood just then.

'You know what, I'll leave you guys to catch up,' I said awkwardly. 'We can do this another night.'

'I won't hear of that,' Carlo said, giving me a mock-stern look. 'You will stay and enjoy the evening. Understand?'

As I walked stiffly in, I prepared myself for a hellishly insecure few hours. But as I crossed my arms protectively around myself, Huck pulled me back, letting Valentina and his parents go on ahead.

He turned me round to face him, and I struggled to stop my eyes from filling up. For some reason it felt like something bad was coming.

'I'm sorry to surprise you like that,' he said softly. 'It totally slipped my mind that Valentina was coming to stay. When I saw you at the front door, I was caught off guard.

I wasn't expecting you . . .' His eyes travelled down my body. 'And looking so unbelievably hot, too.' He lifted his gaze and finally I saw the smile in his eyes.

Inside I breathed a massive sigh of relief. I had worked myself into such a state for no reason. Huck still loved me. It was there, in his eyes.

'Why don't you stay over tonight,' he whispered, leaning in to kiss my nose. 'Tell your mum you're staying with a friend.'

I hesitated. I wanted to be near him. So much. But if I felt pressure before, I now felt that I was backed into a corner. But I had to do this sometime. Why not now?

'Lo?' Huck moved to wrap his arms around me, his lips gently kissing my ear, then gliding slowly to my neck. 'You smell delicious. You're so beautiful, you know that. So sexy. We could have an amazing time. You know what chemistry we have . . .'

He stopped talking, just pulled me close and nuzzled my head with his. I felt a sense of intoxication. I felt myself falling into his words, his touch.

'OK,' I breathed. 'I'll stay. But do you have any . . .'

'Yes.' Huck squeezed me tighter, almost too tight. 'Don't worry. It will be fine.'

25

Daniel

'Just hold on to me,' Paula says, laughing. 'Put your arms around my waist and hold tight.'

I grimace at the floating water scooter and then at the somewhat choppy water. It's been a while since I braved the rough tide on that remote beach. It feels a lifetime ago. Back then I told myself I would try and take more risks. Man up, as it were. But what with the whole Lo thing, and Paula's distinct charms, that plan has kind of fallen by the wayside.

'Daniel,' Paula says firmly. 'Let's go.'

'Sure.' I smile as though I do this sort of thing every day, and climb on the back of the water scooter, the rubber of my wetsuit creaking, and watch as Paula, looking like a rubber-clad young Bond girl, climbs on too. Yep. She even looks good in a wetsuit, her long legs straddling the scooter and her slender back leaning forwards to take hold of the handlebars. She turns back and flashes me a smile. It feels surreal, like I'm in an advert for exotic travel or something.

Don't be an idiot, Daniel, I tell myself. Don't mess this up.

'You ready?' she says, turning all the way round and moving in closer, giving me a soft kiss on the lips. As she pulls away I take in her freckles, her tanned glow, her sparkling brown eyes, and tendrils of damp streaky hair. She is utterly gorgeous. And she's with me.

When the scooter starts moving I suddenly see what all the fuss is about. The wind picks up and blows away the searing heat. I shut my eyes blissfully and tighten my hold round Paula's waist. She's guiding us expertly, weaving in and out of small boats and other scooter travellers, gradually increasing our speed until we're clear of the other vessels and all that is in front of us is a glorious stretch of blue sea.

It is the closest to perfect happiness I have ever got. I press my head against Paula's neck and kiss it.

'I'm going to take you to my private beach,' she shouts above the noise of the engine and the choppy waves.

'Private beach?' I shout back. 'Is this when you tell me you're the heiress to a multi-million-pound fortune?' I kiss her again and she half turns, her hair whipping behind her and smiles.

'Would you like me better if I was?' she says.

'I couldn't like you any more than I do right now,' I tell her. And I mean it. It feels like everything is coming together in this moment. I am relaxed, attached to a beautiful girl and heading for an idyllic private beach.

I can't help wishing Syd and Jamal could see me. They should have stuck around, I think.

Paula takes us round the coast, passing a picturesque little cove, then on past another bit of headland, and then I see it. A 200-foot-long stretch of unspoilt clean sand, bordered by some leafy bushes and a couple of palm trees.

'Wow,' is all I can say as Paula slows right down and we bob closer to the beach. 'This is just . . . beautiful, Paula. Is it really all yours?'

She giggles, cutting the engine as we hit the ground.

'No. But I have been coming here since I was a tiny girl,' she tells me. 'I think I have had every birthday on this little beach.' She breathes in the air deeply. 'It is my special place. And hidden from the tourists. I hoped it would be empty. And it is.'

We dismount and pull the scooter up on the beach together, laying it on its side. Paula peels off her wetsuit, revealing a skimpy black bikini.

I want to stare at her perfect body but the nice boy in me looks away. I've seen Paula naked. The other night we kind of . . . did the deed. And though it was predictably awkward and I wasn't entirely sure if I was doing it right, Paula didn't seem to mind. I mean, she made all the right noises. The thing I enjoyed most, if I'm being honest, was just lying with her on that cramped single bed in Ronnie's box room, thankful that he was over at a suppliers and not liable to barge in at any moment and fire me. It just felt so good to hold her. Thinking about it now, I urge myself to start thinking about something else. A wetsuit does not leave much to the imagination.

'I'm just going to, you know, take this off,' I tell her, indicating my suit. I turn and start pulling it off, with a lot less ease than Paula did. I am a total novice at beach life. Finally I get the thing off and turn to see Paula laying a large towel on the sand. She picks up a bottle of sunscreen and rubs it on to her arms.

I stretch, then flop down on the towel, digging in the cold bag we bought with us for a beer. Once she's finished applying her cream, Paula fishes out a bottle of water for herself.

'Daniel,' she says sternly. 'You should really put some lotion on. You with your fair skin. You will burn.'

'Yeah, yeah, I'll do it.' I smile lazily at her.

'Seriously. I know I laughed at you for all the cream you put on your skin. But you should. Because you are pale,' she goes on. 'I am boring about the skin. I hope to be a, what do you call it . . . beauty therapist one day. I am going to study it at college. Have my own salon if I can.'

'Really?' For some reason I think she is joking, but her expression is pretty determined, so maybe not. 'That's what you want to do for the rest of your life?'

'Uh huh.' She looks at me. 'Why? What is wrong with this? You don't think it is important to know about beauty?'

I shrug. 'Uh, I don't know. I mean, it's not something I've given a lot of thought. As you can probably tell.'

I wait for her to laugh, but she looks even more serious.

'I have a very beautiful mother. She always looks her best. Her complexion, you would not believe how incredible it is. She takes a lot of care for her appearance. I admire her so much. She is who I want to be.'

'So that's where you get it from,' I tell her. 'Beauty runs in the family, I guess.'

I get an appreciative smile for that. But something is a bit off about this conversation. It is suddenly awkward between us. I think I've been clumsy. I should be less flippant. Less rude. But at the same time I can't help feel a tiny stab of disappointment at Paula's ambitions.

'What else do you want for your life?' I say, in as interested a way as possible. 'Apart from your career in beauty.'

Paula finally looks more relaxed. 'I want to get married. Before I am twenty-five. Then I have five more years of the salon, and I have babies.' She sighs. 'I want four babies, two years apart.' She puffs out her cheeks. 'And then I will be a mother. I will look after my children and I will not work. Maybe when they are grown, but not until then . . .'

I am aware that my smile is slightly stretched in a false kind of way. I gaze at her pretty profile, her small freckled nose, her cheeks already sweetly pink. What Paula has just told me is perfectly reasonable. It's the kind of life most of the girls I know back home want. There's nothing wrong with wanting a life like that.

The trouble is, those girls feel like aliens to me. I may be a bit of a nerd, but I kind of imagined myself with a girl who wants something more stimulating than beauty and babies. Someone who runs poetry workshops, perhaps. Or studies for some kind of obscure Masters degree while working for a publishing house.

I want kids, I think. But not for a long time. And marriage? I've only just started enjoying the attentions of a willing female. I wouldn't mind extending that period of grace for at least a decade, if not more.

I feel a bit sick. I am a snob. I should be so lucky that a shiksa goddess like Paula would even look at a weird dude like me. And here I am, judging her for her life choices.

'Daniel?' Paula waves a hand in front of my face.

I focus on her. 'Sorry . . . I was just thinking.'

She cocks her head to one side. 'So, now for you. What do *you* want for your life?'

'Me?' Come to think of it, what *do* I want to do with my life? Up until this point, just being normal, fitting in and not being homeless when I leave uni was the summit of my hopes and ambitions. But now . . . 'Well, I want to get my degree in engineering,' I say at last. 'And then marry a rich widow and spend my days diving off expensive yachts in the West Indies.' I shrug. 'The usual kind of thing.'

Paula's mouth is hanging open, and her eyes are wide with a look of confusion. Or at least certainly not a look of amusement. After several more seconds, when she still hasn't laughed, I decide to put her out of her misery.

'I'm kidding, Paula,' I tell her, gently pinching her cheek.

'Paula . . . that was a joke . . . about the widow and the yacht.'

She grins shyly. 'OK. Sometimes I can't keep up with your humour, Daniel. You're too quick for me.'

She looks adorable in her innocence. And I feel bad. I lie back and put my arm round her shoulders, drawing her in closer to me, and I can feel her delicate breath in my ear.

'You're just going to have to work a bit harder to keep up with me then . . . I mean, you'll have your work cut out—'

Paula digs me hard in the ribs with her elbow.

'Ouch,' I say theatrically, but sincerely, because it hurt.

'You think you are smarter than me, huh?' she teases. 'You think you are the one with the brains? You and your engines.'

I grin up into the air, rubbing at my side surreptitiously. 'It's really all about maths,' I say earnestly. 'Engineering isn't a study of engines, exactly.'

'OK, now I am falling to sleep.' Paula fake-yawns and closes her eyes. 'You lost me at maths.'

I laugh up into the sky. 'That was actually pretty funny. You're catching on. We'll make a smart-arse out of you yet.'

She sighs heavily. 'Clever Daniel,' she says sleepily, turning on to her side and propping herself up with her elbow. 'Shut up and give me a kiss.'

26
Eloise

The sun hits my eyes through the artfully skewed wooden blinds in Huck's bedroom. I open them wider, feeling different to how I felt before. Not in the way I imagined. I feel a kind of landmark has been reached. I sigh and push down the bedcovers, my hands touching my stomach, then moving to cross over my body protectively. It must be early; there is no sound. All I can hear is my own light breathing.

Am I woman now? A grown-up? Huck and I have sealed our relationship. Now there is another layer, another tie, wrapping us together. I need some time to register it all, for now I can relax.

I slowly turn over on my side to watch him as he sleeps. He is lying facing me, his hair curling slightly, messy, his bare shoulders visible. His eyelashes, longer than they have a right to be, beneath his closed eyes. I reach out and gently touch his naked, muscular arm. Loving him in this moment.

At the feel of my touch on him, he opens his eyes. I wait for the smile there, the happiness, the same peace that I am feeling. But what I see makes my skin prickle, my heart freeze.

Huck is staring at me, a blank, emotionless gaze. No recognition, no feeling there. And then he lifts his hand and moves mine away from him, placing it firmly on the sheet, in the space between us.

His words, when they come, slowly, coldly make me shrivel, until I feel as small, as insignificant, as a tiny insect.

'I think you should go,' he says calmly. Then he yawns, as though he is bored. Utterly indifferent to me. 'Valentina is here. She will wonder where I am . . .'

I wake up, a thin layer of sweat all over me, my heart thudding miserably. It was a dream. A nightmare. But it seems to echo all the denial, the desperation I felt towards the last months of our relationship.

The truth is that I woke up the morning after Huck and I had first slept together and he was gone. When I'd got myself washed and dressed and downstairs, it was to find him with Valentina. Sitting at Carlo's big kitchen table, laughing together over something in the papers. They hadn't even noticed me standing there, feeling like a total spare part. When he finally looked up and saw me, Huck's face was impossible to read. Valentina looked sheepish. I'd murmured something about lunch with my family and left. To call it the walk of shame was probably overstating it, but I remember how vulnerable, how confused I felt. It was like I had just thrown away all my power. Like I had nothing left to make things right.

But when Huck had called me later, he was just the same old Huck. Friendly, breezy, relaxed. I had no reason whatsoever to feel insecure. But I did.

I sit up, and for the first time since he died I feel relief. Actual relief that he is no longer here to subtly chip away at me, push me further and further down, until I can't be seen.

My almost empty room, evidence of my imminent departure, mocks me a little. 'See,' it seems to say, 'you have nothing left now. You have nothing left of yourself. Time to go.'

I have never felt quite so lonely in my life. It feels so alien, yet also . . . a bud of something else is there. Freedom from anxiety.

I have finally shaken off the myth of Huck and me. The perfect, idyllic couple. The couple most likely to, as it were. How illusory it all is. How quickly that illusion can be destroyed. I want to talk to someone, but no one who will judge. Just someone who will listen without responding.

I roll over and lean down to grapple in my bag. I locate my phone and find the number.

I'll never know how you really felt about our first time. But you weren't there when I woke up. And you spent the whole of the day with her. It was a big deal for me. And

210

you acted like it was nothing. I wish I had saved it for someone better.

Just typing the words brings a new bubble of anger up in my throat. If Huck wasn't dead already, I think I would be considering killing him.

'Lo.' Jake is outside my bedroom door. 'Mum's going to the hairdresser and she wants you to go with her.'

I stare at the door. 'Why?'

'I dunno. Maybe she wants to buy you a haircut,' he says, sounding bored.

I sigh. 'Tell her no thanks.'

'OK.'

Jake thumps down the stairs, and a few minutes later I hear a new, lighter, pair of feet running up to our floor.

Mum doesn't knock on a door, she raps.

'Eloise,' she says crisply. 'I am not sending you off to university looking like a drug addict. Your roots are atrocious. I've booked an appointment for you with Sasha. She'll have them good as new. Please be ready in five minutes.'

'I'm fine,' I drawl, pulling on my jeans and inspecting my authentic dip-dyed locks in the dressing-table mirror.

'It wasn't a request, darling, it was an order.' Mum clears her throat disapprovingly, and then I hear her rattling the handle outside.

'Mum!' I snap. 'Please, just stop ordering me around. If I want my roots to show, my roots will show. What do you care anyway – you won't have to see me after next week.'

'I want you to look your best, darling. When you look your best you give a good impression. I daresay council estate chic is fashionable amongst a certain kind of girl, but not my daughter.'

Something in me snaps. I grab angrily at a white vest, pull it over my head and stride to the door, yanking it open.

Valerie is in full make-up, wearing a very expensive wool jumpsuit. Looks like Chanel or Yves Saint Laurent. Her hair immaculate, as usual, freshly blow-dried with skilfully dyed blonde highlights. She sort of makes me feel sick. I look her up and down in an exaggerated manner.

'I'm eighteen, Mother. I've done exactly what you wanted, dressed how you wanted, acted like you wanted since I was seven years old. But now I am an adult and I'll do what I want.' I cross my arms over my chest. 'If I want to dress top to toe in New Look then I will.'

'Ridiculous,' she mutters, not bothering to hide her disdain at my dirty white vest and jeans. 'You look terrible. I can't do anything about your depression, of course, but I can certainly sort out your appearance. In fact, it is my duty.'

'No it is not,' I spit out. 'And there is something you can do about my depression actually. You can bugger off and leave me alone!'

I step back from the doorway and slam the door in her face. It feels good for about a nanosecond. But as the sound

212

of Valerie storming downstairs dies away, I climb on to the bed, curl my legs up to my chin and let the angry tears come.

I'm not getting better. I'm getting worse. And apart from Natalie and Sarah, possibly, there is no one in my life who understands me, or who accepts me as I really am. The future feels so scary and I am not prepared for it.

I wish I had never been born.

27

Daniel

It's not my idea of fun, cleaning the bar with sunburnt shoulders and a mild hangover. Luckily Paula was manning the scooter back yesterday. I only had two beers, but you know, lunchtime drinking and all that.

OK, so I'm a lightweight.

Still it was good to go somewhere so empty and peaceful and just lie there with nothing to do but soak up the rays and have some idle chatter. Even if I'm paying for it now.

I am just considering making myself a massive sandwich when I catch a blinking out of the corner of my eye. I realize I left my stolen phone behind yesterday, and it's nearly out of juice. I smile. Maybe I am finally living a little. Normally that phone is practically sewn into my pocket.

I pick it up, and at my touch the screen comes to life and I see a message there.

Whoa, she's angry. Absurdly, I look around me,

ashamed, as though I am being watched. Lo's painful text interests me: a girl's view of the act, and what she expects.

I think of Paula. After we spent the night together, I think I assumed that she was cool. Cool as in content. She never said anything so I thought it was all fine. And me, well, I held her, but then it was getting late and Ronnie was coming back, so I just kind of got dressed.

Neither of us have talked about it. Maybe both of us were too scared to ask: 'Was it OK? Are you OK? How could it have been better?'

But Paula, well . . . Paula seems happy in general. Like her expectations of life are not spectacular.

And there you have it.

See, even underneath all the self-deprecating stuff, there is an intellectual snob in me. I want a girl who wants something more than scraping dead skin off old ladies' faces and applying mascara. I may have simplified the mechanics behind the beauty industry somewhat, but you get the picture.

I want a girl who can discuss a book with me. Or a movie. Who drags me reluctantly to the theatre. Who values her outer shell but doesn't obsess over it.

Not much to ask.

I'm in a bad mood now. And it's all because of her. No, not Paula. Lo. She may not technically be the third wheel in my relationship but it feels like she is. Because I can't help wondering if Lo is going to uni, and if so what she's studying. Is she familiar with the works of Shakespeare? Is she really as pretty as that grainy photo she sent?

Double standards! I hear the collective female cry. He wants beauty and brains – well, what a surprise!

It's at this point that I realize I miss my friends. I miss Syd. I wouldn't mind hearing his misguided advice on the rules of attraction right now, and Jamal's soothing indifference to the whole issue. I want to be grounded. Out here, with no male company, I am floundering.

It's amazing how a little validation in the form of a pretty girl like Paula can make me puff out my chest and raise my bar. I want a little more than I did before.

'Daniel!'

I hold my breath at the sound of her voice. She's standing there, in the doorway, angelic, trusting.

'Paula.' I slide the phone out of sight. 'I was just going to call you.'

She smiles shyly at my lie. Steps forward. She's wearing those very close-fitting jeans that skim like drainpipes down to her ankles and leave very little to the imagination. I can't help my body reacting. I mean, the girl is super-hot. She's also got one of those loose cotton tops on. The kind that only Mediterranean chicks seem to get away with. It's the skin tone.

'You look nice,' I tell her. 'I didn't think I'd see you again so soon.'

Her face clouds over a little. 'You don't want to see me?'

'Yeah, 'course I do. I'm just, you know, working right now.'

'I will help,' she says brightly, her eyes skimming over the glasses and beer caps on the bar. 'Then we can go out. You want to meet my friends . . . my proper friends? They are asking for you.'

'Ah, I'd love to,' I find myself saying. 'But I think Ronnie wants me to stick around here.'

She wrinkles her nose. 'Uncle Ronnie? I will talk to him. He has a soft spot for me.'

I laugh uncomfortably, then shake my head. 'I'm not sure I'm very good company right now.' I tap my shoulders. 'Sunburn . . . possible sunstroke. I don't know. I feel a bit weird.'

'Oh, *madre*,' she mutters. 'Not the weird thing again.' She puts her slender arms on her hips. 'What is it with you boys? You always feeling "weird".'

'What? I'm not feeling weird like *that* . . .' I pause to expand on another lie. 'I'm just feeling a bit tired and thinking about stuff I need to do before I go back to England. Distracted is a better word. Yep, distracted is what I'm feeling. Not weird. Weird is very much the wrong word.' I finally move over to her and put my hands awkwardly on her shoulders, stating falsely, 'It is so nice to see you.'

She eyes me warily but removes her hands from her hips, her lips pouting. It's a clever girl trick that, the pouting thing. And it almost has me giving in to her demand. Almost, but not quite.

'Paula,' I say solemnly, 'you know I adore you. But

sometimes I feel a little . . . serious. You know, like I need to have a think. About all these feelings I'm having. You understand?'

She likes this. I can tell. Her eyes have grown dewy again. Soft.

'I see,' she breathes, and closes her eyes for a second, her long lashes resting beautifully on her bronzed cheeks. When she looks up, a resilient smile has replaced the pout. 'I understand, Daniel. We have a lot of time to meet my friends. We can do it another time.'

This is not the right moment to remind her that in a few days I will be gone.

'Of course,' I tell her, though I am gripping her shoulders a little too tightly. Fortunately Paula takes this as intensity of a more romantic nature. She swoops forward and kisses me lightly.

'Call me tomorrow,' she says. 'When you have had your think.'

'Will do.' I raise one hand lamely, a little blindsided, I must say, at how I melt a bit when she kisses me.

As I watch her go, I decide to give myself some time off from thinking. Contrary to what I have told Paula, I think my brain might explode if I analyse this any more.

When I am certain Paula is a good distance gone, I turn and retrieve the phone. Biting my lip, I start to write.

Forget him. You deserve better than this.

And before I can stop myself I press Send. A hot, prickly feeling, which I'm pretty sure isn't sunburn, travels up my neck and I grab a handful of ice and press it quite painfully to my face.

There's no going back now. Houston, we have contact.

28

Eloise

I am staring at the screen and my heart is beating double time. Treble time. Scrap that, my heart is beating fit to burst out of my chest.

This cannot be possible. Yet apparently it is. Possible. Possible that I have had the wrong number all along. That this isn't Huck's phone. That it belongs to a stranger.

Stay cool, I tell myself.

I swallow, leaning back against my pillows. All around me is evidence of a new phase about to begin. My wardrobe is half empty. Photographs have been cleared from my shelves. There is no rug on the floor. The acoustics are different. I can hear myself breathe in a different way.

I hover over the keypad. What do I say?

I go with the obvious.

Who is this?

I send it and my eyes lift up, I force them up and away from the screen and aim them at the bedroom window. It is a beautiful autumn day, the colours outside are rusty brown and olive green; there is one solitary cloud in the sky. A couple of birds are conducting a conversation on the ledge.

There is no other sound. No responsive beep. It feels acute, agonizing.

Then, after what seems like years but can only be minutes, I get an answer.

Dan. My name is Dan, and you must be Lo. I don't know where to begin, Lo. I found this phone and I kind of held on to it. I am out in Spain and travelling around a bit. I'm sorry. I just got caught up in your conversation.

I frown.

How long have you known?

A pause. Not a long pause, and then:

Since the beginning. I know, I should have found your man and given back the phone. But that's kind of easier said than done. For one thing, he's going to be pretty unhappy that I've been invading his privacy. Your privacy.

I close my eyes, inwardly cringing and type:

221

I feel like an idiot.

A barely perceptible hesitation.

*Please don't. I'm the idiot. I should have said something.
A long time ago.*

I breathe out. Long and slow, and while I'm doing that another text pops up.

For the record. He sounds like a total douche.

I smile then. It feels good to have Huck deconstructed so . . . so succinctly. But the loyal girlfriend in me is compelled to defend him.

He wasn't a total douche. Well, not that I noticed at the time.

I am about to add that it was me – who refused to see any bad in Huck – who was the douche. But before I get the chance, he's back.

Love is blind.

I lean back and feel my whole body relax, just a little.

It so is. So, really, I am to blame.

That's not what I was saying.

Yeah, I know. But I was pretty blinkered about him.

There was a longer pause before I got my next reply.

So who is this guy you put on such a pedestal?

I close my eyes, a flicker of pain strikes me.

He was my first love. My first boyfriend. And he was charming. And good-looking. And he just had this whole South American thing going on.

I touch Send, realizing that what I've just said sounds so lame. I am resigning myself to the end of the conversation when another message pops up.

South American thing?

I smile.

Yeah. He was half-Brazilian. Exotic. And his dad was a successful artist. He was out in Spain on an extended holiday.

I hesitate before I send that. I realize I am now talking about Huck in the past tense. For a second I panic a little.

If Dan reads it, then there'll be a whole thing about Huck being dead. And I am not sure I can get into it now.

I take a deep breath. Maybe it is time to face up to reality. I'll never see this guy again. What does it matter? It might even be cathartic.

So I send my message, then put the phone face down on my bed. My heart is beating hard for some reason.

My heartbeat slows down as the seconds, then the minutes, go by and nothing comes back. I even lift the phone and stare at the screen in case I missed the alert. But there's nothing there.

Maybe Dan had to go and do something?

After ten minutes I have given up on hearing back from him. I am just swinging my legs over the bed to put a sweater on, when the alert sounds. I wait, then slowly pick up the phone.

Was? Has he suddenly become Anglo-Saxon?

I laugh then. Dan's witty question defuses the tension in my head.

Nope. He kind of suddenly died.

I touch the magic icon before I can chicken out. There, I've said it, to a stranger. It wasn't so bad.

Oh my God. I'm so sorry. But you were texting him – I don't think I understand?

Ah yes. Now for the explanation. Which will make me look mentally unstable. Best-case scenario, a sad case.

Yep. I was talking to a dead person. You have my permission to sign off now. Seriously. I know how this looks.

I ping it off, telling myself I really don't care if this complete stranger washes his hands of me. But I'm staring at the screen as though my life depended on it.

And there it is. A reply.

OK. Now I get it. And I'm really sorry. I guess sometimes you have to vent. Even if there's no one to vent off to.

My lips turn up in a half smile. In spite of my humiliation.

There was you. You were listening.

Again. Sorry. I feel like I've heinously invaded your privacy.

Heinously?

Good word, right? I've been wanting to drop that word into conversation for some time now.

I laugh out loud at this.

> *Good usage. Actually, I'm glad you were listening.*
>
> *You are?*
>
> *Yep. It feels like you're my secret therapist.*
>
> *Therapist, huh? If my mother knew about this she would be throwing a party. She always wanted a more meaningful pursuit for her wayward son. Jews make very good therapists apparently.*
>
> *Wayward?*
>
> *I wish. The truth is, Lo, I am disappointingly unwayward. No cool artistic or Brazilian heritage. No charisma. Pretty unspectacular really.*

I bite my lip before tapping out another message.

> *I wouldn't say that.*
>
> *Don't. You're making it more acute.*
>
> *Seriously.*
>
> *Are we getting serious now?*
>
> *I mean, take yourself seriously, Dan.*
>
> *Good point. But that would just undo years of conditioning. I'm not sure my system could handle the shock.*

So this is your way of getting through?

*Oh God. Don't tell me you're perceptive, Lo. Actually, is
Lo your real name?*

Eloise.

Aha. It all makes sense now.

I hate the name. It's just so princessy.

*Not at all. Eloise was a very charismatic child who lived at
the Plaza, as I recall. A self-sufficient, eccentric kind of
kid. I always thought she was pretty cool.*

You've read Eloise?

Could it be I had located the only male who was familiar
with my childhood heroine? Eloise and her Plaza lifestyle
was the only clear validation of my given name.

I know of Eloise. *I had a cousin who had all the books. I
may have gone through a gender crisis when I was five. I
don't recall the context of my familiarity with Eloise and
her adventures. It somehow just sank in to my
consciousness.*

I lean back, fully relaxed, and breathe a sigh. Of relief, but
also of pleasure. I was enjoying myself. I was having
an actual conversation that didn't involve death or
designer dresses.

You're funny. I'm glad I picked you as my voyeur.

*You're welcome. At this point I would add an emoticon.
But we hardly know each other and I am not totally
confident in my powers of emoticon.*

I check the clock. It's dinner time. I don't want our
conversation to end, but I know I have to somehow end it.
Leave on a high, as it were.

*I'd better go now. I have dinner and stuff. Thanks for
listening, Dan. I mean it.*

I send this last message and feel flatness descending.
The thought of getting off the bed and sitting through
another torturous meal with my family seems woefully
unentertaining. For the last half hour I have felt entertained.

I look up and stare into the middle distance.

I haven't felt bereft, or lonely, or angry for a whole half
hour. If you don't count unconsciousness while sleeping,
that is.

And my heart feels lighter. As though a weight has
been lifted.

228

29

Daniel

Paula is taking me to a party. At her parents' house. Apparently they have lots of parties, and the whole of Paula's family goes. And Paula has decided it's the perfect time for her folks to vet me. Sorry, 'get to know me'. She tried to play it down, but I am already having visions of Don Corleone from *The Godfather* giving me the third degree in a locked room in the basement.

It feels like a big deal.

I have procrastinated and deliberated between my five items of clothing for a good hour now, and each ensemble seems less appropriate than the one before. I really don't know why I, a lapsed Jewish boy from Macclesfield, England, is so anxious about meeting Paula's vast, vehemently Catholic family. Like Woody Allen getting to know Penelope Cruz's parents. I mean, what's to worry about?

I finally settle on what is essentially my daily uniform: a more or less clean T-shirt and my skinny chinos, which, as luck and trend tides would have it, are actually not laughable, but accidentally fashion forward. My mother bought them for me when it was Christmas time and the shops were chocka with bargains. Never one to miss a bargain, my ma, even if she does huff and puff over the Christmas thing. She found herself stuck in the Old Trafford shopping mall branch of Gap as local police held down a couple of young male shoplifters outside the JD Sports next door and cordoned off the area. During her half-hour incarceration, sheer frustration drove her to shop above and beyond the sports bra she had actually gone in for. My rust-brown chinos were the result. One Direction were on the brink of bringing this classic staple of the male wardrobe back into vogue. And I was the clueless recipient.

I take a moment to thank my mother for her unwitting genius. Because I actually look almost cool. Respectable, but 'contemporary' as Ma might phrase it.

Enough about her. I have an obligation to meet. A few days ago I would have called it something a little different. A result? An honour? A healthy step forward? But since yesterday afternoon it is now an obligation. Because yesterday I had a breakthrough. An entirely pleasant, entirely unexpected, breakthrough in my fantasy romance.

The girl became real.

It's like having a really nice dream, then waking up to find that it might be true. Am I being naive, or did Eloise and I genuinely have a connection?

Eloise. The little girl who lived at the Plaza. To all outside appearances a spoilt princess, but with hidden depths and resourcefulness. Eloise lived a solitary, self-sufficient life in her hotel, with absent parents and a big imagination. I hardly know the flesh-and-blood Eloise but I can't help fantasizing that, like her namesake, she has more to her than a glamorous dead boyfriend and rich parents. She is funny. Smart. And she actually seemed grateful that I have been 'there for her', albeit secretly, these last few weeks.

But there is something niggling at me about the whole situation. Eloise never actually said the name of her late beloved, but I have spent the whole night putting the clues together in my head, and I have the weirdest feeling that I know who it is. I'm pretty sure it's Huck.

It has to be. The phone I found, the one she's been texting, was under my bed back at Mrs Diaz's hostel. The same hostel Huck stayed in. It explains why no one came to claim the phone. Except I'm pretty sure he had his phone with him the night I last saw him. So maybe it wasn't his?

I spent the whole evening – and most of the night – turning things over in my head, and I still can't be sure. I almost texted her again this morning, but it felt wrong to pursue a dialogue between us . . . now that I am with Paula.

Timing. It can be a bit of a bitch, as they say.

I run a little gel through my hair then stop, examining

got a proper tan (for probably the first time
that hefting of beer crates out into Ronnie's
as given me definition in my arms and, I notice,
up my abs too. I peer closer to inspect my
unexpected reflection. I am no male model but I probably
look as fit as I'm ever going to.

A soft-sounding wolf whistle interrupted my vanity-fest.

'You look hot, boy.' Cristina is leaning against the door, looking me up and down.

'Why, thank you, Miss Cristina.' I turn back to the mirror. 'I've scrubbed up pretty well, if I do say so myself.'

'This is for Paula?' Cristina nods approvingly, then moves towards the table in my tiny box-room bedroom. Her eyes light on the phone lying on top of it. She picks it up.

I frown. 'What are you doing, little busybody?'

'Nothing,' she says coquettishly, putting the phone down again. 'I am just wondering something.'

'What?' If I sound a little nervous it's because I am. Though why exactly, I don't know.

'I am wondering if you have resolved your situation,' she goes on slowly. 'With your girl on the phone.' Her large brown eyes blink innocently. 'Because you can't have two romances at the same time, Daniel. It's not right.'

I am about to lie and tell her I have put an end to my peeping Tom phase, when I realize this is Spain's wisest child-woman I'm talking to. She'll sniff out an untruth if anyone can.

So I sigh, run a hand through my slightly sticky hair and give her a weak smile.

'I spoke to her yesterday. By text.'

Cristina's eyes widen. 'You did?'

'Uh huh. An actual conversation.' I raise one eyebrow. 'What do you make of that?'

'I can't believe this,' she says melodramatically. 'What did she say? How did this happen . . .' She puts a hand on my arm. 'I never thought you would have the courage. I am proud.'

'Really? What about my two-timing?' I say archly. 'Or does dramatic licence trump nobility?'

Cristina regards me with an understandably confused expression. 'I don't know what any of that means. As usual you speak in English riddles. But I think this is one step closer to closure.' She lifts her chin, clearly happy with her statement.

'I suppose so. But she was nice, you know. And most importantly, she didn't have a fit that I'd been privy to her innermost thoughts for all this time. She seemed almost . . . grateful, in fact.'

'This is not a surprise. You are a good listener, Daniel. You are a very nice person.'

'Nice.' I smile tightly. 'Well, that's nice, isn't it?'

'Yes. It is.' She narrows her eyes. 'Paula likes you because you are nice.'

'That's great.' I am trying to keep sarcasm out of my response but frankly I wish someone would change the record.

'Yes.' Cristina nods firmly. 'Don't change on me. Or Paula. We are counting on you.'

'Good old reliable Dan,' I murmur. It's not a bad description, I suppose. Better than Serial Killer, obviously. But it's a bit like being described as a 'brick' by a good-looking girl. Not sexy.

And even though sleeping with Paula didn't leave me feeling like a stud, even though I need a lot more practice, I am beginning to really want that. Sexy, I mean. Not that I want to have multiple girls on the go and behave like a Mancunian Hugh Hefner. I want something serious. But I want something sexy.

And right now, that doesn't seem too far out of my grasp.

'What are you thinking about?' Cristina is staring at me and I find myself colouring up.

'You are thinking about Paula?' She smiles. 'You had better be. You are lucky to be with her. All the boys love Paula.'

This somehow doesn't make me feel like the peacock that it should. Having a desirable girlfriend is meant to be the ultimate, isn't it? So why does it just make me feel uncomfortable? Like a fish wriggling on a hook on dry land.

'I know I'm lucky.' I give her the biggest, most confident

smile I can muster. 'Now, scram. Because I have to go and meet the lovely Paula's entire family, and I need five minutes to prepare myself for an evening of interrogation.'

Cristina tosses her hair. 'Well, we can go together. I am part of that family too, remember?' Her face looks suddenly quite fierce, when she adds, 'So you'd better be on your best behaviour or I will not be happy!'

She's joking, I think. But if I am not mistaken, there is a distinct warning in her words . . .

Paula's house is packed to the rafters with her relations and I arrive to a full-on party. I am hoping it has not been held in my honour.

'Relax,' Paula tells me, squeezing my hand. She plants a dewy kiss on my cheek. 'This is normal Sunday for us. All the family together, eating, drinking, talking.' She steps away to look me up and down. 'You look nice today. I like your trousers.' Her eyes travel over my body and I experience the novel sensation of female desire, with me as its object.

'Thank you.' I take in her floaty white dress, slightly falling off one tanned shoulder. Her tawny hair, curling fetchingly at the ends, the whites of her eyes, as clear and sparkling as a baby's. 'You look nicer than nice, you look—'

'Paula!' a husky voice calls out. We both turn to see a tall blonde lady with contrastingly dark skin moving towards us. She has the same eyes as Paula, and the same hourglass figure, but she is taller and obviously, older.

'Mammy.' Paula beams. 'Daniel, this is my mother, Inez. Mama, this is Daniel.'

'Welcome, Daniel. Paula won't stop talking about this charming English boy she has met.' Inez leans forwards and kisses me once on each side of my face. 'We are all so pleased to meet you. Anyone who Paula likes this much has to be something special, huh?' She gave Paula a conspiratorial wink.

No pressure then. None whatsoever.

'Likewise,' I say. 'I mean, in that I'm pleased to meet you also . . .' I fumble the last bit and feel intensely awkward. I am still holding on to Paula's hand. More as though it were a life raft in a rough sea than as a tender romantic gesture. As this occurs to me I let it go. I decide not to notice the slightly startled look in those deep brown eyes.

Inez laughs, a familiar laugh, like her daughter's, hearty yet feminine at the same time. 'And you are funny,' she says, before casting her eyes around the hallway. 'Let me introduce you to my husband. Andre . . .' she calls to a tall, built Javier Bardem lookalike. 'Andre, this is Daniel.'

Andre nods at me, not quite so friendly as his wife and daughter, I note. I nod back in what I hope is a solid, manly fashion. He excuses himself from the conversation he was having with an older guy and comes over to the three of us. He shakes my hand solemnly.

'I hope you are better than that rascal Tanni,' he

says a little fiercely. 'Seducing my little Pauletta with his charm . . .'

'Daddy,' Paula frowns. 'Daniel is nothing like Tanni.'

'Glad to hear it.' Andre smiles then. 'But you are going home soon, am I right? How do you plan to maintain my daughter's affections when you are back in England?'

'I—' I begin. I have no idea how to end my sentence. I have no idea whether I will ever see Paula again after next week. I hadn't thought about it. I suppose I just assumed it would all end.

'The telephone, Daddy, and the aeroplane,' Paula tells him, mock scolding. 'We will have the long-distance relationship.'

I look at Paula then, her eyes shining hopefully. And it dawns on me that this gorgeous girl really likes me. She isn't humouring me. She is smitten. At this point my heart should be dancing the merengue. Yet what I am actually feeling is mild panic.

And just then I feel the pulse of the familiar device in my pocket. I can't help the quick surge of excitement that comes over me in that moment. I can't help wishing that everyone around me, including the girl I would be lucky to call my girlfriend who is standing so close to me, would all just fade away so that I could take that phone out of my pocket and see what she has sent me.

She. Eloise.

'Daniel, you have to meet my brothers.' Paula tugs my arm, indicating two tough-looking boys about my age standing with a wizened-looking old lady. 'And my grandmother,' she whispers.

'Excellent.' I bite the inside of my cheek. 'I'm good with ladies. They like me, the ladies.'

Paula giggles, pushing me playfully with her elbow. 'She will love you; she is very protective of me. She will tell straight away that you are a good boy.'

'Yes. Of course.' I restrain the sigh that is pushing its way up my throat. 'And she'd be right, obviously.'

'You are funny today,' Paula says, giving me a look. 'In a peculiar way . . .'

I smile at her then. Her cheeks are slightly flushed. It occurs to me that this is a big deal for Paula. And I am indeed being peculiar. It's not Paula's fault I am deep in the throes of a fantasy and not real life. I mean, what the hell am I doing? Paula is lovely. Just lovely. She's gorgeous, she's nice and, as my mother would say, 'she knows what side her bread is buttered'. She likes me. She likes me in a straightforward way.

So why do I hanker after something so far away? Am I scared of what is right here in front of me?

'Paula,' I say with determination, 'I would love to meet your brothers, and your grandmother. I'm sorry if I seem "peculiar" I think I am a bit overwhelmed.'

She squeezes my arm, then slips her hand down to take hold of mine. 'My family will love you,' she says encouragingly. 'Don't worry.'

30
Eloise

'We have to have a leaving party,' Jessica wheedles on the other end of the phone. 'The Girls are splitting up. In a few days we'll be scattered to the four ends of the earth. We need a good send-off.'

I wait a beat. 'I suppose so. But does it have to be so melodramatic?'

'Lo.' Jessica's tone is sharper. 'What is going on? You've been so weird lately. And distant. It's like you're trying to cut off from your best friends.'

Best friends? I ponder this. What is the definition of a best friend? Maybe better not to go there. After all, we are splitting up. Maybe things will take their natural course. We'll just drift apart and that will be that. I should just go with this. Less hassle all round.

'OK, then.' I surrender. 'A leaving party it is. What are you thinking?'

'A few friends round at my house?' Jessica yawns as though, now it's in the bag, no further effort is required.

'Sounds good,' I tell her, then hesitate. 'Mind if a couple of other girls join in?'

That wakes her up again. 'What do you mean? Who?' she asks suspiciously.

'Natalie Yates and Sarah Llewellyn,' I say carefully. 'My friends from years ago.'

There is a tense silence on the line before Jessica responds.

'Um . . . those two squares in biology?' she says at last. 'Who sit by themselves in the common area? The ones with daggy haircuts? Isn't Natalie a disco granny?'

I bite down on her contempt, tell myself not to rise to the bait.

'Yep. I was at primary school with Nat. She's actually really nice.'

'"Nat"?' Jessica can't help the sneer in her voice. 'Since when has she been "Nat"? You normally refer to those people in generic terms . . . I had no idea you'd rekindled your friendship.' The facetiousness is clear. I am determined to ignore it.

'So, you're OK with it, then?' I say at last. 'Don't worry, they're house-trained.'

Jess sighs. 'Right, Lo, very funny. Seriously, you're not really inviting those girls, are you? I mean, they've got nothing in common with us. They shop at Miss Selfridge, for heaven's sake!'

This does make me laugh. But not in the way Jess intends it to.

'I just want to reconnect with my past,' I tell her, once I've recovered myself. 'With people who meant a lot to me, and who I neglected.'

I can just picture her lip curling. But to her credit, Jess's reply is pragmatic.

'Fine, but they'd better not be vegetarian or anything like that. Mum's ordered a meat menu from the caterers, and I can't bear all that do-gooding crap.'

'What does it matter? You won't actually eat anything yourself anyway. You might as well be a vegan.'

'True,' she says. 'But vegetarians make me hungry, and that's what worries me.'

I smile into my phone. Funnily enough, Jess's twisted world view has sent a surge of affection for her rippling through me.

I'm going to miss her. In a way.

'Well, I'd better finish putting all my worldly possessions into cases,' I tell her. 'It'll be wild.'

'God, how dreary,' she drawls. 'If you get bored, come over to the house. Mummy was asking about you only today. Come for supper. You know how she always over-cooks . . .'

'Lucky you,' I say wistfully, thinking of Mum's lacklustre attempts at family catering.

'So you should definitely come over,' Jessica persists. 'It might be the last home-cooked meal you'll have . . . ever.'

I laugh, but I have things on my mind. And they're not edible.

'Thanks, doll, but I'll pass. Say hi to your folks,' I tell her.

'Spoilsport,' she says. 'And just when you were getting back to your old self.'

'What's that supposed to mean?' I say, more sharply than I intended. 'Why do you always have to have a go, Jessica? Can't you for one minute think about the changes I am having to adapt to—'

'OK,' she begins. 'I didn't mean—'

'That's the point,' I say wearily. 'You just don't think.'

'Well, sorrree,' she says facetiously. 'Why don't you go and have a nice cup of cheap hot chocolate with your old friends Natalie and Sarah. Let's face it, those two dullards have so little going on, your tragedy must feel like a welcome distraction from their pathetic lives.'

I lift my chin to the ceiling and count to five before replying.

'Fine,' I snap. 'Go to hell.'

I end the call quite ferociously; my breathing is heavy and overwrought.

My old self, huh? I look angrily around the room, with its bare walls and empty drawers. My old self is disappearing in front of my very eyes.

Ten minutes after my call with Jessica, I am still holding on to my phone. My anger has dimmed and what I think of as the new feeling is emerging again. The feeling I had before

242

I talked to Jessica. Ever since yesterday, I've had this low-lying excited feeling in the pit of my stomach. It's a feeling I haven't had for a long time, not since Huck saw off that bumblebee and captured my heart. A feeling of something beginning. Something new. Something a little bit scary. I don't know why. It's ever since I spoke to Dan yesterday. It felt good to banter with a boy, with no romantic motive, just have a laugh.

I am turning a corner. Ready for my new life. A smile lifts the corners of my mouth and my eyes drift over the two packed suitcases by my bed. I could cheerfully burn the contents. I just don't care about any of my things.

I sigh, take a deep breath, and stare without any emotion at the screensaver picture of me and Huck.

And then I start typing a new message.

Hey. It was good to talk yesterday. Thanks for being there. Take care.

Immediately I regret it. The guy's probably thrown away the phone already, I tell myself. Closure has been achieved. The bubble has burst. I try and recall our conversation yesterday. The more I think about it, the more I think my texts were really lame. Boring. I screw up my nose, irritated with myself. Now I sound like a needy sad-case. I am kidding myself. I am not ready for something new. I should try and enjoy my last days with Jess, Destiny and Laura. I should stop trying to run before I can walk.

But still I am hoping for an answer. I stare at the screen, chewing my lip, before some kind of self-preservation kicks in.

'Right,' I say brightly, sliding over the bed and unzipping one of the large suitcases. As luck would have it, my grey plaid Vivienne Westwood dress is sitting on the top. I pull it out, smoothing out the slight creases.

'I guess I'd better try and have some fun,' I murmur. The new me can wait a few more days.

Jess is dressed in a cashmere onesie when she opens the door. Her normally poker-straight hair is attractively dishevelled and I look down to see a pair of French Sole ballet flats on her dainty feet.

'Lo,' she says, surprised. 'And there was me thinking I was dumped in favour of your "real friends".' She sniffs, taking in my dress. 'But perhaps you're heading out to the local Pizza Express for a goodbye dinner with Rory Gilmore and her mate . . .'

I laugh, holding out the bottle of Pinot Noir I stole from Dad's wine collection.

'Peace offering,' I say, giving her a small smile. 'I'm sorry for being so off.'

Jess lifts her chin in a fake-censorious gesture. 'Well, I guess you have been under some stress lately,' she concedes, taking the bottle off me. 'But take off your shoes. My mother has just had the parquet polished, and woe betide a pair of wooden-soled ankle boots.'

'Copy that,' I sigh, and wrestle with my footwear. Satisfied that my offensive boots are parked on the doormat, she turns to stalk down the hall. 'Brenda,' she calls. 'One more for dinner!'

Jess's parents, unlike mine, have a hospitable, apparently warm attitude towards visitors. Her mum was a beauty technician in Selfridges once upon a time. Until a handsome media CEO walked in to buy a Christmas present for his then fiancée, and a glamorous union was formed. Brenda is as obsessed by 'things' as my own mother, but unlike Valerie she hasn't got a snobbish bone in her body. She must remember only too well how limited her life felt with no qualifications and just a pretty face to get her through . . .

'We haven't seen you for a while . . .' she says brightly, handing me the bread basket. It takes me a couple of seconds to register the willing proffering of carbohydrates before I seize upon a cob roll and put it on my side plate.

'I've been busy with getting ready for uni and stuff,' I say, plastering my roll with butter. 'And I've not been too sociable since . . .'

'Of course,' Brenda says soothingly. 'Of course. It takes time, doesn't it, Tony?' She addresses this last to Jess's dad, whose face takes on a knowing expression.

'Got to give yourself time to grieve, Eloise,' he says solemnly. 'You've got plenty of time to be sociable.'

This is so far from my mother's mission statement that I feel I have stepped into a Martian family dinner. I cast a glance at Jessica, who is looking faintly bored, and wonder how two such seemingly empathetic people could have spawned such an emotionless child. On cue, Jessica yawns.

'Are you tired, darling?' Brenda asks. As she leans across to touch her daughter's arm, I catch just a little too much of a whiff of Dior perfume. Another difference between Brenda and my mother; Mum feels that Brenda's need to douse herself in scent is nouveau, or 'new money'. I hate myself for noticing.

'Can we talk about something less depressing?' Jess says. 'We should be looking on the bright side.'

There's a bright side? I think sceptically. I thought there was one yesterday but today I am less confident. I try not to think about my phone sitting there in my bag, on that chair behind Jess's dad.

'Oh, Jessica! How could I have raised such a hard-hearted child?' sighs Brenda. She pops a last forkful of carbonara into her mouth and I experience the thrill of watching a grown woman swallowing something other than obscure Chinese lettuce.

'I'm pragmatic, Brenda, not hard-hearted,' protests Jess. 'It's just that I don't think Huck was the love of Lo's life.'

'You don't?' I put down the roll I was about to finish. 'Since when?'

Jessica purses her lips and raises her eyebrows in a weary 'since-you-ask' expression. She takes a couple of seconds to stare me out, whilst no doubt composing her own brand of brutal home truth in response.

'I just don't think you were right for each other.' She shrugs.

'Jess?' My eyes dart to her parents, who look intrigued. 'You liked Huck.'

And then I see it, a faint flush in that usually impenetrable olive skin. I see it and some unpleasant cog turns inside me.

'Are we finished?' asks Brenda briskly, clearly sensing the discomfort in the air. She stands and starts taking plates.

'Let's not talk about Huck,' Jess says with distinct nervousness. 'Let's talk about the future.'

I open my mouth and then shut it again. I can't talk to Jess with her parents beaking in on every word. I hand my plate to Brenda and pray that there is no dessert.

'Dessert?' says Brenda over her shoulder as she walks through to their expensively designed Scandinavian kitchen. 'Cheeseboard or lemon meringue pie?'

'Have you maybe just got the lemon, Mummy?' says Jess. 'Without the meringue pie?'

Brenda trills with laughter while she crashes around in the kitchen.

To my relief Tony is rising from his seat. 'I'll help your mother do the dishes,' he says, giving us a wink. 'I'm sure we have some low-fat yoghurt for you girls in the fridge somewhere.'

'Thanks, Tony.' Is it my imagination or is Jess deliberately not looking at me?

Finally he disappears and I grab hold of one cashmere arm.

'Jessica,' I say firmly. 'What the hell was all that about?'

She is chewing her lip and twirling her fork like a dervish now. Distinctly animated, most un-Jessica-like behaviour.

'Jessica?' I let go of her arm and put both elbows on the table. Strictly verboten behaviour according to the Campbell-Taylor Household rulebook.

Finally her eyes meet mine.

'It's just that . . . Huck wasn't the great guy you maybe thought he was,' she says slowly. 'He wasn't all that.'

I hold her gaze. 'Yep. I know that. But how do you know that?'

'You know?' She blinks, her pretty almond eyes still hiding something.

'Know what?'

'Huck, well, he kind of flirted with other girls . . . I don't think he was so straight about that with you. And, I kind of didn't tell you . . . I hoped it was just me.'

'Just you . . .' I sit back, breathing out slowly, though inside my heart is thumping. 'You mean, just you that noticed?'

'No, Lo. Just me that he . . .' She closes her eyes, opens them again, and carries on. 'Just me that he came on to—'

'He what?' My voice jumps up an octave.

'Calm down,' she breathes, glancing over the top of my head in the direction of the kitchen. 'Of course I knocked him back.'

'Well, that's all right then,' I say with studied calmness. 'That makes it all A- OK.'

'Eloise,' she says maternally. 'Do you really think I would betray you like that?'

You already have, I think, my stomach descending like a press. Just by not telling me, you have betrayed me.

'Well, thanks,' I say out loud, after a beat. 'For nothing.'

'Rhubarb or vanilla?' calls Tony with excruciating bad timing.

I swallow, then slowly compose myself, rising to my feet and putting my serviette down on the table.

'Well, it certainly isn't vanilla,' I say evenly, giving my soon-to-be ex-friend a look of fire. 'Is it now?'

Outside Jess's house I wrap my arms around my under-clad body, and stand for a minute on her front step, both trying to not think and think at the same time.

I don't want to go back over every year, every month, every week, every bloody day I was with Huck and examine his and Jess's behaviour towards each other. What is the point? Haven't I already concluded that he wasn't 'all that'? Yet it's funny how you pile on the pain once it lands in your heart. You just keep on adding layer after layer, as though the sheer excess will implode, and leave just fragments too small to pick over.

How could I have been so stupid? So blind? Not just to what Huck was up to, but to my so-called Bestie's disloyal secrecy? A true friend would have told me, stopped me falling so deep. Instead she saved her own arse. And just watched as I made a total idiot of myself.

Jess could do that. She didn't need to have an emotional connection herself, she sucked at everyone else's.

The autumn breeze flashes through me. It's getting cold now. Soon it will be boots and tights, and uni lectures, and awkward conversations with strangers. I stare up at the moon, so beautiful and benign in the sky and I think, bring it on, bring on the winter of my discontent.

31

Daniel

Paula's grandma is sitting so close to me I can practically smell the soap she washed in earlier. I inch very slightly back, only to feel the brawny arms of Paula's brother against my shoulders. I decide on balance that physical proximity to 'Nene' is the lesser evil and lean marginally forwards again.

'So, boy.' Nene's soft, walnut, rippled skin stretches with her smile. 'You like my beautiful Paula?'

'Uh huh . . . Yes,' I say, with as much emphasis as I can muster. 'I like Paula. A lot.'

Nene's eyes narrow with a gimlet-like sharpness. 'You know, she is my little chica. My princess. And her heart . . . it is made of milk.'

I am nodding knowingly, yet I don't want to understand this weird metaphor. I realize I am expected to give a response, though. I sense a lecture is coming and wonder whether to get my answer in first, or afterwards.

Luckily Nene makes the decision for me.

'So she needs to be treated like the *princessa* she is . . . you understand. You give, you will receive. Much in return.' Nene picks up her small glass of sherry and nods slowly at the profound statement she has just made.

One which I don't fully understand, but I get the gist. The subtext. I suspect Nene has had one too many sherries. Whether this bodes well or badly for me, I am not sure. All I know is that I am not too willing to turn and engage with Paula's surly brother behind me.

'I think Paula is . . . amazing,' I tell Nene. 'I can't believe she would even look at a schmuck like me. But I am glad she has. If I wasn't going back to England very soon, I'd probably ask her to marry me.'

OK. This is an exaggeration to say the very least. But I figure that Nene will simply retrieve the sentiment, not take it literally.

Nene's eyes gleam. 'You would do that?' She clasps her hands together. 'Oh, I hope, I hope . . . She has had the bad luck with the boys. They are so selfish and they just want the . . .' She glances quickly at Fernando. 'The sex.' This last is said in a kind of hissing breath. I take a breath.

'I understand,' I say, in what I hope is a soothing tone. 'Boys will be boys.'

'But you.' She stabs one tiny brown finger at me in a not altogether genial way. 'You are not like this. You will cherish my girl.'

This is all sounding way too much like *The Godfather*. I don't like the steel in Nene's eyes. I need to prepare her for the fact that Paula and I may never be husband and wife.

I am about to pursue this line of dialogue when my hand brushes against my pocket and I feel the bulk of my phone, reminding me that I have not opened up the text I got earlier. I hesitate, torn between Nene's piercing brown eyes and my impatience.

'The thing is, Mrs . . .'

'Mrs Corbalan,' she supplies, still fixing me with her nutty eyes. 'The thing is what, young man?'

'The thing is, I'm going back to England in a matter of days, and I don't know when I'll be coming back to see Paula . . . and, don't get me wrong, she's amazing, in every way, but—'

'But what?' Another, younger, familiar, slightly tearful voice interjects.

We both turn our faces up, Nene and I, to see the crestfallen vision standing above us. It's Paula, her adorable white frock falling even further, and very becomingly, off one shoulder, her long, streaky hair tumbling prettily to her waist.

'You are just going to leave and never come back,' she says. 'I thought . . .'

I wince, not even daring to exchange a glance with Nene. For a few seconds, my overactive imagination imagines a Mafioso-like torture at the hands of this passionate Mediterranean family. Beaten black and blue by Fernando and Jaime, denied all sustenance but bread and water by Nene. I halt the thought, and instead think hard about how I am going to get myself out of this situation.

'Paula.' I grab hold her of her hand, which feels limp in mine. 'It's just not practical. I mean . . . we live in different countries.'

'You could move,' chips in Nene. 'Do something important with your life. What is more important than the love of a true heart?'

'Yes,' I nod. 'Yes, that is very important. It's true. But Paula is . . . Paula will be loved . . . A girl like Paula. Any man will feel lucky to have her.'

'Except for you, apparently, Daniel?' Paula's eyes are hard. She wriggles out of my grip. 'I thought you were different.'

I sigh and will the floor to open and swallow me up. How could I have got myself into this situation? One in which I am actually rejecting someone like Paula? It was only a couple of weeks ago that I was dreaming of romance. I have found it, and I am throwing it away.

But you can't fool your heart. OK, if Syd and Jamal knew I had even strung those words together I would be the laughing stock of Manchester, and a good ten-mile radius around it. But it is true. As lovely, as sexy, as sweet as Paula is, I don't feel it. I don't have the connection I want.

'I'm sorry,' I say finally. 'I'm really sorry.'

Paula's dewy eyes glance down briefly before she lifts her chin.

'You had better go,' she says calmly, coldly, her eyes flickering to a distinctly unimpressed-looking Fernando to my left. 'Really, Daniel, you should leave.'

I don't need telling twice. With a ridiculously polite nod at Nene, I get to my feet and stumble through to the hall where Inez is laughing glamorously with a couple of other women by the front door.

'Daniel,' she says, noticing my agitated demeanour. 'Is everything all right?'

I smile, thinking on my feet. 'Upset stomach,' I say. 'Just need some fresh air.'

Inez gives me an odd look, before rubbing my shoulder.

'Of course,' she says kindly. 'But mind out for the goat. We keep her in the front garden at night. She likes to see the porch lights on.'

As I finally close the door behind me, I spot the aforementioned creature prowling noisily by the gate, and can't help a small smile.

I am just deciding how to dodge the goat, who's looking far too interested in my trainers for my liking, when a shaft of light hits the front path, causing both me and my animal friend to blink.

'Daniel,' a familiar voice hisses behind me. For a minute I think it is Paula, come to make peace, but when I turn I see the angry figure of Cristina, hands on hips, glaring at me.

She takes a step towards me, glancing behind furtively.

'So, you are just going to run away?' she asks. 'Just leave my cousin with her heart breaking?'

'Cristina,' I begin gently. 'You don't understand.'

Now she is right up close. 'I understand that you are a fool,' she tells me. 'You have Paula. Paula! I thought you wanted to find love . . . romance. And now you are throwing it away, because of Nene.' She sighs, tossing her long dark ponytail. 'Nene always gives the interrogation. It is her way. She is just making sure you are not a . . . a player. She wants Paula to have the boy she deserves.' Cristina shakes her head. 'I am disappointed. I thought you had turned a corner—'

'Cristina,' I say again. 'It's not like that. This isn't about me being a "player". We all know I haven't got it in me. This is about integrity. About being true to myself. It's about not breaking Paula's heart. Don't you see? It would be fake, because . . . well, because I don't—'

'You don't love her,' she says calmly, more softly.

I stare at her earnest little face, and wish more than anything to see that impish grin. But I've started this mad process. I have to follow it through.

'No,' I say finally. 'I don't think I ever will. She's the most amazing, beautiful, lovely girl. But it's not there. It doesn't feel right.'

Cristina sighs. 'I see,' she says, looking down at the ground for a second. When she lifts her head up again, there is a different, more accepting look on her face.

'This is about Lo, isn't it? You hold a torch for this mysterious sad stranger.'

I take a second to marvel at the articulate way this child has summed it up. Considering English is most definitely her second language she is doing a pretty good job at nailing my feelings. I'll say this for the female species, they don't half get to the heart of the matter, however uncomfortable it makes everyone else. Some of them can see right through to your soul, it seems. It's comforting really. To know you are seen clearly. How on earth would us boys ever manage to achieve anything without a girl to push them in the right direction?

I can almost hear my mother cheering.

'I am not sure,' I say in answer to Cristina. 'But it felt . . . easier with her. We haven't met, but we just seemed to connect. You know what I mean?'

Cristina smiles a little sadly, but she puts one delicate hand on my arm.

'Yes,' she says. 'I suppose I do. I think you have to try and find out if your connection is real. You need to see how this story ends. I understand.'

It occurs to me that in a short time I will be leaving this place, and Cristina, maybe never to return. The thought makes me feel sad. I have made a friend here.

'Thanks, Cristina,' I tell her, taking hold of her hand and giving it a manly squeeze. 'For everything.'

Even in the dark I can see her cheeks flush.

'No problem,' she says, lifting her little chin, her eyes

bright and dewy. 'Now, go . . . Go and find your future.'

I let go of her hand and turn to navigate my way around the watchful goat. I don't look back.

I find myself on a deserted, silent street, with a few crickets serenading the dying summer. I feel a bit dazed by the past hour. Dazed and sad. I really did like Paula. She was very sweet. And I suppose I could have got used to her family after a while. But there's no turning back now. I owe it to myself to find the right girl.

Just thinking this I can hear my mother's voice in my head. 'You wait for perfect, you wait for ever.' She might well be right. But hell, I'm young, I'm idealistic and I am going to aim high.

As I tell myself this, I can't help but think how I have changed in the space of the past few weeks. The old Daniel would never have dared to dream he could have what he really wanted.

The new Daniel thinks it could be a real possibility.

I dig into my pockets and take out my phone.

Hey. It was good to talk yesterday. Thanks for being there. Take care.

When I see her message, I can't help breaking out a pleased smile. I reply.

You too. Don't be a stranger, stranger.

Pleased with my suave invitation, I wait at least two minutes for a message to come back to me, but nothing. I went too far. As usual I don't know when to leave well alone. She was just being polite. She's probably got herself a new boyfriend already. All thanks to the stupid pep talk I gave her yesterday. What was I thinking?

I stuff the phone away and give my head a little shake, as though it will rattle some sense into my naive brain, and then I start walking to find a cab to take me back to Ronnie's. I just hope that news doesn't travel too fast. If Ronnie is anything like Nene, he'll have me out on my ear before dawn.

Eloise

I am sitting in the town centre Pizza Express, fiddling with a napkin. My eyes glance at the clock on the wall. 1 p.m. They'll be here soon. The girls. I feel nervous. And I am tired.

I left Jess's house and walked all the way home the other night. But I still felt wired when I got in. Thankfully my parents were out with my aunt, and Jake was shut off from the world in his Xbox turret. I crept upstairs, brushed my teeth and tried to get to sleep in my cold, bare bedroom.

I didn't sleep. I just stared up at the ceiling, tears clouding my eyes, trying not to go over what Jessica had said. The look on her face. All this time, she had flirted with Huck. He had come on to her. And she didn't bother to tell me. It didn't occur to her that she should warn me.

Maybe I had known this about Jess all along. That she

goes where the wind blows, as my grandma used to say. My mind grappled for clues that I hadn't picked up on at the time. Huck never seemed to show much interest in Jess when I was around. Other than his usual brand of friendly charm, he seemed indifferent to my friends. But maybe I didn't want to see him watching them . . .

It was about midnight when I finally remembered my phone. I was so wrapped up in Jess's betrayal I'd completely forgotten about Daniel. I hadn't checked to see if he had replied to my forlorn little message.

Even wider awake, I got out of bed and upturned my bag, the contents scattering over the floor. I grabbed my phone and it flashed to life.

And there was a message from Daniel. In the midst of the crappy night, it was like a little piece of driftwood in a rough sea.

I had a sudden crazy thought, pushed it away, then retrieved it again. I figured I had nothing to lose.

So I dialled his number. And it went straight to voicemail.

I was totally alone.

'Hey.' Natalie brought me back to the present, her cheeks flushed, her arms drooping with bags of shopping. Out of sheer habit I note the names on the bags. Marks and Spencer and Topshop. I look away quickly and smile at her as she struggles past tables to reach mine.

'Hi,' I say, getting up, nearly knocking over my fizzy water in the process. 'It's so nice to see you.'

I must have sounded utterly pathetic, because her eyes flash anxiously when she looks at me, dumping her bags on an empty chair and easing herself out of her coat.

'Are you OK?' she asks, half smiling.

'Fine . . .' I begin, but the fact that Natalie reacts within seconds to my obvious not OK state has my eyes brimming. A tear splashes out and on to my nose. I rub it away with my sleeve but it's too late.

'Lo?' Natalie is sitting now, and she reaches out her hand, putting it over mine and squeezing it. 'What on earth is the matter?'

'It's nothing, it's just . . .' But it's too late, I am breathless, and the floodgates have opened. Before I know it my whole face is damp with a stream of tears. I don't bother to wipe them away, I just give little gasps. It feels like they'll go on for ever. I decide to let them.

Natalie's hand is still holding mine, but a little more tightly. With her free hand she reaches for a spare napkin, then leans forward and dabs gently at my cheeks.

'There,' she says softly. 'It's all right. I have more tissues in my bag somewhere.' She smiles, and it goes up to her eyes, like proper smiles should and she still hasn't let go of my hand. She isn't trying to stop me, or get me to explain. She's just . . . here. Listening.

'I should stop,' I say, recovering a little. 'Sarah's going to be here soon, and just look at me. I must look like such a freak.'

Natalie sits back a little. 'When we were at Parkway,

I was so jealous of how you cried. Because you never looked puffy or weird, you always looked so . . . pretty and sweet.' She sighs. 'You've not changed in that respect. I promise.'

I smile. 'Thanks. For being so kind,' I tell her. 'I don't deserve it. I haven't been kind to you.'

Natalie looks seriously at me. 'I missed you,' she says. 'Me and Sarah. We both missed you.'

I sniff away some residual wet stuff around my nose. 'I'm sorry. I can't believe I just dumped you two like that.' I sigh. 'I let my mum take over. I thought she knew best. I didn't realize she was a shallow, misguided fool.'

Natalie laughs. 'Your mum thought she knew best, too, I reckon. She's all right. She's just lonely.'

'Lonely?' My eyes widen. 'My mother? She doesn't have the time to be lonely . . . or the space. Every minute is filled. Every shop is raided. Seriously, she is not lonely.'

'But that's why she does it. She can't keep still, because then she'd have to face up to it.'

I stare at her. 'You really think that?'

She gives a small shrug. 'It's just a theory.'

I think about it. I guess I've never thought of my mum as anything other than a somewhat bossy control-freak, with a little too much self-assurance. And how can she be lonely? She has my dad, who obeys her every command. But then I remember what her life was like once. She had a good job, a clever job, she did something useful with her life. Unlike now – unless you count single-handedly

263

keeping the local economy buoyant through her incessant consumerism. Could all that stuff, those clothes, those shoes, those house renovations, be a substitute for that early ambition? The dreams she had before she had us – Jake and me.

I am so lost in thought that I don't notice Sarah come into the restaurant until she taps me on the shoulder.

'Hey you, lost in your own world,' she says smiling. She plants a kiss on my cheek and sits down. 'So how are things? All ready for uni?'

'Not really.' I sigh. 'In fact, not at all. Everything is changing so fast. It's all a bit overwhelming.' I see them exchange a look.

'This isn't just about uni, is it? What's really wrong?' Sarah waves at a waiter who is hovering nearby. I wait till she's ordered a drink before I respond.

'I don't really know where to begin. Obviously it all started when Huck died . . .' I hesitate. 'Though actually, it didn't start then. It was before that even.'

Sarah frowns. 'What do you mean?'

Natalie is looking a bit nervous. I remember how cagey she was when we talked about Huck before, about what her mum implied when she worked as Carlo's cleaner. I direct my answer at Sarah:

'Since he died I've been thinking a lot about us. About our relationship. And things have been coming back . . . memories. Kind of bad memories. Which is exactly what you don't want when someone dies. You

264

want to think the best of them.'

I pause. They sit and wait for me to go on.

I take a deep breath and continue. 'Huck wasn't quite as . . . devoted . . . as I believed he was. I think I didn't want to see the way he flirted—'

Natalie takes in a distinct sharp breath then and my eyes flicker over to her, but she is recovering herself, smiling weakly now.

'The way he flirted with other girls,' I continue. 'Even Jessica. My supposed best friend. Only I didn't notice at the time. I never saw it. She only told me the other night, and made out like it was nothing.' I realize my eyes have filled up with tears again. Weeks of no crying, and suddenly I am crying all the time.

'Sorry.' I fumble. 'I'm not making sense.'

'Yes you are.' Natalie's voice is clear, serious. 'At least, I know exactly what you're talking about.'

'You do?' For a horrible moment I think Nat's going to tell me she slept with Huck. But she reaches out and takes my hand again.

'My mum's always had a soft spot for you, you know. I think she was even more gutted about us not being friends than I was. She always asked about you . . . and I told her about you and your glamorous new friends, and your boyfriend. And then she got a job as Carlo Rafael's cleaner. And that's when she saw what went on at Huck's place. She used to come home a bit angry actually. On your behalf. Huck used to have girls round. Mum was never sure whether they spent the night or not, but they were sometimes there when she cleaned in the mornings, and one time . . .' She hesitates. 'She did see Jessica there. With Huck. I mean, it was early. Like eight a.m. or something . . .' She bites her lip. 'I'm really sorry, Lo. I should have told you before. But I mean, we weren't friends any more, and you would have thought I was interfering or jealous . . . and then, the other week I nearly did tell you, but I guess it didn't seem worth hurting you more than you were already.'

I open my mouth and let out a small gasp. Of shock, but also of realization. My best friend and my boyfriend. It's such a cliché. It's almost funny. Except it isn't. It's hideous. And humiliating.

'Lo . . .' Natalie gets up and puts her arms around me, holding me tight. 'You were always worth more . . . more than the lot of them put together. None of this is your fault. You know that, don't you?'

I nod, but I am clinging to her, my head buried in her jacket.

'I just feel like such a mug,' I say, finally wrenching myself away from Natalie. 'And Huck isn't here to confront . . .' I squeeze my eyes shut to stop another barrage of tears. 'Though I've tried.'

Sarah looks confused. 'What do you mean?'

'I've been texting him . . . I still have the number of the phone he was using while he was in Spain, and I know it's stupid but I just needed to talk to him, even though he's obviously . . . he obviously can't respond. I thought it would help. But I'm not so sure it has. It just seems to have made me madder with him. And with myself.' I look at the two of them, listening patiently. They don't appear to think I'm a lunatic. Maybe they're just humouring me.

'I can understand that.' Sarah turns to Natalie. 'It's like that therapy I had a couple of years ago. In lots of ways it's like talking to a brick wall, but it's good to vent. Even if stuff does come up that you don't like.'

'You had therapy?' I cut in, blinking at her. 'When? Why?'

'Oh, it's nothing. I'll tell you another time.' Sarah waves my questions away with a smile. 'We're talking about you.'

'OK. Well, yes.' I nod. 'I suppose it is a kind of therapy.' I take a deep breath. 'And the really weird thing is . . . that the other day, I got a message back.'

'You what?' Nat and Sarah chime in together.

I smile a bit then. 'Well, it wasn't a message from the dead, if that's what you're thinking. It was from a guy called Daniel – he's got Huck's phone. He found it and no one came to claim it.'

'Wait a minute.' Natalie leans over the table. 'Are you saying he's been getting all the texts you sent? Like, every single one?'

I shrug. 'I think so. I mean, not that I didn't feel a total prat. And annoyed at first. But he was really nice. And funny. And we had this really normal conversation by text.' I realize just saying that makes me feel better already. Just talking about Daniel.

267

'Oh my God.' Natalie grins. 'This is like a really great rom-com. It's like fated love. That's so cool, Lo. Who is this boy? How old is he? Is he single? Does he have a girlfriend?'

I wave her away, but I can feel myself blushing.

'You're blushing!' Sarah states the obvious.

'I don't know the answers to any of those questions! It's nothing . . . I mean, it's not like we're ever going to speak to each other again. What would be the point?'

Natalie raises an eyebrow.

'Seriously. It was just a weird fluke-ish thing. There's no romance. I know nothing about the guy.'

'So why are you looking so excited?' Sarah says. 'I mean, minutes ago you were in floods of tears over Huck and that hussy Jessica . . . and now look at you. Your whole face has lit up just talking about Daniel.'

'Shall we order?' I say, forcefully changing the subject. 'I fancy an American Hot.'

'Are you sure?' whispers Nat loudly. 'Are you sure you don't fancy a Hot Daniel instead?'

I laugh, and realize I am blushing even harder.

'Good one, Natalie.' Sarah nods appreciatively. 'I mean, not one of your best; it needs a bit of polishing, but you should work that into your routine when you get that gig.'

'Gig? What am I missing?' I stop smiling and look from one to the other, confused.

'I'm kind of trying out some comedy stuff,' Natalie explains a bit shyly. 'I started writing some things down and I did this ad-lib stand-up at the pub where my dad goes, and everyone seemed to find it quite amusing . . . So, I'm giving it a go.'

'Natalie, that's amazing.' I think of how withering my ex-best-friends would be about that kind of ambition, but I mean what I say. 'And you've always been the funny one. I always thought you'd be an actress, actually. This seems so right for you.'

'We'll see,' says Nat, picking up her menu. 'Let's just order. Then we can hatch a plan for you and your new man.'

'Natalie,' I say warningly. 'He's not my new man.'

'We'll see,' she replies maddeningly. 'We'll see.'

33

Daniel

Ronnie helps me with my rucksack en route to the station, somewhat humiliatingly, I should say, but I'm not going to protest. I'm just grateful he has been so good-natured about my behaviour with his niece. I put this down to the power of little Cristina, who must have told him to cut me some slack.

Still, I manfully relieve him of my luggage when we reach my destination. I'm catching a train back to Madrid. I'll stay another night with Mrs Diaz, who insisted I stop off and say goodbye before I leave Spain for good, and then I'll be flying back to Manchester. In a week or so, I'll be starting the next phase of my life in Bangor.

Considering how much I have been looking forward to flying the family nest and reinventing myself with a whole new set of people, I don't feel as exhilarated as I should. Not since last night.

Last night everything changed.

Let me backtrack a little.

I spent the whole of yesterday feeling like a total hound. And not in a good way. In a sad, slightly regretful way. Even though I had walked away from Paula, I missed her. I missed her good nature, and her laid-back attitude, and of course I missed her smoking beauty. At moments throughout the day I felt like sprinting over to her house, despite the inevitable unwelcoming committee that would have greeted me, and begging her to forgive me.

But then I had remembered. It would never have worked.

Ronnie had grunted at me at first, but he warmed up. He even told me he was sorry I was leaving.

'You been the lifesaver, chico,' he told me as I washed and polished my last glass and arranged it carefully on the shelf above the bar. 'Me and the little one . . . we have liked having you around the place.' He slapped me on the back, still too hard. 'You come back and see us, you promise?'

'Of course,' I told him, grinning. I knew I probably never would, but it felt nice to be wanted. Even if it was by a gnarly old guy with a stick.

'You going to be a big-shot, huh?' he said, parking himself on a stool and lighting up a slim cigar. 'Once you get your fancy degree?' He blew out some smoke. 'You never work in a bar again, I bet.'

'Don't know about that,' I said wryly. 'I've got to pay off

my student loan somehow. You've set me up for a job in the student union bar, I reckon.'

'Glad to help, chico.' He smiled paternally. 'You always need the back-up plan, see?' He nodded. 'Always good to have the back-up.'

'Absolutely.' I hang up the cloth I've been using and take a last, lingering look over what has been my kingdom for the past few weeks. I'll miss the routine. But I've served enough beers and washed up enough sticky glasses to last me a few years yet.

'Promise me something else, Daniel,' Ronnie says more seriously. He puffs on his cigar and puts it down in the ashtray. 'Promise me you will relax about the chicas, yeah?' The lines around his eyes are crinkling kindly. 'Find the right one and be happy. Is the best thing in the world, the love of a good woman.' He rubs his chin. 'Never a day passes when I don't thank Jesus for Eva, the only woman I ever love. Even now she has passed these last five years. Every time I look into my Tina's face, I see my Eva.' He smiles distantly. 'She was an angel from heaven.'

I gaze at him, moved. Another bit of perspective comes into view.

I nod slowly. 'You got it,' I say. 'One day I'll come to my senses, I promise.'

'Excellent.' He winks quickly and shifts himself off his stool. 'I have phone calls to make. I need a new barman,' he says over his shoulder as he picks up his stick and limps back to the door.

'Cool. See you later,' I tell him. 'I'll help you celebrate my departure.'

'Yeah, yeah, yeah,' he mutters gruffly. 'No fuss, no fuss.'

Ronnie cooked a huge meal later. Cristina, her friend Rosa and a huge photograph of the late beloved Eva gathered in his large kitchen diner for roast pork and cinnamon, and an unbelievable amount of patatas bravas. I had secured a bottle of champagne. Not exactly a Spanish delicacy, but a fitting tribute to the friends I had made here in this beautiful country.

'Cristina and me, we are coming over to England one day,' declared Rosa, sucking her home-made lemonade through a straw. 'I have English cousins in . . . Sessex.'

'Sussex?' I suggest, as Rosa shovels some patatas into her mouth. 'Cool. You'll have to give me a little warning though. Wales is quite a distance from that part of Britain.'

'Wales is not English, is this right?' Cristina enquires. 'So you will be in a different country.' She looks pleased with herself.

'Yes, technically,' I tell her. 'But even then it's all part of the same mainland. The whole of Britain is pretty small really. You can get all the way across it in a few hours.'

'So, you will take the train to see your mysterious friend?' Cristina exchanges an impish look with Rosa.

'Somehow I don't think that's going to turn into anything,' I say quietly. 'All a bit daft really.'

'If you don't find out for sure I will be very cross,'

Cristina says, waving her fork somewhat threateningly in the air. 'I simply must know what happens.'

Rosa is nodding feverishly. I look helplessly at Ronnie, who is shaking his head, hopefully clueless.

'OK, OK. I'll try,' I say, to shut her up for a moment. 'Could you pass me the champagne, please, bossyboots.'

She grins and obliges. 'You must get drunk tonight, and do something daring,' she says. 'It's your last night; you make it count.'

'Righto,' I reply, making a mental note to pass out in a blissful alcoholic sleep instead.

'She is right,' Ronnie butts in. 'You should let go a little. We could go dancing – the flamenco club in town is open late. I know José who owns it. I will call him for a special table.'

'Yay, yes, Pappy!' Cristina is in raptures. 'I want to go dancing!'

'Not you, monkey,' he says laughing. 'You and your little friend will watch the television.'

'I don't know,' I start. 'Dancing isn't really my thing, and—'

'I will not take no for the answer,' Ronnie states, mopping up his plate with a hunk of bread. You have never seen proper dancing until you see the flamenco. It lifts the soul. It is an art!'

I smile. 'OK. Why not? I could do with some soul-lifting.'

'Excellent.' Ronnie gets up to take his plate to the sink.

274

'Tina, Rosa . . . you are in charge of the dishes tonight. I will make the phone call.'

Cristina doesn't look happy but she nobly begins gathering the dirty plates on the table, while Rosa turns on the sink taps.

At the sight of these industrious, delightful people, I have a weird lump in my throat. I haven't got a little sister, but if I did, I could do a lot worse than Cristina. And living with a family where fun is an order is kind of infectious. I'll miss them.

'I'm just going to have a quick shower,' I tell them, and head upstairs to my room.

And that's when I see it. The missed call.

I forget about the bathroom and flop on to the bed, the phone in my hand and find my heart beating just a little too loudly.

She called me. Last night. Late. Should I call her back? It's 9 p.m. and I'll have to rush it. I'll do it on the train tomorrow. No, there'll be people listening on the train. It will be awkward. It can't be awkward . . . It has to be right.

I could text her. Maybe that would work? But I want to hear her voice. I just want to hear her voice.

This is stupid. This is not real, I tell myself. You're over-thinking it. She probably did it by accident. In a flash I am inspired.

Did you call? Or was it an accidental DUI?

I ping it off, my heart still thudding a little. I'm not so sure flamenco is such a good idea any more. I'm not sure I can handle the excitement.

I fully expect to be ignored. I have moved on to the pre-emptive catastrophic thinking that is my strong suit. I am already taking off my T-shirt, determined to have a quick shower. But just as I've tossed the T-shirt on to the bed and started taking my jeans off, the phone begins ringing.

Stuff the shower. I grab the phone and try hard to breathe normally.

Yes, ladies. Some men are actually from Venus too. Remember that.

'Hey,' I say, before she has a chance to speak. 'It's you.'

'It's me . . .' There is a tiny silence. 'And now I don't know what to say.'

'Well . . . what did you want to say last night? When you accidentally called me at two a.m.?'

Lo laughs. A sweet, slightly nervous laugh. For some reason it is the nicest sound in the world.

'I . . . nothing really. I just wanted to call. I wanted to speak to you.' She stops, and I am summoning every witty, yet reassuring response I have ever given. Not surprisingly, my repertoire is thin. I decide to play it straight.

'I'm glad,' I tell her. 'I enjoyed talking the other night. And again, I apologize for crashing your love life.'

'Nothing to crash,' she says. 'Nothing worth crashing.'

'You sound stronger.'

'I don't know if stronger is the right word,' she answers

thoughtfully. 'I guess I just don't feel the same. It's funny how a one-way street can do that to you . . . along with the odd skeleton that falls out of a cupboard.'

'I'm sorry,' I say. 'I'm trying to keep up with the metaphors. There's a skeleton falling out of a cupboard in a one-way street?'

She laughs loudly, catching her breath before she speaks. 'Forget it. It doesn't matter. I don't want to talk about any of that awful stuff any more. None of it matters now.'

'Well, good.' I am nodding at the phone. Slightly confused, but kind of enjoying it. 'I'm glad we sorted that out, then.'

Lo's laugh is cute, husky yet feminine. 'You're funny,' she says.

'So I'm told.' I put on a mock-weary voice.

'No. You're sharp . . . smart. And you've got a nice voice.'

'Thanks.' I feel a warmth spreading through me. No, not that kind. A more innocent kind. It feels strangely like I have come home, where I belong. 'You too.'

'So, Daniel.'

'Yes, Eloise.'

'Your turn. Tell me something about you. How old are you? Where do you come from? What's your favourite colour?'

'Uh, I'm eighteen, nearly nineteen actually. I come from a little town outside of Manchester. And blue.'

'Blue?'

'My favourite colour.'

'What colour are your eyes?'

'Um, kind of a sludge colour? Sort of brown with a bit of green. Kind of a non-colour really.'

'Don't knock sludge,' she says seriously. 'Sludge has substance.'

'Yeah, it's very like mud in that respect.' I laugh. 'I can tell you're determined to put the best possible spin on things today.'

'It beats the alternative,' she quips, a slight quaver to her voice. 'It beats texting a dead person, for instance.'

I hesitate. 'About that,' I say tentatively. 'You know, not to freak you out, but I might have met your man. What was his name?'

She is silent for too long and I curse myself for my crassness. I mean, how insensitive can I be? I am working out how to make it better when she finally replies.

'Huck, Huckleberry . . . What do you mean, you knew him? How?' She sounds a little less friendly now. Defensive. I can't say I blame her.

'It's not what you think . . . It's, well, I didn't know him. But a while back, he was in Madrid the same time as me and my friends. We got talking . . . but it was just a couple of times. And I didn't . . .' I wince, wishing I had just kept my mouth shut.

'Didn't what, Daniel?'

'I didn't really like him. He seemed a bit full of himself to me.'

Another silence. Then, 'That sounds like him.'

I breathe out a silent sigh of relief. 'But, like I say, I didn't really know him. We hardly spoke to each other.'

It's her turn to let out a sigh, audibly.

'I'm sorry, Eloise. I shouldn't have said anything.'

I've blown it.

'Daniel!' Cristina is thumping on the door at the worst possible moment. 'Pappy is ready to go. Are you fresh yet?'

'I'll just be a sec!'

I wait for Cristina to disappear, hoping she won't decide to barge into the room and see me with my top off and my jeans undone, on the phone to the mysterious stranger. Luckily she retreats downstairs again.

'I'm sorry about that,' I tell Lo.

'Who is that? Who is "Pappy"?'

'That was Cristina. She lives here with her dad, whom she refers to as Pappy . . . I've got a live-in bar job with Pappy, whose name is Ronnie. Well, I did have. I'm leaving tomorrow . . . But listen, Lo . . . I hope I haven't upset you. Sometimes I really don't engage my brain before I speak.'

'No. It's fine, you know. In a way, it's good to have some closure. I've been hanging on too long . . . trying to remember all the good bits, and it's just upsetting. Better if I think of him as an arrogant, dead douchebag.'

There is a split second of silence before neither of us can stop bursting out laughing.

'You know,' I say, recovering first. 'If *one* more person says that to me, this week, I swear—'

I stop just listening to her laughing – which sounds like the kind of panting laugh you do when you finally let go of a lot of pent-up tension.

'Anyway,' she says eventually. 'So I dated a dirtbag for a few years. Not like it was a total waste of my time or anything . . .' She sighs, and I can tell she's feeling just a bit sad again now. Now that the hysteria has died down.

'But it wasn't all bad, Lo. It can't have been. How long were you together?'

'Four years.'

'Well, that has to mean something. I mean, four years is a massive achievement as far as I'm concerned.'

'I take it you haven't been in a long relationship then?'

'Uh . . . not as such.' Try I've only had one girlfriend, for about two weeks, I think, but I am not a complete idiot, so I don't say it out loud.

'Have you got a girlfriend now?'

'Hey, wait a minute. Let's stick to you for the moment,' I tell her, laughing.

'Aha!'

'What does that mean: "Aha"?'

'It just means . . . you have got a girlfriend, but you don't want to admit it because then you couldn't . . .' She doesn't finish her sentence, but gives a nervous little cough instead.

'I couldn't . . . ?'

'You couldn't F.L.I.R.T with me.'

'OK. Were we F.L.I.R.T.I.N.G then?'

She gives a cute little 'grrr' in response. I smile, happy.

'I'm kidding,' I tell her softly. 'I totally was. Or at least attempting to. I'm not so sure I'm pulling it off so far, though.'

'You're not doing so badly,' she says. I like to think she is smiling, because I am. I have a ridiculous grin on my face. God knows what I look like.

'Anyway . . . I did have a girlfriend. Until recently. But I broke it off.'

'Oh . . .' She is trying to sound like that is bad news, but even I can tell it's a bit of a fake 'oh'. I'm certainly hoping it's fake anyway.

'It's fine. There wasn't any real connection.'

'I'm sorry.' Again with the fake condolences. Excellent.

'I'm not,' I tell her swiftly. 'But back to you. You and Huck.'

'Fine. But while we're on Huck, when did you figure out you knew him? And why didn't you tell me before?'

'I don't know. I was kind of caught up with other stuff,' I say truthfully. I'm not going to lie, I was. I was happy with Paula for a while there. She may not be the one, but while I was working that out, I was kind of into her. I'm not prepared to elaborate to Lo, though. Some things are private. And though I can't say 'I never kiss and tell' – primarily because there hadn't been all that much kissing in my life before Paula – I've been brought up to be respectful toward the female sex. 'I also didn't think it was going to achieve anything. I mean, I was there the night he died, and—'

'Hang on. You were there?'

And I've done it again. If Lo decides to instigate the three strikes and out rule then I'd better tread very carefully from this point.

'I wasn't actually right there; I didn't witness it. But my friend Syd, who I'd been travelling with, was in the same club as Huck, and he saw it happen. He came back to the hostel in a total state. It was a shock. I mean, he was our age and . . . you just don't expect it. I mean, well, you'll know. He was fit. He was healthy. He must have . . .'

'He took something,' she says flatly. 'I mean, I think Carlo – his dad – knows what caused his death, but he hasn't told me. He made out it was his heart. And I guess it could have been. It happens. Rarely. But if he was in a club then he must have taken something bad.'

'I guess.' Suddenly the fizz has gone out of our exchange. Not surprisingly. Death kind of has that effect. 'But it could have been any one of us, you know.'

'Do you take drugs?'

'No!' I say, a little too vehemently perhaps. 'It's not my thing. I'm more into the natural high . . . or maybe I am too cowardly. But that's not what I meant—'

This is like a kind of emotional *University Challenge*. And I appear to be letting my team down spectacularly.

But to my relief she laughs. 'OK, OK. Sorry, Daniel. I

know what you meant. And you know, I really am done with talking about Huck. To be honest, I am much more interested in you.'

And it's back. The fizz. Thank you, Jesus.

'You know, Lo . . .' I tell her. 'You're not going to believe this but I have to be somewhere. Ronnie is downstairs, waiting to take me to his friend's flamenco club. It's kind of a special treat for my last night.'

'Oh, oh . . .' She starts laughing again. 'I wish I could see that.'

'See what?'

'You flamenco dancing. I mean, how cool is that?'

'If you mean you would enjoy laughing at me attempting to flamenco dance, then no, Eloise, that would not be cool as far as I'm concerned. In fact, I can't believe I agreed to it. And the timing sucks entirely. It means I'll have to end this conversation—'

'Which is costing one of us a fortune,' she cuts in.

'Which is costing one of us a fortune,' I echo. 'But which I would gladly pay for, possibly even twice over. But Ronnie's been good to me, and I will probably never see him again after tomorrow. So I'm going to have to go and endure it.'

'Respect,' she says seriously. 'And it actually might be fun. You never know.'

'I'll tell you all about it, I promise.' The words are out of my mouth before I know it. I think about qualifying that with something casual and non-committal, but I decide just to shut up instead.

'You'd better.' Lo sighs in a contented kind of way. 'I'll be on tenterhooks.'

'Right you are.' I drag my T-shirt towards me. 'It's a date.'

Another, this time pretty delicious, silence.

'Daniel,' Lo says after ten seconds.

'Yes, Eloise?'

'You're nice.'

My shoulders droop. Just when I thought I'd got away with it too.

'And,' she says. 'I can't see you, but I'd like to . . . one day. Maybe.'

'Likewise,' I say, grinning like a fool again. 'I'll say goodnight now.'

''Night, Daniel. Break a leg. Well, not literally, obviously.'

'Goodnight, Eloise,' I say, chuckling. '*Hasta mañana*.'

So, I never made it to flamenco. By the time I got downstairs Ronnie was asleep on the sofa, his mouth partly open, snoring quite loudly. Cristina was dead to the world too, her head resting on his arm. Rosa must have gone home.

I was relieved. I picked up a rug from the back of the sofa and draped it over the two of them. Then I crept back upstairs, whistling badly to myself, to finish my packing.

So here I am, standing on the platform, sad to be leaving, but looking forward to getting home – via Mrs D's.

You know that feeling, that fluttery, slightly scared feeling you get when something unexpected but immediately precious happens to you. You get what you wanted for Christmas, you get what you wanted for dinner, you're let off Sunday dinner at scary Aunt Naomi's house, you meet an amazing girl on the phone . . . that feeling. Well, I've got that feeling. Right now. And frankly, it scares me more than walking into a tempestuous sea, or accidentally walking in on my mother in the bathroom after she's done her hair in curlers and applied a pointless, yet hideous, mud face mask.

Pretty scary.

'Sweetheart.' My mother pours me a cup of tea and brings it over. Typically it is black and just looking at it makes the insides of my mouth dry. Still, it is a rare thing, Mum being domestic, or maternal, so I smile in appreciation.

'Thanks, Mum. You didn't have to do that.'

'It's your last cup of tea at home,' she says mournfully.

'What are you going to do with my room?' I ask, to lighten things up a little. 'Turn it into a gym?'

Instead of the barbed comeback I am accustomed to, Mum gives me a benign smile. 'I'm not going to do anything with it,' she says mildly. 'You'll want somewhere to sleep when you visit, I assume. And I can't have you sleeping in the pool house.'

'It looks strange now,' I say sadly. 'Empty and alone.'

She frowns. 'I'll redecorate,' she suggests brightly. 'What would you like?'

'You don't have to do that.' I gaze sadly down at my black tea. It has that dirty, slightly oily look to it. 'It doesn't need to be redecorated.'

But when I look up I see a slightly helpless look on her face. And I realize that her offer is her way of making me feel cared about. Worth making an effort for. That never would have occurred to me if Natalie hadn't offered her own theory on the mysterious creature that is my mother.

'But if you want to . . .' I smile. 'I mean, you always know what works.'

'Good.' She brushes at an invisible speck on the table. 'Well, I'll have a think about it. It's always good to bring some metaphorical fresh air into a room. It helps . . .' She trails off. I see, with panic, that my mum is upset.

Emotional.

'Mum.' I put my hand out. She hesitates, before extending her own hand to wrap around mine.

'I do love you, Eloise,' she says, widening her eyes. It's a trick I've also used to stop myself crying. It looks incongruous on my mum.

'I know.' I grip her hand. 'I'm sorry I've been so horrible and weird lately.'

She shakes her head and I see a tear snaking down her cheek.

'Ladies.' Dad appears in the doorway. 'Jake and I have got all the cases in the car.' He looks over at me. 'Ready to rumble?'

I am still holding Mum's hand, and he glances down. A

small smile appears on his face. 'But we don't have to leave immediately . . .'

'We should get going.' Mum is brisk again, and her hand loosens out of my grip. She sniffs, then quickly, subtly, runs her hand over my hair. Before I can blink, she is back to business again, moving towards the window to close it.

The fridge hums, breaking the preciousness of the moments just gone.

'OK then.' I get up and pour my un-drunk tea down the sink, placing the dirty cup in the poignantly empty dishwasher. I walk over towards Dad and let him wrap his arms around me, enjoying the solid warmth of his chest.

'Let's go,' I tell them. 'Get this over with.'

Four hours later, in the heart of London, I am watching my family – my mum, my dad and my brother Jake – drive off down Charlotte Street. Unable to watch them any longer, I look in the other direction, at the regal coolness of Fitzroy Square. A few tourists are taking pictures of the BT Tower, ignoring the imposing and beautiful houses ringing the square.

I smile.

My room is small and spartan, with only the faint remains of old Blu-Tack on the walls. There's a large single bed, a cheap wooden desk and some distinctly Argos-looking free-standing bookshelves against one wall. The previous occupant has left a fairly hideous fake purple gerbera daisy in a plastic pot on one of the shelves.

It's hardly the romantic Oxbridge suite I had imagined for myself before I understood what uni living is for most people, but it is mine. Mine to clean, decorate, eat kebabs in at two in the morning if I want to. Mine to do, within reason, exactly what I please in.

It feels pretty good.

I start taking stuff out of my cases, hanging up my clothes first, stuffing my shoes under the bed for the time being. It doesn't escape me how little reverence I give to this expensive sartorial collection now. Where once I would have maniacally bagged and de-fluffed every item before I hung it, now it doesn't matter to me if my Miu Miu coat has creases in it. They'll drop out, eventually.

I sink down on the bare bed. Just a lumpy mattress, which at least looks clean. I decide to make the bed up in a minute. I threw into my luggage my faded Cath Kidston rose print duvet cover set this morning. I haven't used it for years, but it pre-dates Huck. It's the old me.

I get out my phone. Five message notifications. All from hours ago:

You never said goodbye. I'll be home for Christmas, unless the Hamptons makes me a better offer. Come over for a girls' reunion. XXJ

I sigh. Typical Jessica. Emotionally obtuse as ever. Weirdly, I'm not angry any more, just detached. I have already dismissed her from my life. I click on to the next one:

*Lo, Lo, Lo. I can't believe you went without seeing me. I'll
come to London soon. Clubbing? Laura xxxx*

Destiny's is next. Less emotionally retarded, I'll give her
that.

*I wanted to tell you what went down with Jess and Huck.
But she had me believing it was better I shut my mouth. I
regret that. I'm sorry, kid. Still wanna be friends?*

Not sorry enough, I murmur, deleting her. I feel a twinge
of sadness. I really thought those girls had my back.
Underneath the glossy veneer, I thought they were on my
side. Turns out, not so much.

Natalie sends me a text wishing me luck, hoping I'm
settling in. She's temping locally, hating every minute of it.
Wondering if she should take a risk and move to the big
city. I reply:

Do it! Nothing to lose. And I'll be here.

The last text, the one I have been saving for last at least, is
from him. We haven't spoken since that night he was due
to go flamenco dancing. But we have texted. Loads. Daniel
will be in Manchester now. Too far. I feel a kind of
emptiness when I think about it. Ridiculous, really. I don't
even know what he looks like. He could be hideous, with
out-of-control acne and a hump.

Hey. Settled in to your new home OK? I'm at Madrid airport, just about to get on a plane home. Going to be a day or two in Mancs, where my mother will overfeed me. Hopefully that will keep me going until I learn to cook when I get to uni. Talking of uni. Did you know that Bangor is only six hundred miles from London?

I smile, feeling a nervy little jitter shoot through me. I am just about to respond when someone hammers loudly on my door.

'Hey! Anybody in there?' It's a female voice. Kind of loud, but maybe I'm about to make my first friend here.

'Just coming.' I drop the phone on the unmade bed and open the door.

A tall girl with short red hair, pale make-up and red lipstick is standing in front of me. She's wearing a tartan shirt, leather shorts, tights and metallic-blue Dr Martens. She has several piercings – a hoop in her nose and a silver stud above her lip. I gaze at them, wondering if they hurt.

'Hi,' I say, waiting for a smile back. Or something vaguely less hostile than the look currently on her face. 'Do you room down the hall?' I stick out my hand. 'I'm Eloise.'

'Stella.' She relaxes a little, takes my hand and gives it a quick shake 'Yup. Just unpacked. Thought I'd check out the neighbours.'

'Well, hi, neighbour,' I say shyly. Stella looks like the kind of girl who might eat me for breakfast. 'Where are you from?'

'Norfolk born and bred,' she says. 'And not proud of it! How about you?'

'Just outside London,' I tell her. 'A boring little town in Kent. Not proud of it either!'

Stella's expression softens slightly at my lame copy of her joke.

'You sound posh,' she says. 'I bet you had a pony growing up?'

I open my mouth to respond when a boy shuffles into sight behind Stella. He's about her height and dressed in an old-skool Adidas tracksuit with a beanie pulled down over his hair.

'Hey,' he grunts at me.

'Eloise, this is my boyfriend, Jonah.' Stella raises an eyebrow. 'Who has been asleep on my floor for the past two hours in an effort to get out of helping me unpack.' She pushes him. 'Well, now you're awake, you can go out and get us some beers.'

Jonah looks resistant, but he does smile at me.

'You're not a ball-breaker too, are you?'

'I'm pretty sure that's not how my friends would describe me,' I tell him, laughing. 'Is that going to be a problem?'

'I think that's a plus,' he replies, giving me a genial two thumbs up. 'Stella likes to rule the roost wherever she goes. Isn't that right, dear?' He leans into her and kisses her on the cheek.

'Ignore him.' Stella's lips twitch at me. 'I'm a softie really. It's only Jonah that needs discipline. Like most men.'

It's my turn to raise an eyebrow. 'I wouldn't know. My experience in that area is pretty limited.'

'You're a virgin?' Jonah asks outright. 'Wow. A virgin.'

'Jonah!' Stella pushes him again, harder this time. 'That was totally out of order. Just go and get the beers.' She rolls her eyes at me as Jonah slopes off down the corridor.

'Seriously, though. Are you?' she asks as soon as he is out of earshot.

'No,' I say calmly. 'But I've only had one boyfriend. And I wasn't too good at bossing him. Or anyone else for that matter.'

'Meh.' She shrugs. 'It gets a bit tedious after a while, anyway, the bossing. Sometimes a girl just wants a guy to tell *her* what to do.'

'Well,' I say, 'I certainly didn't expect to be having this kind of conversation before I'd even unpacked. It beats asking for a cup of sugar, I'll say that.'

We grin at each other. We couldn't be more different on the surface, but we've managed to communicate more significantly in five minutes than I have in years of talking to Jess, Destiny and Laura. No frills, just straight to the point.

I like it.

'So . . .' she says, craning her head and seeing my cases and unmade bed. 'Where is he, your boyfriend? He at uni somewhere else?'

'Um, not exactly,' I say uncomfortably. 'We're not going out any more. In fact, he died this summer.'

293

'Jesus!' Her eyes widen. 'I'm such an idiot. Me and my big mouth. I'm sorry, kid. You must be a mess.'

'I . . . Actually I'm not,' I say, realizing that I feel normal for the first time in years. 'I was. But I'm OK now.'

'Uh huh.' She nods cautiously. 'Still . . . take it easy, yeah. That's a huge thing.'

'It is, isn't it?' I nod. 'And thank you for not brushing it off.'

She shrugs. 'I tell it like it is. It's one of my specialities. And not always appreciated . . . as Jonah often reminds me.'

'Come in. I'm just going to unpack a couple of things.' I open the door wider and turn back into my new home. 'Sit down, make yourself comfortable.'

'Thanks,' she says, plumping herself down on my bed. She has very long legs and the kind of firm, boyish figure my mother wants for me.'

'You been together long?' I ask her. 'You and Jonah.'

'A year or so,' she says. 'He's a bit of a stoner and kind of odd-looking, but he's funny . . . and he's kind. And he puts up with me, accepts me. Loves me for who I am. We met at a gig and kind of kept things up since then.'

'Huh. That sounds nice. That sounds just right,' I tell her, my thoughts wandering to someone else who might just fit that description. But who is a bit of a long shot, if I'm being honest with myself.

'Has Jonah got any single friends?' I ask her wryly.

'I wouldn't inflict Joe's friends on you, honey. You look a little upmarket for that lot. Unless you have a secret skateboarding habit and smoke weed.'

I laugh. 'Maybe not. I'm a little on the square side. Not very brave or adventurous.'

'From where I'm sitting – quite literally sitting,' she laughs, 'you seem pretty brave to me. I mean, you're here, you're getting on with your life. After what happened to you. Well, I don't think I'd be doing so well.'

'What choice is there, though?' I ask. 'You either get on with things, or you . . .' I shake my head, as it suddenly occurs to me that in fact I could have slid down into something darker than I did. I could have slept for two months, as opposed to two weeks. I could have stopped eating altogether. I could have . . . It's not worth thinking about what I could have done, I guess. Maybe I haven't done so badly, after all?

'Anyway,' Stella says brightly, after a pause. 'Fresh start and all that. There are bound to be a few glamorous alpha males knocking around the uni campus. You'll be coupled up before you know it.'

'No. No alpha males,' I answer firmly. 'I'm done with them.'

Stella crosses her legs underneath her and gives me a wide grin.

'You know, Eloise, I think we might just be friends, after all.' She eyes my Cath Kidston bed set. 'Even if your taste in bed linen is a bit Chelsea for my liking.'

'Get over it,' I tell her, as I throw a floral pillowcase at her head.

A couple of hours later I am slightly tipsy from two bottles of lager and have made little headway with sorting out my room. At least my bed is fully made now. I suddenly feel so exhausted, all I want to do it collapse into it and start again tomorrow morning. I have a few days before my first lecture, and though there is some kind of orientation thing happening, and a few freshers' week activities, I'll have plenty of time for myself.

Then suddenly I am wide awake. I remember what I was about to do before Stella came knocking on my door and we got talking, and then Jonah came back with the beers, and . . . I realize have no idea where my phone is. I also realize I am panicking slightly. It is of the utmost importance that I find that phone.

Twenty minutes later I am resigning myself to its disappearance when it comes to my rescue. I hear the blissful sound of a message arriving in my inbox.

I roll my eyes as I see it peeking out from under a pillow on my bed. I sink down and grab it like the lifeline it has become.

I realize my heart is beating fast. Because I am so hoping it isn't my mum, or Natalie, or Sarah who's texted. God love them, but they're not who I want to hear from right now.

I haven't felt like this since, well, since I first started

seeing Huck. I am like a lovesick teenager. Maybe I am a lovesick teenager. Which is crazy. And delusional.

It's funny how, as soon as you start to feel a certain way about someone, you start expecting more from them. It's so difficult not to hold yourself inside your bubble, hoping it won't burst.

But the number that comes up is not one I recognize. My heart sinks. It's just some random who's texted me by mistake. Forget the bubble, I am like a balloon whose air is slowly leaking out. I check it anyway.

> *Back in England, on a train to Macclesfield. It's so cold in this country! Anyway, Lo. You never replied to my last update. Anyone would think that my travel itinerary is not that interesting…insert smiley face. And I am feeling somehow not as excited about uni as I was. I don't know why that is. What do you think, Eloise? D x*

OK, so my bubble is intact, my balloon is inflating once again. I am absurdly happy. I know it's totally sad, and I am really going to try not to analyse his last two sentences.

But if I am reading them correctly, then there is someone out there who is feeling exactly as I am.

35

Christ, I'd forgotten about the miserable weather in the north of England. I don't know why, since I have spent a good eighteen years enduring it. But a few weeks in the balmy Spanish climate has spoilt me. This train is like a travelling refrigerator. I get down my rucksack from the luggage rack above my seat and take every item of warm clothing out. I put them on and sit down. I will overheat shortly, but my major concern now is keeping hypothermia at bay.

My phone rings and I smile, recognizing the number.

'Sydney.' I settle back into my seat and possibly for the first time ever put my feet up on the one opposite me. I take risks now, see?

'You're back.' Syd sounds like he has flu. On cue he lets out a deafening chesty cough. 'You know it's been, like, raining here for weeks, and freaking freezing. I feel like

298

crap and I'm supposed to be leaving for Brighton first thing tomorrow.'

'Uh huh. Well, enough about me, let's talk about you,' I say drily.

Syd coughs again. 'Sorry, mate. How was it? I don't want to hear any really good stuff, mind you. Biggest mistake I made was coming back. Jamal started seeing this chick at computer club and it's all he talks about. He's turned into a right bore.'

'Jam's got a girlfriend?' I raise both eyebrows at once. 'How on earth did he manage that? He never speaks to girls.'

'She's French.'

'Mystery solved then. Is she attractive?'

'Uh . . . kind of. Actually, she's gorgeous. Looks like Natalie Portman. She's besotted with him. It's obnoxious.'

'I can imagine.' I shift my legs. 'So . . .'

'Yeah. Sorry I haven't been in touch. My phone ran out of credit, which was great because I'm skint, but then my mum took pity on me and gave me a fiver. I'm back in the game.' He coughs again. 'So, what did you get up to after we went? Wandered listless and alone around the Spanish coastline?'

'Er . . . not so much. I mean, I stayed in Madrid for a week or so, then I headed over to San Sebastian and got work in a bar in a place nearby, just up the coast.' I decide to leave out the fact that I didn't have to lift a finger to get the job because a seventy-year-old woman did it for me. 'It was cool.'

'Cool?' Syd blows his nose. 'In what way? The thrill of long hours and meagre tips, huh?'

'Um . . . No, I mean, yeah it was hard work but it had its moments.'

There is silence. 'Don't tell me you copped off?'

'Well, I wasn't going to phrase it quite like that, but yes, I met a girl.' I have a flash of Paula's tanned smiling face, but it only registers as a pleasant apparition. Nothing more. 'Her name is Paula.'

'Oh . . . God.' Syd sounds depressed. 'Am I the only adolescent boy in the world considered untouchable.'

'Well, no, but you might want to consider thinking and talking about someone other than yourself for a moment . . . you know, the virtuous circle theory?'

'Yada yada yada,' he says grumpily. 'Anyway, about this Paula. She has a hunchback, right? Kind of stumpy? Partially sighted?'

I laugh. 'No, no and no. She's beautiful. Tall, slim, kind of sporty . . .'

'So. She obviously has some kind of mental disorder.' Syd pauses. 'Sorry, mate. I'm just jealous. Please continue. Do tell me about this gorgeous creature. Please. I really want to hear about the crazy time you two had, fooling around with each other on the beach, falling in love . . .'

'We didn't. I didn't,' I say, hesitating. 'I didn't fall in love with her.'

'OK, so you're the one with the mental disorder?'

I sigh. 'Possibly. I don't know . . . there wasn't enough of a connection, you know?'

'Mate. I don't think I would recognize a connection with a girl if it hit me in the face,' Syd says. 'So, I don't know. But I'll take your word for it.'

'And, there was . . . is . . . kind of someone else.' There, I've said it. Out loud.

'Your mother. Yes, we know that, Dan.'

'Give it a rest, Sydney.' But I am laughing. 'Not my mother. A female of my age. Except . . . well, it's a kind of bizarre situation. We've not actually met.'

'OK. Now I'd better warn your mother,' Syd tells me. 'Because something happened to you out in Spain. You appear to be speaking in riddles.'

'It is kind of a riddle.' I pause. 'Remember that kid who died?'

'Of course. Pretty memorable, that. It's the reason I foolishly cut short my trip.'

'Well, this girl . . . she was his girlfriend.'

Another pause while Syd puts the pieces together in his head.

'So . . . how? I mean, how?'

'Huck dropped his phone in the hostel. He must have been staying in our room and I found this phone under my bed. I meant to hand it in, but then you left and it was all going off, and I kind of forgot. So . . . I have this phone – Syd?' I pause. 'Are you keeping up?'

301

'Yep. You had the phone.'

'Right. Anyway, texts start coming through on the phone and they're from a girl. And she's obviously totally pissed off with whoever she's texting, but she never calls him by his name, so I don't know it's Huck . . .'

'Hang on. At this point, why have you not handed the phone in?' Syd chimes in, quite reasonably.

'Yeah. It looks bad. But I figure that this guy clearly hasn't come to find his phone, and when I ask Mrs Diaz she confirms it. And I also figure he's a total douche for just leaving this girl to worry about him.'

'And of course, you're not going to put her out of misery?' Syd says, again reasonably.

'I know. And I don't know why. Except that I was lonely and this girl was my only source of conversation. Pretty one-sided conversation, I know. But I was selfish. And then it was too late. And I couldn't face putting her straight. I thought she'd give up. And then I was glad she didn't give up.'

Syd sighs heavily, followed by another coughing session.

'Bad Daniel,' he says when he's recovered. 'Bad, bad Daniel.'

'But, see, it was the right thing to do. Or not to do. Because, now . . . me and this girl – her name is Eloise – are kind of having a thing.'

As I finish my explanation it strikes me how delusional and ridiculous I sound. It's like a moment of clarity. It is so ridiculous.

'That is so ridiculous.' Syd echoes my thoughts. 'I mean, totally and utterly sad. And kind of cool. Stuff like that only happens in films.'

'Yeah . . .' I breathe, turning to look at the dark countryside flashing past. 'But I feel kind of silly now. I mean, just telling you about it.'

'So. What are you going to do now?' Syd asks after a bit. 'I'm assuming Eloise is British. So now you're in the same country . . . you can finally meet her.'

'Not so sure about that. She's just started uni in London and I think she thinks I'm a pain in the arse. I just sent her a text, before you called, and she hasn't replied.'

And as if by magic, my phone pings with a text notification. I take the phone away from my ear to glance at the screen. And there's her name, shining up at me.

'Mate, I just got a text – it's her. You know what I'm going to say now, right?' I say.

'Yep. Speak later.'

'Later.' I end the call, and wait for a feverish beat and there it is. Lo's reply. Never has a little blue box with someone's name written on it looked quite so good.

Sorry so long to reply. I was entertaining my new neighbour. And after a couple of beers, I lost contact with my phone. So, what does excite you then, Daniel?

Whoa. I re-read the text. If I'm not mistaken that was a distinctly flirtatious question. More than that it was downright provocative. And very heartening. Maybe I'm not such a pain in the arse after all. I need to come back with something good. Calm but encouraging. I think for a few minutes, running lines from films through my head. Consider some kind of Bogart quip, then dismiss it. 'Here's looking at you, kid,' would be better used at some other, less crucial moment.

Oh, you know, mysterious blondes, long-distance relationships . . . something like that? Insert emoticon of your choice. D

The train is pulling up at the station and I get up, grab my bag and peer through the window. I am surprised to see the figure standing on the platform waiting. It must be way past her bedtime. She's usually stretched on the sofa with her hundredth cup of tea at this hour.

For there, wearing an oversized sheepskin coat and wellington boots, stands my mother, her face set in the standard expression that most people in the north of England have. It comes from years of standing outside at freezing bus stops or on windy train stations. It's an expression of discomfort mixed with endurance. Somewhere beneath the scowl beats a heart of pure gold. It just takes a little time to find it is all.

I am surprisingly pleased to see her. I mean, I will be desperate to get away from her in approximately two hours, but for now I enjoy the warmth that comes from arriving home, to the safe and the familiar.

Stepping off the train I give Mum one of my dazzling smiles, prepared for her outstretched arms. Instead she rolls her eyes, looks me up and down and pushes a bulging plastic Tesco bag at me.

'Mum?' I shift the heavy bag more comfortably on my arm. 'What are you doing here? I didn't expect anyone to meet me.'

'You've lost weight,' she says, by way of answer. 'And my back is killing me. We'll need to get the bus. I stopped off at Linda's place for some poker at five and I got waylaid. Sheesh, that woman can talk. The car's at the garage again. Your dad is still too mean to buy a new one . . .'

'Nice to see you too, Mother,' I say brightly. 'Missed me?'

'Pah. I didn't have time to miss you,' she tells me, turning round for the exit. 'Life goes on, Daniel; the world doesn't revolve around you, you know.'

Staggering under the weight of my rucksack and what feels like a bag full of hand grenades, I marvel at the woman's knack of bringing a person brutally down to earth.

'You can tell us all about it over hot milk,' she puffs over her shoulder.

'Shall we get a cab?' I ask tentatively. 'We'll be waiting ages for a bus.'

'Look at you, fancy-pants,' she tells me, a hint of a smile on her grumpy face. 'Well, just this once.'

At last, the heartfelt gesture I have been holding out for.

'Great,' I tell her as we exit the station. 'Good to be home, Mum.'

36
Eloise

I'm in Regent's Park, watching a crowd of geese arguing with each other on the park river, and I am just exulting in the chilly October sun. Above me is blue sky; around me are tall regal trees topped with browning leaves. It's end of school time and a few kids are circling round and round each other on bikes.

I've made it through my first two weeks at uni. And already I feel home; my mother, along with the three witches, have faded into an almost distant memory. Of course, Mum has been on the phone. 'Shall I get Marco to come and give the walls a lick of paint?' or 'Are you sure you don't want a little studio flat in Bloomsbury somewhere?'

I refused, of course, though my humble little room is looking more humble by the day. I'm used to being well away from the street when I sleep, separated by an electronic gate and a decent gravel drive, for a start. But here, just after last orders, the whole of Fitzrovia is like the Notting Hill carnival.

Sarah and Natalie came down at the weekend. Natalie's still intent on getting a job in London. And Sarah is flying off to Peru in December to do some voluntary work. Despite the fact that my old friends are making a real effort to move into their adult lives – without the help of their parents – they both want to know all about uni, and of course, all about my mysterious phone friend . . .

Talking of him. We've kind of lost contact. After my first night, when he sent me a bunch of nice texts, there has been nothing. I texted him a few more times, but when he never replied I gave up. I was surprised how flat, disappointed – OK, how hurt – it made me feel. But then I forced myself to get immersed in uni life and try not to think about a boy I'd never actually meet. Even if he had made me feel happy again when we talked. I have spent the time since telling myself he is very likely deeply unattractive, and the disappointment would have been way greater if we ever did meet. Better, I convinced myself, to end on a high.

Except, seriously? We all know it doesn't work like that.

There are a couple of guys in my building who seem OK. Hot hipster types, who probably have hipster girlfriends somewhere, but one of them, Tom, asked me to an installation exhibition at the Whitechapel gallery next week. Well, he asked me, and Stella, and Jonah, and Jonah's friend Arthur, but still . . . he asked me.

That's another thing. I am so not the cocksure princess

308

I was before. Back in the day I never had a moment's doubt that I was pretty and that a boy might like me. I was used to giving the knockback, not quite so ruthlessly as Jess, Laura and Destiny, but I've done my time making guys look small. Too much time. And looks like I'm getting my just deserts right now.

If ever there's somewhere to put you in your place, then it's uni. There are hordes of fit girls, likewise cute boys. I am just one fairly pretty blonde in a maelstrom of beautiful youth. I've learned that being better looking than average does you no favours when it comes to making an effort. I'm not used to it. But I know I have to. I have to trade on my sparkling wit now. Not my Swarovski iPhone cover and expensive beauty routine.

I've already had all my Clinique stuff nicked anyway. One of the hazards of a bathroom shared with impoverished strangers. Doesn't really bother me, but I won't tell my mother just yet. I'm going to see how I do with Boots own-brand products for a while.

I smile into the distance when I picture the horrified faces back home.

'Yo, Princess!'

I turn to see Stella marching across the grass towards me, and I wrap my leather jacket closely round my cold body. I smile at her long legs encased in purple tights and black suede creepers. Her short red hair is framed by a bright-pink velvet bow. On anyone else that ensemble would look appalling. On Stella it looks like she was born in a technicolour rainbow, and it suits her.

Stella picks up a bit of pace as she gets closer. 'Thought I might find you sitting morosely on a park bench,' she says. 'I've been looking everywhere for you. I tried calling you, girl. Are you screening?' She puts a hand theatrically on her heart. 'Jesus, I haven't had this much exercise since I stupidly offered to take the dog for a walk back in 2002. It was a bad idea then, and it's a bad idea now.' Stella adjusts her velvet headband, drops down next to me and catches her breath, squinting at the geese, who seem to have made their peace and are sharing a bit of stale white bread.

'I'm honoured,' I tell her. 'My phone's out of battery, sorry . . . So what's the occasion?'

'Huge fight with Jonah,' she sighs. 'I've been in the library, getting some peace and quiet. Then I call Joe, thinking we might have a bit of alone time. But as usual he has all his weirdo friends round and they're all in my room!' She sighs heavily. 'All of them, crowded on my bed playing old-skool Saints Row on his Xbox. I'm sick of that thing. Just because my room is bigger than his craphole bedsit, he thinks he can use it as his own personal hangout space with the rest of his immature "homies".' The quote marks she does in the air make me laugh, then shiver as another gust of autumn wind slices through me.

'Boys, huh?' I say drily. 'They say that you should always date a guy at least five years older than you are. Only then will they be of equal maturity to you.' I wrinkle my nose.

'Or, you just put up with it, I guess. They're all children underneath.'

'S'pose.' She inhales, more contentedly now, then her eyelids flutter and she jerks to sit up straighter. 'But I almost forgot. Joe said some guy was asking for you?'

My heart skips a little beat. 'Who? I don't know any guys.'

Stella shrugs. 'Apparently he was ringing all the bells outside the building. Sophie on the floor down from us went mental. She and her girlfriend were in the middle of some studying of an intimate nature . . .'

'Sophie's gay?' I blink, thinking of the preppy girl downstairs who I could have sworn had a boyfriend called Blair, or Brendan, or something like that.

'Apparently.' Stella shrugs again. 'And she didn't appreciate being interrupted by your caller. Gave him a bit of an earful. Jonah came down to see what the fuss was about and found her stabbing her precious little fingers a little too close to his grille and claiming to have no idea who you are.'

'Feisty.' I smile. I am holding off asking who my visitor is because I don't want to know that it's not who I pathetically hope it is. And I also realize it must be Jake. He did say he was coming to London with his mate Laurie this week and might come by and see me.

'My brother,' I say flatly.

'Mystery solved!' she exclaims.

I raise an eyebrow. 'So where is he?'

'Jonah rescued him,' she says. 'I'm not sure which is worse. Being screeched at by Sophia, or being trapped in a room with that Jonah and his crew. Poor guy.' She grins guiltily.

'He won't mind.' I nod. 'Jake lives inside his Xbox at home, I swear. And it will do him good to converse with live human beings for a change. Was he alone? He told me he was bringing a friend with him.'

'Unless he was accompanied by the Invisible Man, then yes, he was alone.' Stella tugs on my leather sleeve. 'Come on, kid, better get back. Jonah was giving me grief about having to babysit a a stranger, which was what sparked our massive row.'

'Sorry, hon.' I smile at her.

Of course it wouldn't have been Daniel, I told myself, feeling stupid for even briefly thinking it. Daniel has clearly lost interest. I need to get real.

37

Daniel

One day earlier . . .

'No it's fine. Really, Mum, I've got myself one of those pay-as-you-go phones in town. I really don't need a smartphone . . . No, Mum. It's not a big deal—'

I hold the phone away as another wave of anxious chatter hits my earlobe. I decide to wait for a pause before I cut in. But the guy in the room next door to mine has appeared behind me making his presence felt by the sheer odour of stale lager and roll-ups emanating from his pores.

I turn slightly and give him a tight smile. 'Another couple of minutes, mate, then it's all yours,' I tell him before channelling back into the tinny diatribe coming from the communal payphone in this freezing corridor.

He sniffs, taking a moment to register, before shuffling off back to his room.

'I can find all the numbers again,' I tell her. 'It's not like there were that many. Seriously, mobile technology is a little wasted on me. This is not a problem.'

No, it's only vaguely catastrophic, I am thinking. Because I've lost her number and have no way of getting it back.

But it's not my mother's fault. She was only doing what mothers do. And I am not about to tell her quite what a personal disaster it is that she chucked all my clothes into the washing machine without checking the pockets. No, that would only trigger another stream of angst and fuss, not to mention an interrogation on the nature of my relationship with this girl, whose precious number is lost for all time.

I finally get off the phone and return to my spartan little room, sinking down on to the bed and switching on my laptop. I consider Googling Eloise or searching for her on Facebook, but without her surname it's impossible to narrow the search.

Instead I continue researching for my 'Engineering in Construction' essay. As usual I am a model student already. Way ahead in terms of all study. I don't let a little thing like thwarted romance thwart me. Oh no. I am far too unfamiliar with romance, and far too familiar with immersion in homework. It has been my friend over the years, after all. Staving off many cravings and validating my existence, in the absence of any other, obviously more important, validation, such as, as Ronnie might put it, 'the love of a good woman'.

I am wasted on this century, I tell myself as I click through to the website I need. Seriously, Jane Austen modelled one of her emotionally isolated male heroes on me, did she but know it.

But then a brainwave hits. Well, it was obvious, you're thinking. But not to a dating novice such as myself. I Google University College London. It's vast, with study halls and campuses stretched over most of central north-west London. Like the veritable needle in a haystack, tracking down my girl will not be easy.

But, I figure, if I can just locate the Student Union or something . . . the secretary, perhaps? Then maybe if I beg, someone will give me something. I look harmless enough; it's possible.

I note down a couple of addresses and search my memory for clues from Lo's texts. Did she say something about her room overlooking a pretty square? I believe she did. Yes, London is chocka with pretty squares, but eventually I will find the right one.

I stand up feeling a little bit feverish. Crazy. Is what I'm thinking of doing crazy? A long shot? Or is it just another stepping stone in my ultimate quest to take a few risks and stand a cat in hell's chance of winning my heart's desire?

I decide on the latter option. Worst-case scenario: I make a complete fool of myself. I've spent a fair portion of my life so far doing that so, hey, water off a duck's back.

I check my wallet and find my new bank card. I have around five hundred pounds to play with – or, more accurately, to pay back somehow. But it should get me to London and back and if necessary a dismal single room in a Holiday Inn somewhere. It's Thursday night and my next lecture isn't till Monday afternoon. If I leave tomorrow I can do some study catch-up on my laptop on the train.

'Eloise . . .' I screw up my face in concentration, feigning a memory trawl. I have no idea what Lo's surname is. Typically, it didn't occur to me that this was important. Not until I am face to face with a middle-aged woman whose glasses hang from a vivid green cord around her neck. She looks a little bit like my Aunt Sandra, whom I like and who likes me. I am hoping that this lady, like Aunt Sandra, has a soft spot for foolish youth and their romantic whims.

She sighs. Leans forward across her desk and takes in my frantic demeanour.

'There are ten students named Eloise who are first-year undergraduates this term,' she tells me, putting her glasses on and running her finger down a list for emphasis. 'You expect me to give out each address?' She removes her glasses and blinks at me. 'You don't honestly think I would do that, do you?'

'Well . . . No. I can see you are a responsible employee of this university,' I say earnestly. 'And I totally understand. It's just that my future happiness kind of depends on finding a very specific Eloise. And if I lose that opportunity over a matter of . . . of legal obligation . . . well, it just

316

seems like a heavy load for you to carry with you into your future years. Your retirement in that idyllic Cotswolds cottage might be smeared by memories of my miserable face, pleading with you one chilly afternoon—'

'OK. Cease!' She holds out a hand and shakes her head slowly, a hint of amusement in those eyes. 'That was a performance worthy of the Royal Shakespeare Company, young man. Perhaps it's really RADA you're looking for?' One sanguine eyebrow is raised.

'Possibly,' I say brightly. 'But I've heard that RADA is notoriously biased against the Mancunian accent. My ambitions would be much better served by a handful of, say, street addresses . . . buildings, house numbers . . .' I trail off, feeling futile and desperate.

The secretary stares me out for thirty seconds before her facial expression alters — to something a lot more sympathetic.

'I've got a mountain of paperwork to get through before my break, and I really don't have the inclination to argue with you for another hour. And . . . you do remind me of my nephew,' she says wistfully. 'Edward. Clever, articulate, resourceful . . . a trifle idiotic.' She lowers her voice to a conspiratorial whisper. 'I wouldn't do this for just anyone, you understand. But I would only want happiness for Edward, and I expect no harm will be done.' She pauses then adds, 'It might help if I had an idea of what this particular Eloise looks like . . . ?'

Ah.

'She's blonde . . . and very pretty,' I offer lamely. 'Prettier than average?'

'Aren't they all,' she sighs, thinks and then looks down at her list. She taps a line, and hands me the piece of paper. 'Try Eloise Campbell-Taylor.'

'Great.' Oh God. She's posh. Eloise has a double-barrelled name. I am doomed. 'Are you sure?'

'Prettier than average, you said.' She is already eyeing somebody waiting in line behind me. 'So, be gone.'

'Thank you,' I whisper hoarsely in return. 'You have no idea what this means to me.' I push the list into my jacket pocket. 'Edward is proud to have an aunt like you, I'm sure.'

This earns me a gratified smile, before the eyes narrow ever so slightly once more. 'You ask politely and you take no for an answer,' she says. 'Understood?'

'Understood.' I straighten up, pat my pocket. 'God bless you,' I tell her gratefully. And then I scarper before she comes to her senses.

38
Eloise

'Why don't you come for a pizza with me and Jake?' I ask Stella. We're approaching Great Portland Street and have been standing waiting for the traffic to stop on the Euston Road for about twenty minutes. Or so it seems.

'That's nice, hon, but at this rate, by the time we make it back it'll be around midnight,' she says wearily as three Harley Davidsons thunder past us followed by a filthy lorry. 'Jesus, I hate this road. Is there any uglier road in the whole of the world? I feel like I'm high on carbon monoxide.'

'Yup. It's pretty ugly . . .' My eyes drift over the road. Behind the rows of cheap Indian restaurants and dirty modern builds sits the historic haven of Fitzroy Square. It's one of the things I already love about London, even though I've been here less than two weeks. I love the little pockets of grand beauty sitting serenely behind soulless office buildings. You turn a corner and you are suddenly back in time.

'Well, come on . . .' says Stella, grabbing my arm and pulling me across the road with her. 'The traffic lights will change back in about five seconds. Get a shift on.'

Finally we make it across to the right side of the street and I am grappling in my bag. 'I need to get some cash,' I mutter, locating my purse. 'Jake eats for about four and I've only got a tenner.'

'Fine,' she says wearily. 'But seriously, hurry up. We need to rescue your little bro before he becomes initiated into the cult of the stoner society.'

We find a bank on Great Portland Street, then wander through the back roads to Charlotte Street and our humble abode. Stella hands a pound coin to a homeless man propped up against some railings.

'God bless you, sweetheart,' he slurs, giving us a rotten-toothed smile.

'You're welcome.' Stella turns to me. 'That'll def go straight down his gullet, but whatever gets you through the night.'

I stop walking and smile at her.

'What?'

'Why, you've got a heart of gold, Miss Stella, ain'tcha?' I tell her in my best Cockney ragamuffin, looping my arm through hers. 'Not one of my so-called best friends back home would have done that. They'd probably have kicked the poor guy.'

'Good job you've got me now then, Princess.' Stella pats my hand. 'I'm giving you a guided tour of the milk of human kindness . . . or something.' She shrugs and we both laugh.

'I feel good being around you,' I say. 'I feel kind of real.'

'Yo, sister,' she teases.

'Seriously. For the first time I'm thinking of something other than designer clothes and mani-pedis and whether my ex-boyfriend was really a lying cheat or simply misunderstood.'

She frowns, and now it's her turn to stop.

'Are we speaking of your "late" boyfriend?' she asks carefully.

'Sorry, didn't meant to spew that out,' I say. I start moving again but Stella pins me where I am with her remarkably strong left arm.

'We should talk about this sometime,' she says. 'Because I heard a lot of pain just then.'

'Really, like I said, I'm over it now.' I smile as brightly as I can. Stella doesn't look ready to drop it though, and is just opening her mouth to verbalize that when three police cars scream past us to the entrance of Fitzroy Square.

Stella and I turn to the scene of the action. A policeman has got out of the car and is taping over the road.

'What's happening here?' Stella calls.

'Bomb scare, sweetheart,' says the policeman. 'Whole area is cordoned off. If I were you I'd go and get yourself a cup of tea somewhere else.' He points over to the direction from which we've just come.

'No, we have to get back home,' she protests. 'It's kind of an emergency.'

He gives her a distinctly sarcastic smile. 'Has a bomb gone off somewhere else then?' he asks, slipping his walkie-talkie out of his pocket.

'No.'Course not,' she says quickly. 'We'll go and get a cup of tea then . . . Officer.' She gives him the full Stella smile, and he puts his walkie-talkie away and shakes his head before giving his attention to matters of a slightly more important nature.

'Cup of hot chocolate more like,' says Stella grumpily. 'It's turned Siberian all of sudden.' On cue a gust of wind hits us.

I am shivering in my leather jacket and Stella opens up her coat and puts it half around me. It smells of perfume and ever so slightly of weed. I don't mind it, really. One can get awfully tired of Miss Dior, after all.

'And this will give me a chance to get to the bottom of these unresolved feelings of yours,' she says as we shuffle awkwardly along, back to the top of Great Portland Street, and the little Meze cafe at the back of the tube station.

It's toasty in the cafe and I cup my hot chocolate in both hands, warming up. Stella is on the phone to Jonah.

'What do you mean, you're going out?' She frowns into the phone. 'You've got to take care of Lo's brother . . . you can't just leave him there. And anyway, I doubt you'll get far; the whole place is cordoned off because of the bomb scare . . .'

She listens for a moment, then her expression changes. 'No, he's called Jake, you fool. How much weed have you been smoking?'

My ears prick at this development in the conversation, and I crane forward, as though this might help me hear what Jonah is saying. Stella's eyes flicker over at me, a new look of confusion on her face.

'Well, maybe it's a joke then. You know what these suburban kids are like. Too much time on their hands . . . vivid fantasy lives . . . ?' She laughs at her own joke for a second and then I hear Jonah's voice raised, unusually for him.

'Keep your hair on, Joe,' she sighs. 'Hold on a sec.' She leans toward me. 'We may have an imposter scenario on our hands, babe,' she tells me. 'Now, just to be clear. Your brother's name is Jake, right?'

'Right.' My eyes narrow. 'Why? What's Jonah saying?'

'Jonah says the kid isn't called Jake. But he has, most insistently, come to see you.'

I feel a weird fuzzy feeling inside me. A kind of scared feeling. Suddenly I am not cold any more.

'What does he say his name is?' I ask slowly. 'This kid.'

'Daniel.' She says slowly back. 'D. A. N. I. E. L.'

'Oh God.' I'm pretty sure my face has been drained of all colour.

'What? Who's Daniel?' Stella raises both eyebrows at once.

I sigh, quite heavily. 'It's a funny story. And we may need more hot chocolate . . .'

Daniel

'Who was that?' I ask Jonah, who snaps his phone shut.

'My girlfriend. She and Eloise are trapped over in Great Portland Street.' He frowns for a moment. 'She seemed to think that you're Lo's brother . . .' He studies me. 'But that's not right, is it?'

'Uh . . . No.' Last time I checked I didn't have a sister. Or any siblings at all. I think for a moment. 'So, Lo has a brother?'

'Yep. Name of Jake. But . . .' He eyes his mates. 'How well do you know Eloise?'

'Not very. I kind of met her while I was in Spain recently.' I realize that I am about to give a pretty lame explanation for how we actually met, or rather the fact that we technically haven't met at all, except by phone. And judging by the thinly veiled hostility these boys have shown me so far – having crashed their game-fest – I somehow don't think they're going to care. 'Anyway,' I add. 'Another game? Darts? Cluedo?' I smile weakly at the blank faces around me.

'Listen, mate. I don't want to be a prat or anything, but we've kind of got things to do,' says Jonah. 'It's been nice having you visit and all, but . . . we're thinking of heading off to Forbidden Planet as soon as we get the all-clear, and I get the feeling you're not really into all that.'

'Fine.' I stand, feeling a slight cramp from one leg. 'But can you tell me whereabouts your girlfriend and Eloise are? Did they say?'

His eyes narrow. 'Not really. A cafe somewhere. Maybe it's not such a good idea to just walk in there. Is Lo expecting you?'

'Not as such.' I know this looks shady but I didn't reckon on having to get past this bunch of bodyguards, shambolic as they look. 'But . . .' I sigh. 'I'm going to tell you the truth, and it might sound a little far-fetched, but just hear me out.'

Jonah sighs but he looks interested, I can tell. His mates grunt at each other, settling back in position on the overloaded bed.

'OK, then,' says Jonah. 'I'm listening . . .'

Twenty-five minutes later I am outside Eloise's block of flats and facing a square. A pretty square. Looking up I see the iconic BT Tower and take a moment to wonder at London's eclectic skyline. The old and the new jostling together quite happily.

I feel nervous, suddenly wondering what on earth I am doing here, pursuing a long shot like Eloise. I am also freezing and pull my scruffy old Carhartt jacket round me. Talking of which, I am not exactly dressed to impress. And I should have had a haircut; my buzz cut is already growing out and my dark hair is getting dangerously close to curling. What with my glasses, because I left my contacts behind in Bangor, and the fast-fading Spanish tan, I don't look how I wanted to look.

I can't think about that. I put one foot in front of the other and stride in the general direction Jonah told me to take. I am swinging past the square, past some remaining police cars and abandoned tape, now trodden into the ground, and keep my head down against the bitter wind.

'Hey!'

I bump straight into a pair of purple legs. As my eyes travel upwards, I see a scowling redhead, her arm linked through that of a pretty blonde girl.

'Hey, sorry.' I try and smile. 'Wasn't looking where I was going.'

The redhead nods. 'Cool glasses,' she says.

'Thanks,' I say, my eyes drifting to her companion, who does look vaguely familiar and whose eyes catch mine for a minute, then look away. 'Um, is this the way to Great Portland Street?' I ask Red.

'Straight through the square then turn left,' she says.

'You can't miss it; it's on a little island next to the main road.'

'Thanks again,' I tell her.

'Where you from?' she says. Her friend looks fractious, as though she is in a hurry to get away.

'Manchester, thereabouts,' I reply.

'Cool. I'm Stella, and this is—'

'Stella!' breathes the blonde. 'What are you doing?'

'Just making introductions,' says Stella. 'Being friendly.' She nods at me. 'What's your name then?'

Ignoring her interrogative tone, I open my mouth to reply when her pretty friend nudges her, rather unsubtly.

'We've got to get going,' she says, and gives me an apologetic smile. 'Sorry. But we're in kind of a hurry to get home.' She prods Stella's ribs lightly with her elbow. 'Right, Stella?'

Stella sighs. 'I was just wond—'

'Stella . . .'

'Fine, fine. Well, goodbye, whoever you are,' says Stella, allowing herself to be dragged away.

I watch them go.

'Dan,' I tell her. 'That's my name.'

But my words are lost in a sudden gust. I look at the two of them retreating, the redhead – Stella – legs that go on for ever and some crazy old dress sense, and the blonde – small, hair tumbling down her back, gripping hold of Stella's arm to stop herself from being blown away.

Shrugging, I turn up my collar and continue to my destination.

But the cafe, when I get there, is empty aside from an old man reading a newspaper and a woman with a crying baby. No girls.

I sigh. I am really tired and my plan seems sillier by the moment. I check my watch. It's two thirty.

I think of the work I should be doing. Of the long journey back to Wales. I order a coffee to take away, and head back outside, watching the cars zipping up and down, feeling, cold and, yeah, just a little bit lonely.

40

Eloise

'What do you mean, he's gone?' Stella is prodding Jonah, who looks half asleep. At least his mates have disappeared, though the room smells toxic.

'Where did he go?' I ask. 'I mean, did he say?'

'Uh. Well, yeah. He was heading off to find you guys.' Jonah scratches his head. 'In the cafe?'

Stella and I look at each other.

'That boy . . .' I breathe. 'The one we just bumped into in the square.' I put my hands up to my face. 'I am so thick! He said he was from Manchester.'

'Wait . . .' Stella blinks. 'That was him?' She turns back to her boyfriend.

'What was he wearing, Daniel?' she asks slowly.

'I dunno.' Jonah frowns. 'Clothes?'

'Jonah! For God's sake, you're useless.' Stella crosses her arms across her chest.

'Glasses?' I ask. 'Was he wearing them?'

'Yeah, yeah, he was wearing glasses. Pretty cool glasses actually. He was kind of ordinary-looking though, really. The kind of kid you forget about the moment he's out of sight.' He smiles, as though this statement will somehow throw a huge amount of light on the issue.

'It was him. It was Daniel,' I say, colour coming into my cheeks. 'And I just more or less ignored him.'

'See. That's what I mea—' began Jonah.

'Shut up, Jonah,' Stella and I tell him in unison.

'I need to go back and find him,' I say quickly. 'Back to the cafe.'

Stella starts putting her coat back on. 'Come on then. If we run, he might still be there.'

'No,' I say firmly. 'I'll go on my own. But thanks.'

'Aw,' she says, hugging me. 'This is brilliant! I love it! It's like *One Day* or something!'

'I don't get it.' Jonah is clueless.

'Shut up then,' Stella tells him again. She grabs hold of my shoulders and practically throws me out of the door. 'Go, Lo, and hurry!'

It starts to rain as I start running, little drops at first then full-on pelting down. By the time I get to the little island where the tube and the cafe are, I am soaked. I squeeze some water from my hair as I push through the cafe door and realize I am totally out of breath. At least it's warm in here. I take a moment to recover myself, before looking around me hopefully.

There's no one here. Only the bored-looking waitress and a guy chatting on the phone behind the counter.

I walk round, searching pointlessly in every corner.

'Can I help you?' asks the waitress, looking with disapproval at my wet footprints on the floor.

'Did you have a boy in here?' I ask. 'I mean, did a boy come in here about ten minutes – twenty minutes – ago?'

'A boy?' She puts her hands on her hips, thinking. 'Gio? Did you see a boy?'

The man making the phone call ends his conversation and nods.

'Yes. A boy with glasses. He bought a coffee to take away.' He shrugs. 'And he had things on his mind because he paid with a ten-pound note and left without his change.' He smiles a little guiltily and opens the till, taking out some money. 'Here.' He hands it to me. 'You give it back to him, yes?'

'I . . .' I am about to tell him that there isn't much point, but instead I take the money and stuff it in my pocket, because it's easier.

Maybe one day I can return it to Daniel.

'I don't suppose you saw where he was going?' I ask them.

'I'm too busy to stalk customers, sweetheart,' says the waitress, despite pretty clear evidence to the contrary. But she smiles at me kindly. 'Maybe try the tube station?'

'Thanks,' I say miserably. 'I'll do that.'

But as I step outside and see the main road, lorries thundering down it, rain dashing off windscreens, my heart slumps. I feel as though something important has just slipped out of my grasp.

I decide to trudge back home, to my building, and this time I walk slowly, my eyes down on the ground. Adrenalin is fading, leaving just a horrible flatness. As I enter the square, the rain stops and the clouds part to reveal blue sky again, and a shaft of bright October sun casts a kind of filmic light over the fenced-off grass in the middle. A man appears, with a dog. He bends and lets the dog off its leash and the animal comes bounding towards me, relishing its freedom. It runs round me and I laugh.

'Hey there,' I say softly, rubbing its velvety ears. 'Hey, you.' As I bend to give it a proper stroke, coins drop out of my pocket, followed by a load of other crap I've got in there, including a Chanel lipstick, which rolls away. I am just retrieving it and my Oyster card when I feel a hand on my shoulder.

'It's good luck to drop money in the street,' says a vaguely familiar voice. 'At least, that's what I'm hoping . . .'

I turn, and feel a flush of colour shooting up to my cheeks.

Daniel.

'It's you?' I say stupidly.

He pushes a hand through his hair. It's kind of scruffy and dark, with a hint of a curl. He looks like a real boy.

'It's me . . . And it's you,' he says, equally stupidly.

We laugh together, in a nicely awkward way.

He hands me the money he picked up and smiles a little shyly.

'Actually, it's your money,' I say sheepishly. 'The guy in the cafe said you left your change.'

'Aha. Well, I was feeling somewhat distracted,' he says. 'I was looking for someone and I didn't think I'd ever find her.'

'I thought you'd lost interest,' I say quickly. 'I sent you some texts.'

'I lost my phone,' he says. 'Actually my mum washed it. Seriously.'

I giggle. 'That is lame. In fact, it is so lame that I actually believe you.'

'So, I had to come and find you,' he says. 'Because I couldn't call you, or text you. All I knew was that you were here, somewhere. And when I thought about never talking to you again, never finding you . . . I don't know. It felt like a big deal.'

'You came all the way here? How did you know where I live? How did you find out my name? How . . . ?'

I feel an absurdly pleased, fluttery feeling.

Instead of answering, Daniel looks up at the blue sky pushing the clouds aside.

'Shall we go for a walk?' he asks. 'While the rain has stopped? I feel like we have some catching up to do.'

'Of course.' But I shiver spontaneously and then Daniel is taking off his jacket and putting it round me.

'But you'll be freezing,' I protest.

'I'll be fine,' he says cheerily. 'I feel a bit warmer now, as it turns out.'

41

Daniel

I was so convinced that my mission had been a complete and utter failure that I thought I was seeing things, like a mirage, when I saw her, bending down to pet a dog in the square.

This was Eloise. The mysterious blonde. Here, right in front of me.

And now that it came to it, I didn't know what to do.

But fate came to my rescue in the form of some dropped coins and I seized my moment.

And while we were standing there, having this surreal conversation, I looked at her properly. And believe me, I felt totally out of my depth.

She had to be the most beautiful girl I had ever seen. One of those girls who never looks rough, whose skin always glows, even when she's been rained on, and her face is flushed from scrabbling around on the ground, and her hair is hanging in dark-blonde tangled strands.

Totally out of my league.

But in keeping with my new life mantra: He who dares, wins. Or gives it a good go, anyway.

I needed time to explain, and even though the weather was in its most volatile of moods, we went for a walk.

We passed by her university and sat on the steps outside in the main quad.

'It was the truth about my phone,' I said. 'You've no idea how frustrating it was for me. I realized that your phone number was all I had of you. And then I got embroiled in the first week of Bangor and I felt as though maybe it wasn't meant to be. You know, that we'd had our moment, and it was kind of over.' I looked across at her. 'And you know, it hasn't been long since Huck . . . well, maybe I am just being selfish. And stupid. You guys had a serious thing going on.'

Eloise is fiddling with her bracelet. 'I thought that. But you know, the more I remembered about us, the more I realized that it had always been a little one-sided. Like I was the one who had all the feelings, and Huck was like this wall that they bounced off. He was so perfect on paper. But I never felt he really knew me. The real me.'

I cast my mind back to the Huck I had met. He did have that aura about him, a kind of bland aura. Like everything had to be a good time. Everything always went his way.

'So, in a funny way . . . the texts I was sending him, knowing he couldn't read them, that was the most honest

337

I'd ever been with him. See, I wasn't scared to tell him the truth. I was the real me.'

'Huck was one of those golden people, I think,' I tell her. 'And those kinds of people are hard to get to know. You need a chink . . . you know what I mean? Something less than perfect. Otherwise what's to love?'

'Uh huh. And it turns out that Huck's imperfections, when I finally saw them . . . well, they weren't so lovable after all.'

'What an idiot,' I say, without thinking.

'But I went along with it,' Eloise sighs. 'I was the golden girl. It's my fault. It's like I didn't know how to step down a little. Even though I wanted to.'

We fall into a short silence before she looks up at me again.

'But how about you. You said there was a girl?'

I nod slowly. 'There was a girl. Her name was Paula. I met her in Spain. She was gorgeous, kind . . . a happy person, you know.'

Eloise is nodding, but I notice she hugs herself a little, a hint of anxiety in her eyes.

'But . . . she was just too mapped out for me. She wanted to settle down and have kids and that was pretty much it.' I hesitate. 'You know, she is the only girl I have ever kissed.'

Eloise stops hugging herself and her eyes widen out. 'Seriously?'

'Seriously.' I laugh. 'I mean, I wait all this time for a girl like her, and when she comes along . . . I don't want her. Talk about messed up.'

'That's not messed up at all,' says Eloise. 'That's being true to yourself. Holding out for what you've really been waiting for. I think it's noble.'

'Noble, huh?' I sigh. 'Like a kind of valiant knight? Or the guy that a girl might only want as a friend? You know, reliable and nice.'

'Reliable and nice, for sure,' she says, a slight quaver in her voice. 'But also kind of sexy.' She looks away and I am pleased to see the blush spreading over her cheeks.

'Well, thank you, miss. I guess that's what I really wanted to know.' I pause. 'From you, especially.'

She turns back, and our eyes meet. And I wonder. I hope. That what I've really been waiting for is here, right in front of me. On these steps.

'I should have been more like you,' she says. 'As honest and less afraid of being alone. I want to start again, Daniel.'

Suddenly all the background noise fades away, and it feels as though it's just me and Eloise in all the world.

'So you're not disappointed?' I ask her. 'Now that we've finally met? I mean, I am pretty boring. And I'm no Brad Pitt.'

She laughs. 'Brad Pitt? He's, like, a hundred years old!' She shakes her head, reaching out one hand and squeezing my wrist. 'Not disappointed,' she says. 'Lucky.'

42

Eloise

Daniel and I make our way back to my building in another bout of rain and under a darkening sky. I glance sideways at him, in his white tee and grey V-neck and jeans, trying not to look like he's cold without the jacket that I still have on. And I keep thinking about how much it must have cost him to get here from Wales, and how he tried to find me, and tolerated an ear-bashing from Sophie, and hours of mind-numbing computer-gaming action with strangers, not knowing whether I would be pleased to see him or not. I am thinking that he is really something. Even more so because he has no idea that he is. And that has to be the most seductive thing ever. Not glamorous parents, or parties. Not flashy moves, or chat-up lines. What Daniel did . . . well, it's the ultimate romantic gesture.

As we turn off Tottenham Court Road and head for my building I realize I don't want him to leave. I try not to think about him heading back to Wales, and the whole long-distance thing.

'I still can't believe that you went to all this trouble to find me,' I tell him quietly.

'I can be pretty resourceful when I put my mind to it,' he says. 'Or when I want something enough.' Daniel takes off his glasses and I allow myself to eye him properly. Dark-lashed eyes, and the hint of a tan, and a face that, though it isn't Orlando Bloom's (or Brad Pitt's), is most definitely cute. In a boy-next-door, serious kind of way. There is something about his eyes, a kind of smartness, kindness. A twinkle, my grandma would call it. He rubs at his lenses and then puts the glasses back on. And he looks nervous suddenly.

'Eloise, I know we know nothing about each other, and technically we've only just met, but I can't stop thinking about you. If I'm being honest, I've been thinking about you ever since you sent that first text. I'm not a romantic, I like certainties and tangible facts, and I never, I mean never, act on instinct. Not until now. And I would understand if this is all too soon, and too weird, but I just like you. A lot more than I liked Paula. And nearly as much as I like my mum . . .'

He shoots me a sweet, impish smile at that.

'Me too,' I say, grinning. 'And for a non-romantic, that was a pretty damn romantic confession. I mean, I can't imagine—'

'Shhh,' he says and puts one cold finger gently on my

341

lips. 'I'm working up the courage to kiss you as my next romantic gesture, and I need to do it quickly, before I lose my nerve, or you run away, or both.' He takes his finger away and then moves closer, his face moments from mine.

I can feel heat coming from him now, and his hands when they gently take hold of my waist feel strong, but not forceful.

'You're so pretty, with your hair all wet and your eyes a little smudgy and your cheeks all rosy,' he says, letting go one hand and brushing a strand of damp hair off my forehead. 'Way prettier than I deserve. And you're smart, and funny and I want to get to know you better, Eloise.'

No suave seductive routine, no clever remarks. Just straightforward. It's not what I've been used to. I realize that I've been used to games. Just skirting around feelings.

All at once I can't wait any longer. I take Dan's face in my hands and I kiss him, long and soft, then harder as he responds hungrily, his hands gripping hold of my waist, pulling me into him. I get the strangest feeling then, a feeling of safety and excitement rolled into one. A feeling of belonging.

After a long few moments we slow down our kissing and pull gently away from each other. He's tall. Taller than Huck. I feel a faint satisfaction in that. Not that Huck is on my mind any more. Actually, that's not true . . . he is. Because Huck never really kissed me like that. Never really made me feel like this. Like my stomach is doing giant cartwheels in my stomach.

'Well,' says Daniel. 'Well.'

'Well?' I demand lightly. 'Well?'

'Well.' His hands are back around my waist. I can feel his hands pushing carefully but persistently underneath the layers I have on. I can feel his fingers circling the flesh above my waistband. It gives me a surge of feeling I haven't felt for a long time. 'What do we do now, Eloise?'

'Lo,' I tell him. 'Eloise is so . . . so princessy.'

'I like Eloise,' Dan says softly. 'I like the girl, and the name. It suits you. It's a great name.'

I smile, almost sadly. Huck always insisted on calling me Lo.

'What are you thinking about?' Dan says, tracing the tip of my chin with his finger.

'Nothing . . . just how I kind of like Eloise too. Now.'

He grins, and it makes me want to start kissing him again. But the rain is coming down now, and we can't stand here all night.

'I feel weird,' I say suddenly. 'I mean . . . good weird.'

'Me too.' We stare at each other, as though we can hardly believe each other. It has to be one of the best feelings ever.

'I'm sorry you got stuck with Jonah and his mates,' I say, grimacing. 'They're pretty one-dimensional when it comes to conversation.'

'They are,' he agrees, laughing. 'But they were less scary than that screaming girl who answered the door . . . and they tried their best.'

'You've had quite a day, haven't you?' I sigh.

'I think we both have.' His eyes when they meet mine are serious. They make me catch my breath.

'You want to come back to my room?' I ask, biting my lip. 'Hang out for a while?'

'You're inviting me back to the Plaza?' he says solemnly. 'I'm honoured.'

'I can't promise room service,' I say, laughing. 'But we can pick up a pizza on the way.'

'Perfect.' His hand slips into mine and squeezes it. 'Perfect.'

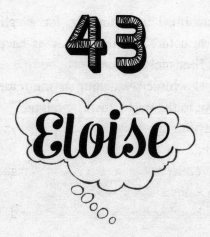

43

Eloise

I press my face comically to the train window, and then kiss it. I have no make-up on, messy hair, and I'm wearing Daniel's scruffy grey jumper, Stella's Primark leggings and a pair of fake Ugg boots.

And I feel the hazy, lazy, don't-care feeling you get when nothing else matters but the boy you're falling in love with.

Inside the train carriage, Dan leans towards the window and kisses it.

We are kissing through glass.

The train starts to pull slowly out of the station and I move with it.

It is speeding up and I start waving.

'Hey, Daniel!' I shout at his face, still pressed to the window.

He is grinning, and mouthing, 'What?'

But the words I am shouting, for everyone on the platform to hear, are lost to my boy as he pulls out of London and heads for Bangor.

'Call me,' I whisper, watching as the train disappears round a curve in the track. 'Just . . . call me.'